What others are saying about...

Sand Castle Dreams

"Sandcastle Dreams deals beautifully and honestly with the realities of teen life and struggles. Sprinkled with humor, romance, and raw emotion, this is a book both teens and adults will enjoy."

Krista McGee, award-winning author of the Anomaly Trilogy

"A refreshing story brimming with friendship, first love, and forgiveness."

McCall Hoyle, M. Ed., award-winning author
Meet the Sky (HarperCollins/Blink 2018)

"From the opening line of *Sand Castle Dreams*, readers will be swept away on a wave of Taylor Bennett's rock-solid storytelling. Her words are golden, bringing authenticity to every page. Facing heartbreak and learning to hope, Bennett's characters are relevant and real. Don't miss this one! *Sand Castle Dreams* will tug at your heartstrings and keep you reading well past midnight."

Sara Ella, award-winning author of the *Unblemished* trilogy and *Coral*

Sand Castle Dreams

The Tradewinds Series

Sand Castle Dreams

Book two in the Tradewinds series

By Taylor Bennett

Sand Castle Dreams
Published by Mountain Brook Ink
White Salmon, WA U.S.A.

The website addresses shown in this book are not intended in any way to be or imply an endorsement on the part of Mountain Brook Ink, nor do we vouch for their content.

This story is a work of fiction. All characters and events are the product of the author's imagination. Any resemblance to any person, living or dead, is coincidental.

Scriptures taken from the Holy Bible, New International Version®, NIV®. Copyright © 1973, 1978, 1984, 2011 by Biblica, Inc.™ Used by permission of Zondervan. All rights reserved worldwide. www.zondervan.com The "NIV" and "New International Version" are trademarks registered in the United States Patent and Trademark Office by Biblica, Inc.™

ISBN 978-1-943959-58-7
© 2019 Taylor Bennett

The Team: Miralee Ferrell, Nikki Wright, Cindy Jackson
Cover Design: Indie Cover Design, Lynnette Bonner Designer

Mountain Brook Ink is an inspirational publisher offering fiction you can believe in.
Printed in the United States of America

To Maui, God's magnum opus,
for inspiring the story of my heart.

Acknowledgments

Writing a second book, a sequel to the story of one's heart, sounds like a piece of cake (coconut, preferably) doesn't it?

It's not.

Sorry to spoil your optimism, but writing a sequel is (at least in this case) more like baking a ten-layer wedding cake than cutting a simple slice of carrot cake. But, thanks to the circle of friends, family, and supporters surrounding me, that wedding cake turned out bigger—more beautiful—then I ever could have imagined.

First of all—Miralee Ferrell. The one who believed in me enough to send me down this path to *Sand Castle Dreams*. The one who wasn't afraid to tell me that what I had planned for this book *wasn't working*. The one who didn't even bat an eye at my three-day-editing-turnaround. Thank you for everything you've done to help me share my heart, my stories, with the world. I couldn't have asked for a better team than you and the rest at Mountain Brook Ink.

Thank you, Aunt Janice, for posting oodles of pics every time you go to Maui, for being one of the first people to share your love of Hawaii with me, and for being the best aunt I could ever ask for. Thanks also to Dr. Freeh, who might as well be family—I'll forever be grateful to you and your generosity. Your Hawaiian condo will always remain one of my favorite places on earth.

Dad, thank you for being one of the only guys who will ever read my book, for understanding my need to go to Hawaii for "research," and for shamelessly tooting my horn wherever you go—even when it does embarrass me.

Sara Carrington, thank you for always being there when I have a question, and for helping me brainstorm when my mind's gone numb. Your gentle and kind encouragement in this season of my life has been such a blessing.

I could say a million individual thank-yous to all of the wonderful staff and faculty at the Oregon Christian Writers Conference but sadly, space is short. Still, allow me to say THANK YOU here, and know that I'm thinking of each and every one of you right now.

Huge thanks to everyone on my street team, my "Porch Swing Girls"—I wish there was a way I could name all of you and remain within my word count! You all are amazing, and I'm so blessed to have such a caring and supportive online community surrounding me.

To all of my endorsers: thank you, thank you! A few years ago, I never could have dreamed that some of my favorite authors would be reading and endorsing *my book*. You are all amazing inspirations to me, and I'm so, so grateful that you took the time to read my work. I pray that someday I might pay it forward to a young teen author like me.

Most of all, to Mom—for everything you do and everything you've done. Thank you from the very bottom of my heart. Thank you for letting me call you my best friend, for being my faithful proofreader, and for crying at the end of everything I write. I wouldn't be where I am today without your unwavering love and support, and it blesses my socks off to know how much you care about me.

And dear Jesus—thank you for never leaving my side, never

giving up on me, no matter how many mistakes I manage to make in a day (I'm sure it's a greater number than I could ever imagine). Thank you for guiding me with Your hand and for giving me gentle nudges that keep me walking evermore toward You. Let this book do Your work in the world, Lord, and no matter what success I see in my life, let me forever be reminded that it comes from You and You alone.

Chapter One

"WE'RE GOING TO LIVE *HERE*?" MY words bounce off the walls of an empty, bare-walled apartment, and I raise my brows at Dad. "How do you expect us to fit?"

I cross my arms and stare at a kitchen that is barely big enough for my six-year-old sister, Macie, to fit in. She must not care, because she makes a beeline for the fridge and throws open the door.

"There're no snacks in here." She throws back her head of brown curls and whimpers. "Daddy, you said there'd be snacks."

The real estate lady narrows her eyes and rests a finger on her blood-red lips. "Can't she settle down? I'd hate for us to disturb the other residents. This is a very respectable establishment, you know." Her tone is cold as steel in the dead of winter.

I hurry over to console Macie before a full-on tantrum can break out, pulling a granola bar from my sweatshirt pocket as I do so.

When I dreamed about coming home to Boston, this was *not* what I had in mind. I've only been here a month and, already, Dad and this real estate lady have taken Macie and me on a tour of every available apartment this side of Newbury Street.

But this one is by far the worst.

Macie goes to work on the granola bar, and I level my gaze across the room at Dad, who's standing next to the lady, his hands wadded tightly in a ball. "This place is a joke, right?"

The ticking of my watch echoes in the empty room as Dad makes impressive eye contact with the floor. Finally, he looks up. "Let's see the rest of the place first, before we make any rash decisions."

Macie bobs her head and crams the rest of the granola bar into her mouth in one huge bite. She races across the room to the microscopic window overlooking—is that what I think it is?

I cross the room in a few short strides.

A parking garage.

I swallow past the near-permanent lump in my throat and close my eyes, picturing the view from my old house in the suburbs. The beautiful, glorious suburbs, where the air smells like freshly mowed grass. Not exhaust and smog.

A wave of fury builds inside me, and I nearly kick the doorframe as we're paraded into the master bedroom. A cramped little breadbox of a room.

Why did Mom have to die?

The question that has haunted me for the past few months chases after me, nipping at my heels, as we go from room to room. Before Mom died, everything was perfect—at least, as perfect as life with a scatterbrained professor dad and high-maintenance little sister *could* be.

Now...

I scrub at my burning eyes as the woman gives Dad the full rundown of the place—including its top-of-the-line appliances and unique, space-saving design. Not that there's much space worth saving.

Why did I ever try so hard to get home to Boston, anyway? Staying with Gramma in Hawaii was a million times better than *this*.

Inching over to the far corner of the room, I pull out my phone and text Jazz, my best friend from the island.

On the apartment hunt. Again

I sigh and lean against the wall. The air is tinged with

the stench of fresh paint and the polished wood floors glint up at me, sneering at me and my pathetic predicament.

If only I could magically teleport back to Hawaii, to the cluttered coziness of Gramma's beach house, to the Shave Ice Shack with—

"Olive?" Dad waves at me from across the room. "Time to see your room."

"Great." The word tastes like cardboard in my mouth, and I pocket the phone, crossing the hall in two steps. My phone buzzes but I ignore it as the real estate agent crosses the threshold into a dim room with a window barely bigger than last year's history textbook.

"This is it." Her words are singsong-y, her pasted-on smile a little too welcoming for my personal taste. "It'll be nice and cozy, but you should be able to fit two beds in here."

"But I don't need—*oh.*" The realization tumbles over me like the monster waves of Maui. Not only is this room cramped and ugly, but Dad expects me to share it with my six-year-old sister.

The woman launches into another monologue of specs and upgrades, but I cut her off with my nicest smile. "No, thank you. I don't need to hear about any of that."

The lady's lips quirk up in a sort of icy smile, and she peers at me through a pair of dainty glasses. Keeping a smile pasted on my face, I turn to Dad and whisper through gritted teeth: "I shared a room with Macie at Gramma's all summer. Don't you think it's time I had my own space again?"

"You mean you don't *like* me anymore?" Macie appears at my side and tugs my hand, her voice dripping with the threat of tears.

Dad cuts his eyes at me, and I wince. What happened to the amiable, fun-loving Dad of my childhood? Ever since Mom died, it's like he's been replaced by Eeyore the Donkey. Everything in his life is woe and desperation, but he doesn't dare pay a bit of mind to anyone else's troubles.

We finish the tour in eerie silence, and our footsteps slap against the bare wood floors as the real estate agent ushers us out of the mausoleum and into the crystal-studded lobby.

"Shall we see another?" Her voice is blindingly bright, her tone pathetically fake. *This* is one of Boston's premier real estate agents? I scoff out a laugh as we step out onto a busy side street.

"No, thank you. That's all for today." Dad takes Macie's hand and presses his other hand against my back, propelling me toward his sedan.

The real estate lady waggles her fingers at us as we climb into the car. Macie returns the gesture with a *shaka*, thumb and pinky extended in the traditional Hawaiian way. I do the same and smirk when the lady wrinkles her brow. She probably thinks it's some sort of gang sign.

"Olive." Dad's voice is steady—too steady—as he turns the key in the ignition. "Would you like to tell me what that was all about?"

"What? The gang sign?" I tear my gaze from the window as Dad zips out into a lane of fast-moving traffic.

"*Gang sign*?" His brows jump up. "What are you—"

"Never mind." I roll my eyes, more at myself than anything, and stare out the window as Dad pulls onto the main road. We're headed home—but how much longer will I be able to call it that? How much longer before that *Sale Pending* sign turns to *Sold*?

Shivers run races up and down my spine. When I imagined coming home, I imagined coming *home*—not spending every day combing the city for a house that will never, ever become a home.

According to Dad, we need to downsize. Simplify. And he wants to be closer to work. That might all be true, but there's got to be more—like he's trying to run away from everything we had Before.

Before Mom died.

Before I went to Hawaii.

Before Jazz and Brander and—

"So?" Dad switches off the radio, and his gaze flicks over to me. "You were extremely rude to that woman. What do you have to say for yourself?"

"What do you want me to say?" I raise my hands in defense. "I hated that place. What possible reason is there to sing its praises? It's miniscule, for one, and did you see the snobbery in the lobby? No thanks."

"My room barely had a window." Macie's voice is watery. I twist around and find her, eyes wide, lip pooched out like a tiny blimp, glaring at me like all of this is my fault.

"Hey. *Our* room, remember?" I turn around and cross my eyes at myself in the rearview mirror.

"You mean we really have to share?" Macie's voice creeps up toward a full-blown howl.

"Unless you want to sleep on the couch, squirt." Which would be fine by me. If she did, maybe that would mean there'd actually be enough space in the bedroom for me to, you know—*breathe.*

"I don't want to sleep on the couch. I want to sleep in my flower fairy bed in my real house. Don't make me sleep on the couch, Daddy." With that, Macie bursts into tears, her wails piercing my eardrums as Dad continues down the street.

His gaze is fixed straight ahead, and he doesn't even bat an eye at Macie's hysterics. He's off somewhere, floating in another world. Who knows what will drag him back to earth this time?

"Dad?" I step into his office later that night, gripping a piece of paper in my hands, fresh from the printer.

"What?" Dad swivels around and dumps a huge stack of encyclopedias into a box before wrenching his wire-framed reading glasses off of his nose. "Are you done packing your sister's things? Because someone needs to start on the living room, and I doubt it's going to be me." He waves a hand over the calamitous state of his office.

"Macie's stuff? I haven't even started packing my own room. Listen." I clear my throat, as though that can somehow muffle the sound of my heart beating out of my chest. "Do you seriously think that apartment we saw today could be a good fit? Because I don't think it would be a good fit for a midget, let alone the three of us."

Dad cocks his head to the side, as though questioning whether he should correct my word choice or get straight to the point. He pinches the bridge of his nose and sighs. "The apartment we saw today was not ideal."

Not ideal? Give me a break.

"But." Dad holds a finger in the air before I can object. "The price was."

"You mean..."

"Sit down." Dad's gaze flickers as I ease into a leather-backed chair across from his desk. "We need to talk."

"I'm listening."

"The only way your mother and I were able to afford a house this size, in this neighborhood, is because we relied on both incomes. Now that she's...gone, we don't have that second income." Dad raises his brows at me. "Do you know where I'm headed with this?"

I swallow against a bitter taste in my mouth. "You're going to tell me that all of the apartments we looked at are at the top end of your budget. Except for—" the rest of the words pile up in my throat, threatening to choke me.

"The one we saw today." Dad nods and brushes his jacket. "It's not just the house—we had a lot of medical bills that insurance didn't cover, so I'm dealing with that. Besides, a smaller space would be ideal for downsizing and simplifying. Think of all the togetherness. Try to keep an open mind, okay?"

"An open mind. You want me to keep an open mind about a closed-off cardboard box?" I sit, glued to my chair. Blinking at the stranger my father has become. "When I said I wanted to come home, I meant—"

"Olive." Dad's voice rumbles like the growl of a lion. It bounces off the bookshelves and echoes in my ears. "You were the one who pushed so hard to come home. You're here now. So chin up and *deal with it.*"

I gulp back a nasty response, the taste of my unspoken words bitter when I swallow, before laying my paper on the desk in front of him. "All I'm saying is, if you honestly want to move into a place as cramped and miserable as *that...*"

Dad slips his glasses onto his nose and stares at the sheet of paper. "Flight schedules? You can't be serious."

"I have friends on Maui. And Gramma. I have a life."

"You have friends here."

"Who, my literature club buddies? They've probably forgotten all about me. Think about it. I could spend junior year on Maui with Grams and Macie. You could simplify. It would all work."

Dad shakes his head and runs a hand through his hair. "I've already lost my wife. Now you want me to give up my children?"

I snort at Dad's melodrama. "The way I remember it, *you* were the one to leave *us.*"

"I was grieving." Dad waves a hand in the air, as though that excuse can magically wipe away the blow of pain he dealt us all when he dumped Macie and me at Gramma's house this summer.

"And I had to beg you to let us come home. As soon as school starts again, you're going to be at the university all day anyway. It's not like you'd have that much time to miss us."

"That's beside the point. I don't have money to keep flying you and Macie halfway around the world. Plus, you two would have to share a bedroom again."

"Even if I stay here, that's what I'll end up doing. At least this way I'd be sharing a room in paradise. If you let us go, I'll even—I'll pay for the flight." The words tiptoe out of my mouth, as though Dad will be more apt to listen if I whisper.

"Where do *you* have money?" Dad runs a hand over the stubble on his jaw and glowers at the paper I handed him.

"My college fund." I lock my gaze on him as he stares at me, his mouth wide as a gaping cavern.

"You'd be willing to—no. Seriously?" Dad shakes his head at me.

I grit my teeth and nod. Ever since I was little, the money I got—be it for my birthday, from Christmas, or a lemonade stand—went into my college fund. So I could go to school at my dad's domain.

Harvard.

My dream school.

But two plane tickets won't wipe out my entire account. Put me back a couple semesters' worth of textbooks, maybe, but I can always apply for a few more scholarships when the time comes. And if my SAT scores are high enough—

"I'm willing." I force the words out before I can lose my resolve. "It's my money. I can do what I want with it, right?"

Dad sighs and runs *both* hands through his hair. "What does your grandmother think of all this?"

Hope blooms in my chest as I spring to my feet. "I don't know. But I'll call her right now."

Chapter Two

Two Weeks Later

"ALOHA, LADIES AND GENTLEMEN, THIS IS your pilot speaking. We're about ten minutes from Kahului International Airport." The speaker crackles, jarring me from my half-doze. I jerk to attention, my heart pounding. *Almost there—almost to Maui. To Gramma. To Jazz—and Brander.*

The pilot continues blabbing, reminding us to put our tray tables up and store our electronic devices, but I tune out and push up the window shade. My breath catches at the sight below me—a vast expanse of ocean, stretching as far as the eye can see. A strange, crescent-shaped reef protrudes from the azure waters. Several boats are docked around it, and they bob in the gentle waves.

"Macie." I poke her pudgy arm and she stirs, rubbing sleep from her eyes.

"What?" A string of drool dangles from her bottom lip.

I wrinkle my nose and wipe it away as I peek out the window again. "We're almost home."

Home.

A few months ago, *home* was Boston. Now, there's no place I'd rather be than on the beach with Brander and Jazz or sitting on the front porch with Gramma.

The West Maui Mountains come into view, and goosebumps prick at my arms. Every second seems to last an hour as the plane takes a long, leisurely loop around the island. I crane my neck, tracing the coastline with my eyes, trying to spot the road that leads to Gramma's house in

Lahaina. Before I can find it, we begin our descent. Macie's hand worms its way into mine, and she leans into me as the ground comes rushing up to meet us.

She gives me an extra-tight squeeze as we make contact with the runway. The jet bounces once—twice—before slowing and drawing to a stop. I uncross my legs and jiggle my foot against the floor as the pilot comes on again, reminding us to stay seated until we arrive at the terminal.

Wind buffets a stately line of palm trees, the tops of which are visible beyond the terminal building, and I focus on them as the old man sitting next to Macie lets out a horrifically loud, long snore. Macie giggles and snorts out an imitation, but I shush her as we pull into the gate.

"That's all for today, folks. Your luggage should be delivered to the baggage claim area shortly. Have a nice day, and *mahalo* for choosing Hawaiian Air."

"Mahalo!" Macie returns the Hawaiian thank-you and swings her legs as we wait our turn to get off. "We're really in Hawaii. Are you excited? I want to see Gramma. And Jazzie. And—"

"Yeah, Mace. I'm excited." I ruffle my sister's corkscrew curls. *Excited* is a major understatement. We're finally here—in this strange place I've somehow come to call home.

Thankfully, Grams was all for my return—in fact, she even offered to cover our luggage fees. Dad still isn't crazy about the whole thing, but I am, and Macie practically dances down the aisle as we make our way off the plane. As soon as we step into the terminal, she falls to her knees and...*ew.*

"Macie, did you seriously *kiss* the floor?" Without waiting for an answer, I grab a sanitizing wipe from my carry-on bag and run it over my sister's lips.

"Stop, Olive." Macie sticks out her tongue and sputters. "It tastes like soap."

"Then don't put your mouth on the filthy floor next time."

I cross my arms and shudder, but I don't fault my sister. If there was any way I could jump out of the terminal and wrap my arms around a palm tree right now, I'd do it in a heartbeat.

But I can't. Not yet, anyway.

Instead, Macie and I navigate a million walkways before finding the baggage claim. I plant one hand on Macie's shoulder as we weave through a crush of people but let go when we reach our luggage carousel. "Stay here, okay?" I stare at her and cross my arms.

Macie nods and plops on top of her carry-on suitcase. I stand there a moment, watching her, before crossing to the baggage carousel.

I'm doing a pretty good job of keeping one eye on her and one eye on the bags rolling by, but then Macie jumps to her feet and takes off at a run.

"Grammy!" Her voice is barely audible as she disappears into a thicket of pasty white tourists.

Rolling my eyes, I huff out a breath, grab her abandoned carry-on, and take off.

I squeeze between two guys so big they *must* be sumo wrestlers, and one of them gives me the stink eye. Bad. "Whoa, cool it. I'm trying to keep my sister from disappearing is all, buddy." I toss the words over my shoulder and pick up the pace as Macie's head of dark curls disappears behind a kiosk advertising snorkeling excursions.

"Macie!" I round the kiosk as Macie screeches to a halt in front of an older lady clutching a scrawny, nearly hairless little dog. "Macie!"

My little sister turns and raises her hands, palms up. "What?" Her tiny voice is nearly lost in the din.

"Come on. Get over here." I wave her toward me, but I don't dare take a step closer toward that lady—or, more specifically, her dog. "That's not Gramma. She said she'd wait for us out front, remember?"

"So*rry*. Her muumuu looked like Grammy's. And they both have big bottoms." Macie kicks at the floor and scuttles over to join me. Not ready for any more escapades, I forgo the lecture on tact and keep her close by my side as I gather our bags. By the time we catch sight of Gramma out front, I'm nearly ready to collapse at her feet. I don't know how Mom did it—this parenting stuff isn't easy.

"Grammy!" Macie bounces on her tippy-toes and waves her hands over her head, and I'm nearly ready to join in when Gramma sweeps in and wraps us both into a giant hug.

"You're home." Gramma pulls away, her vibrant blue gaze extra-sparkly. Are those tears glistening in the corners of her eyes? Before I can decide whether they are or not, my vision clouds over and something wet trickles down my cheek.

"Sorry." I swallow hard and swipe at my face.

Gramma doesn't even blink—just reaches out and places a warm, soft hand on my shoulder. "It's okay to cry, sweetie. It only means you have a heart so full it doesn't have room for tears."

I squint at Grams, the platitude blowing over me like a soft breeze. The words are pretty and all, but how can they be true? Tears aren't something to embrace, to be proud of. All they do is show I'm not as strong as I'd like others to think.

My tongue itches to argue the point, but a lump in my throat keeps the words at bay. Instead, I throw my arms around Gramma's neck and breathe in her ubiquitous sugarcane-and-plumeria smell. She lifts a hand and strokes my hair for a minute before pulling away and gesturing to the suitcases surrounding me.

"Are you ready to get going?" Gramma waves us toward her rattletrap station wagon. "I'm sure you'd like to get settled soon."

I nod, sniffling as I grab one of my suitcases. Most of my stuff will stay in storage in Boston, but I brought all of the necessities—and some non-necessities too, like a certain shave ice necklace...

By the time we've all piled into the car and made our way to the main road, the light has begun to fade. Gramma's station wagon weaves around the curves of the shoreline as we follow the oceanside highway's winding path home.

I dig my phone out of my pocket, check the time, and groan—by the time we get to Gramma's, it'll be too late to swing over and surprise Jazz. Somehow, I've managed to keep my return a secret from both her and Brander. But now that I'm here, I can hardly wait to see them. I twine my necklace—the one made from a sunrise shell that washed up on the shore of this very island—around my index finger as excitement fizzes up in my stomach.

I don't know what's going to happen this year, but I can't help believing it'll be good. After flicking through Instagram for a few minutes, I let my eyes grow heavy. I'm about to pocket my phone when a text from Jazz pops up.

I know it's late, but I have big news! Call me!

I bite my lip to keep a laugh from slipping out. It would be late in Boston, but here it's barely past dinnertime—though Macie must not have gotten the memo. Her breaths come in rumbly little puffs, her head lolling against the window. There's no way me talking on the phone with Jazz would wake Macie. *But* there's a chance Jazz would hear the road noise—or at least Gramma's favorite ukulele-melee radio station. And there's no way I'm tipping her off now. I text her back:

Busy now. Tomorrow?

Her reply is almost instant:

What time?

I fidget in my seat and watch out the window as we pass through a tunnel carved into a sea cliff.

9AM your time?

Jazz shoots me a thumbs-up, followed by a string of emojis, then adds a final note. Can it be a video chat?

I respond with a thumbs-up, then add:

I'm excited to see you

She has no idea.

I pocket the phone, lean against the seat, and gaze at the rolling ocean beyond the highway. This is where I'm supposed to be. This is where everything will return to normal—not like what I had *Before*, when Mom was alive, but a new normal.

A good normal.

I can't wait.

"Aloooha!" Jazz waves into the phone, her voice tinny through my speaker.

"Good morning to you too." I turn the phone so Jazz can get a good look at me—or, more importantly, what's *behind* me. She's getting that video chat she wanted. Except she might be getting even more than she bargained for.

"Are you ready for my news?" Jazz leans forward and squints into the phone at me. "Wait...where *are* you? Are you—on Aunt Ruby's porch?"

"Why would you think that?" A lone giggle slips out, and

I pan the phone to show Ruby's porch, complete with its sagging floorboards and rickety railing. I still can't believe Jazz has been staying *here*, in this decrepit little breadbox.

"You are!" Jazz stares at me with wide eyes, then shakes her head, almost as though shaking off her optimism. "You mean you're—?"

"Why don't you come outside and see for yourself?"

"No. Way." Jazz's face lights like a tiki torch, and she squeals into the phone. A grand total of three seconds later, she's barging through the front door and hurling herself into my arms. "You're here! You're—wait. How did you get here?" Jazz pulls away and stares at me like I'm a hologram.

"I swam." I wink and pocket my phone.

"And you're here for—" Jazz gasps, then gapes at me like a hungry *humuhumunukunukuapuaa*—the Hawaiian state fish. "Wait. Did your dad sell the house? Are you moving *here*?"

I lift up my hands. "Yes and no."

"You'd better come—" Jazz snaps her mouth shut, as though biting back the rest of her words. When she speaks again, her voice is quieter, cooler. "You'd better come with me to the beach. And tell me *everything*."

"The beach?" I cross my arms and peer into her aunt's house. "Why not inside?"

"Because...it's the beach." Jazz shakes her head and links her arm through mine. "Come on. It's been forever since we hung out by the water."

"But how can you—*oh*." I look at Jazz's legs and gasp. A warm glow runs through me as I stare at her. "Is that *the* leg?"

When I showed up at Gramma's earlier in the year, Jazz was battling bone cancer. I didn't know about it at first, but I sure did when Jazz ended up having part of her left leg amputated a few weeks after I met her.

Jazz's friend from youth group, Brander, and I ended up

launching a fundraiser to get Jazz a prosthesis. And now...tears spring to my eyes for the second day in a row. Not good. I duck my head and blink half a dozen times.

"That's the leg all right." Jazz bends and knocks on its compact metal frame. "I was going to show it to you when we video chatted today. But now you get to see it up close and personal."

"Does it—you know—work?" A sudden swelling in my chest keeps me from saying any more as I examine Jazz's new leg—a sturdy pole ending in a freakishly real-looking foot.

"It works all right." Jazz beams and lifts her new foot. "Check out the bottom. It's got special traction on it so I can go barefoot at the pool."

I nod, then point to the space between the toes. "Can you wear flip-flops?" Jazz would croak if she had to spend the rest of her life in sneakers.

"You mean *slippas*, right? Remember, you're in Hawaii now." Jazz winks at me. "And yeah, I can."

"Wow." I breathe out one long, slow breath, my chest heavy with emotion. Seeing Jazz's leg is neat and all, but still—it's one more reminder that life for her will never be the same.

Fortunately, Jazz, the queen of positivity, doesn't seem to view it as such. Instead, she lowers her foot, barely reaching out to steady herself against the wall. "I can't believe you're really here. This is *so* cool." She lets out another little squeal before glancing back at the house.

"Is everything okay?" I shoot a peek at Jazz as we start down the porch steps. Her long stride is shorter, her steps more cautious than they used to be, but other than that, she's moving like a pro. "With your aunt and stuff?"

Jazz blinks at me, her eyes stretched into sand-dollar sized circles. "We're fine. I didn't want to...wake her. People like to sleep in on Saturdays, you know. Come on, let's go."

"Are you sure you're up to it?" I trail after Jazz as she weed-whacks her way through the overgrown front lawn. "Is this even good for you? What would your doctor say?"

"Doc Freeh?" Jazz shakes her head. "He'd be thrilled. I've told him so much about what you and Brander did with the whole fundraiser thing. Plus, Doc says walking on wet sand helps me build muscle quicker."

"Really?" I arch a brow at Jazz. She'd better not be pulling my leg—so to speak.

"Really." Jazz motions down the street.

I'm not sure I believe her, but if there's one thing I've learned about Jazz during my time on the island so far, it's that she won't take no for an answer. Some people call that stubbornness. Jazz calls it persistence. "Let's go. I want to hear *everything*."

I laugh, and we continue on. Overhead, the midmorning sun is bright and warm. A barely-there breeze kisses my face. The air is sweet, perfumed by plumeria and saltwater. I haven't even been here a day and already I know—

It's good to be home.

Even so, I can't help but glance over my shoulder at the place Jazz is staying before we turn the corner. What is she hiding in there? I've never actually met her aunt, only heard mention of her. Is there something wrong—something I don't know?

I shake myself and refocus on the beautiful Hawaiian morning. I have all year to worry about Jazz and her aunt. And, though I know I'll have to get to the bottom of this sooner rather than later, all I want to do right now is breathe in the wild sea air, walk with my best friend, and bask in the glory of my new town—my new *home.*

Chapter Three

"YOU'RE SERIOUSLY STAYING FOR A *WHOLE year?*" Jazz stops walking and stares at me, frothy waves splashing against her prosthesis. "That is one *big* vacation. How long have you known?"

"Not long." I launch into an abbreviated version of my talk with Dad, ending with Macie's dramatics at the airport yesterday.

Jazz shakes her head and shoves my arm when I'm done. "I can't believe you managed to keep it a secret. And"— Jazz's eyes squinch into slits, and she flashes her trademark Cheshire-cat grin—"does this mean even Brander doesn't know you're here?"

I shake my head, bending to pick up a near-perfect square of white sea glass and slip it in my pocket. "You're the only one who knows. Except for Grams, I mean."

"Wow." Jazz starts walking again, her prosthesis leaving the wet sand with a *slurp.* She stumbles a bit, and my pulse accelerates as I reach to catch her, but she waves me away. "Brander is going to flip when he sees you."

"You think?" My cheeks grow warm at the thought of seeing Brander again.

"Totally." Jazz lowers her voice and leans in close. "I think he missed you."

"Yeah?" I'm about to admit that the feeling was mutual but, if the cocky lift of Jazz's chin is anything to go by, she already had that one figured out. After all, it would be hard *not* to miss him. We spent almost every day working at the Shave Ice Shack together, and then we started the fundraiser for Jazz's prosthesis.

Plus, there were those kisses...

My face grows warm as I'm swept back to that day he kissed me on Gramma's porch swing. Up until that point, we were nothing more than friends. We still aren't, as far as I know, but ...

One doesn't easily forget something like their first kiss. Even if it *was* on the forehead.

"So? Should we?" Jazz stares at me, as though waiting for an answer.

"Should we..." I tilt my head at her. Obviously I missed something.

"I said we should go surprise Brander. He's got a wacky weekend shift at the Shave Ice Shack now that it's the off season, but we could catch him before he leaves for work."

I twine my fingers around my necklace. "You mean go to his house? Now?" An image of Brander's mangy mutt, Rosco, flashes through my brain. My mind's eye instantly zeroes in on the beast's sharp, white teeth, and I cringe.

"You got a problem with that?" Jazz pulls out her phone. "I'll text my aunt to give us a ride."

"But she's sleeping—you shouldn't have to wake her. I can see Brander another time. Or we could just wait for him at the Shave Ice Shack." I reach to grab Jazz's phone, but she's too fast—and tall—for me. With a sweep of one long, toned arm, she's able to hold it out of my reach by a good inch or two. I jump for it, but my five-foot-two-inch frame is no match for Jazz's skyscraper build.

"It's fine. She won't mind." Jazz fires off a text. A few moments later, her phone pings with a response. "She's on her way."

"Great." I choke the word out. After all, Jazz's aunt is getting up early on her day off to drive us. It's the least I can do to be thankful.

And who knows?

Maybe Brander's family has finally decided to ditch Rosco—or at least start locking him away in their dungeon when visitors come.

"Aunt Ruby, this is Olive." Jazz nearly has to yell to be heard over Ruby's heavy metal CD as we climb into her rig and snap on our seatbelts. "The one I've been telling you about."

"Cool." Ruby chomps on her gum, and she glances at Jazz in the backseat before pulling onto the highway and squeezing her massive mega beast—excuse me, minivan— between two luxury sports cars in the next lane.

"Nice to meet you, Ruby." I smile long enough to be polite, then nibble on my lower lip. Ruby's younger than I expected, probably in her mid-twenties, and she has her half-shaved head of hair dyed an outrageous shade of Heinz ketchup-red. An uneven line of sea turtle tattoos parades down the back of her neck, and the only thing that likens her to Jazz is her lithe, lean figure.

I meet Jazz's gaze in the rearview mirror, and she lifts her palms, as if to acknowledge Ruby's eccentricity. My stomach twists, and the smile I offer in return feels plastic.

This is who Jazz has been staying with since I left? I swallow a groan as Ruby's van chugs along the highway at the pace of a lazy sea slug. If only I'd known, I never would have gone back to Boston to begin with. I would have convinced Grams to keep looking after me and Macie—and take Jazz in while she was at it.

"Can Brander give you a ride home? I have to work at noon." Ruby's scratchy voice grates on my nerves like a piece of steel wool, but I nod and glance at Jazz.

"Sure." Jazz leans forward to whisper to me. "So, how are we going to knock this guy's socks off?"

"What do you mean?" I turn and peer at Jazz through the

space between the seat back and the headrest.

"You can't show up at his door and yell 'surprise.' You need to wow him. Let's think." Jazz's enthusiasm is contagious, and I shoo away any lingering thoughts about Rosco as we concoct a plan.

Before I know it, Ruby pulls up in front of a glass-walled monstrosity perched atop a mound of perfectly manicured lawn. "See ya, squirt." She yanks her niece's braid as Jazz clambers out of the car. I jump out and offer my arm for support, but Jazz waves me away.

"I'm not an invalid. Just a peg-legged pirate." Jazz's nose crinkles when she smiles, and she waves for me to follow her up the path leading to the mansion.

Brander Delacroix is one of the most humble, down-to-earth guys I've ever met, but I never would have known it if I hadn't spent the summer working with him at the Shave Ice Shack. Not when his parents own one of the island's most exclusive resorts, and *definitely* not when he runs around the island in any one of his numerous pairs of freshly polished Oxfords.

A dog barks, its low, rumbling *woof* sounding much too near for my own liking, but I wad my hand into a fist and lengthen my stride. I can do this. There's no way I'm going to let Jazz know what a baby I am about—

"*Ruff!*"

A huge, hulking beast with four legs and a wagging tail careens around the side of the mansion, and my heart gives a kick so strong I'm surprised it doesn't launch right out of my chest. Tremors run up my spine as the brute races toward me, studded collar jangling, tongue lolling from his mouth.

My breath escapes my chest in short, frantic puffs as the massive German Shepherd makes a beeline for me. I clutch my necklace and close my eyes. *Please, God, can't he get distracted by a squirrel? Do they even have squirrels in Maui?*

"Oof!"

I open my eyes to find Jazz struggling to keep her balance. Rosco's elephant-sized paws are planted on either side of her chest, and she's patting his oversized head. "Careful, buddy." She gives Rosco a gentle shove, and he drops to all fours. "My balance isn't that good yet."

Rosco plops on his haunches and stares at Jazz like she's the last doggie treat in the pet store. Jazz ruffles the mutt's pointed ears. "Don't you want to say 'hi' to Olive?"

As though he understands, Rosco jumps to his feet and galumphs over to me. He extends his neck to sniff my leg, teeth bared. My pulse kicks up another ten notches, and I flinch before he even has a chance to bite me. I breathe in deep—in and out, in and out, exactly like Mom used to tell me to do—but it doesn't work. Rosco takes one more step toward me, and my terror bursts out in a scream rivaling that of a character in a horror flick.

Rosco screeches to a halt.

"Go away! Shoo!" I flap my hand at him and take a backward step toward Jazz. He cocks his head and lifts a paw, as if to draw near again. Another scream rips my throat, and I turn tail and run, making it almost to the edge of the yard before stopping to catch my breath.

"Olive?" Jazz's voice carries across the way, and I whirl around as she starts toward me, Rosco close on her heels. "You're spoiling the whole surprise."

Before I can explain, flip-flops *phwap* against the ground. Brander appears, almond-shaped eyes stretched into coconut-sized circles, navy button-down hanging loose over a pristine white undershirt. "Rosco, get over here. What are you doing? Whatever you smell, it's not worth tearing up the lawn over." Brander screeches to a halt at the end of the walkway and turns to Jazz. "Are you okay? I heard screaming."

My heart thuds again. Whether it's because of Rosco's

glint-eyed gaze or Brander's low, concerned tone, I can't decide. I strain to catch Jazz's reply, but it's drowned out by Rosco's rough, ragged panting as he draws near. *Easy, boy.* I hold up my hands and step away as Brander and Jazz keep talking.

After what seems like an eternity, Brander turns toward Rosco. He takes a step forward, then stops. Glances at Jazz. Takes another step forward. "Olive?" His voice is tight. He squints at me.

"Yeah, it's me. Call off your beast, and I might even come say hello." The words fly out of my mouth before I can consider them, and I cringe. That was pretty harsh. I'd like to think that Brander would take it as a joke, but it definitely didn't sound that way. In my defense, it's pretty hard to be funny in the midst of a panic attack.

But...

Thankfully Brander doesn't seem to mind. Instead, he races over and shoves Rosco out of the way. "Go home, boy." Rosco dips his head and retreats, but his pace is far slower than I'd prefer. At least he listened to Brander's instructions—doggie day-school must finally be paying off.

"Olive?" Brander's voice rumbles in my ear, and I focus on him. Brander's cowlick, absent of its usual gel, flops over the side of his head. He swallows before taking a step toward me.

"Sorry about all that. Your mutt freaked me out." If Jazz wasn't standing, watching us, this whole scene would be an instant replay of the first time Brander and I met, earlier this year.

"It's okay. For the record, I would have had him locked inside if I'd known you were coming." Brander steps forward and gives my shoulder a pat so soft, so gentle, he might as well be touching a china doll. His hand is warm, and I catch a whiff of his citrusy cologne as he whispers in my ear. "It's good to see you again."

"You too. Sorry again for the commotion. Jazz and I planned on surprising you."

"You definitely did that." Brander pulls away. "Though I'm surprised you managed to get Rosco to cooperate."

I laugh. "Nah, we had a way better surprise for you than me screaming in your front yard. Balloons, fireworks, the whole bit. Blame it on the beast." I lift my hands and shrug. "But whatever. I'm here now."

"For how long?" Brander's hand brushes mine as we turn and start toward Jazz.

"A year." I keep my tone light, airy, and wait for Brander's reaction.

"A year?" His jaw drops so his expression is eerily similar to Jazz's when I first told her. "You're staying all *year*?"

"Yep. Broke into my bank account to pay for the tickets myself."

Brander pounces forward and wraps me in a hug that is neither soft nor gentle. Instead, he practically squeezes every drop of air from my lungs before pulling away. "You *paid* to come here? When you spent the whole summer trying to get away?"

I step toward Jazz. "God has a way of showing people what they really need. And Boston wasn't it."

"How long have you known?" Brander shakes his head as we pull alongside Jazz, who winks and slings her arm around my shoulders.

"Now that you two have had your *moment*, or whatever that whole thing was, care to go inside? My stump is killing me."

"Some moment." I laugh as we walk toward the house. Brander leads the way and I follow along, slowing my stride to match Jazz's slightly less ambitious pace.

"That mutt isn't going to be inside, is he?" I lean close and whisper to Jazz, but Brander must hear me anyway, because he glances over his shoulder at me and pulls out his phone.

"Let me text the housekeeper. She'll make sure Rosco stays out of our way."

The last of my anxiety leaves my chest in a *whoosh,* and I finally let my shoulders drop. It's great seeing Brander again, but if hanging out at his place meant hanging out with Rosco, I would've had to make my escape.

Even without the threat of Rosco looming, my heart rate kicks up as we draw near the house. From my vantage point on the sidewalk, I grossly misjudged the vastness of the Delacroix estate. It's even bigger than I could have imagined, and—I peer past Brander as he slips off his shoes and steps inside the house—is that a *fountain* in the entryway?

Sure enough, it is. And past the fountain is an immaculate, glass-walled living room, which looks out over— the ocean? I blink a few times and squint.

Not the ocean, but one very large, very clean pool. Beyond which is a perfect view of the ocean. I shake my head at the magnificence. My house in the suburbs was nice and all, but this place is on a whole other level.

Jazz doesn't seem to have any qualms about kicking off her worn flip-flops—*slippas*, as she and the other locals call them—and joining Brander inside. I, on the other hand, take my time removing my high-tops and arranging them, toes pointing forward, right beside the doorway.

"Make yourselves comfortable. We can open the doors if you want." Brander waves a hand at the glass windows.

"But how—"

"They're hidden doors. They fold up and turn the place into a patio." Jazz leans in to whisper to me, then backs off and snickers as my breath catches.

Good grief, I've stepped straight into an episode of some rich-people reality show.

The tips of Brander's ears flush red as he leads us into a spotless, stainless-steel kitchen that looks more like the galley of a five-star restaurant and points to an intercom system on the wall. "Want me to call Abigail? She can make us a snack."

"Thanks, but you don't have to."

"Come on, Olive. Let's do it. I'm starved." Jazz bounces on the balls of her—would it be feet, now that she has her new leg? After all, the lump of tanned plastic at the bottom of her prosthesis *is* foot-shaped. With toes and everything. "I was going to make breakfast but then—" Jazz's gaze flits over to me and she frowns. Something is definitely up with her.

But what?

Brander takes me on a mini-tour of the mansion, but with Jazz's secret hanging over my head, I have a tough time paying attention to the twenty-foot soaring ceilings, hand-carved teakwood paneling, or even the hydraulic elevator.

I keep one eye fixed on Jazz as we head outside. Aside from her slightly uneven gait, she looks better than ever—her skin has lost most of its sickly pallor. Her gaze is bright and alert. Maybe she's fine after all—maybe it's me, overthinking it. I mean, she's recovering from *cancer*, for crying out loud.

"So." Brander motions to Jazz with his glass of lemonade after Abigail has supplied us with enough "snacks" to feed half the island. "Have you told Olive your news?"

News? "What's up?" I start to reach for a cheese-stuffed jalapeno, but my hand falters. It can't be bad news, if the way Jazz is grinning is anything to go by—right?

She leans into the cushy chaise and pops a teriyaki meatball into her mouth, chewing for one painfully long moment. "I'm joining the swim team." Her eyes glint at the admission, and her pearly whites sparkle in the late-morning sunshine.

"The..." I bite my lip as my gaze flicks to her prosthesis. "Swim team? Are you sure that's a good idea?"

"Pfft." Jazz blows out, ruffling her bangs, and turns to Brander. "I told you she'd say that. Olive, you're such a worrywart. I'll be fine."

"But why go out for the swim team *now*? I mean, when you've only got—you know." I nod towards Jazz's leg—the fake one.

"I was team captain last year. We would've gone to state, but my leg gave out at the qualifying meet last spring. That's when the doctors found my tumor." Jazz's voice is steady as she says the words, but a cloud falls across her face. "I let them all down. And now it's my chance to make it up to them."

A bird trills in the still morning air, and I stare at my clasped hands. Why hasn't Jazz ever told me this before? I roll my neck from side to side. A million different responses tumble around in my brain, but none of them seem *right.*

Jazz rests a hand on my arm. "Don't feel weird, okay? All I care about is getting in the water again. Doc Freeh gave me the go-ahead."

"You're sure this is something you want to do?" I look into Jazz's smiling face.

She nods and gives my arm a shove. "And, if I want to be ready for team tryouts, I need to start training soon." Something wells beneath the surface of her gaze. She licks her lips. "I think you'd be the perfect training partner."

"Me?" I can practically feel my eyes ballooning on my face. I can do a pretty good freestyle, but I'm far from athletic. "I don't know. Maybe I could time your laps or something, but I'm not—"

"Oh, come on." Jazz clasps her hands in front of her chest and pooches out her lip. She looks so pathetic that I have to laugh.

"Fine." I extend my hand as though shaking on an important business deal. "I'll help." After all we've been through together, I'll do anything for Jazz.

"For real?" Jazz's face is a sudden rainbow of emotion, and she reaches over to give me a hug. I return the gesture, then pull away as she starts rambling about breaststroke and flip turns. I don't know what a flip turn is, but it sounds like something that would make me get water up my nose.

As Jazz continues on, I let my eyes wander over to meet Brander's. He winks at me, and his foot nudges mine underneath the low-slung table. I return the wink, then focus on Jazz again. What is it about her—this entire place— that makes me say yes to the things I'm most opposed to?

I don't know, but I sure hope Brander never asks me to puppy-sit Rosco. Or hang out in the same room as him, for that matter. Because, when it comes to dogs, I will never compromise.

Ever.

Chapter Four

"GRAMS, CAN I TALK TO YOU?" I cross my fingers on both hands, as if for luck, as Gramma pulls out of the driveway to take me to youth group on Wednesday.

"Sure, sweetie." She lowers the volume on her crackly radio and glances over at me. "What about?"

"School." The word is dry in my mouth, but this is a conversation we need to have—sooner, rather than later.

School in Hawaii starts way earlier than it does in Boston. If I get enrolled in the public high school now, I'll be more than the new girl. I'll have half a quarter's catch-up to do.

"Olive?" *Oh. Right.*

The car rocks as Gramma turns a corner, bringing us that much closer to the church. Better get right to the point. "I do *not* want to go to public high school."

Gramma glances at me, forehead scrunched into a washboard of worry lines. "There's no way you can skip school for a whole year. The state wouldn't allow it. Neither would I, for that matter."

"What about Brander's school? He said classes don't start until next week." *Come on, Grams.* I bite my lip, waiting for her response.

A brisk evening breeze blows through the open windows of the station wagon. I pull my sweater tighter around my shoulders as Gramma merges onto the main road. "Brander goes to Lahaina Christian Academy, right?" I nod. "I don't know, Olive—I hear tuition there is pretty expensive. And I'm already readjusting my budget now that I'll be taking care of you girls long-term."

Oh.

My stomach plummets. "I didn't think about that. Public school is"—I choke the words out around a lump in my throat—"fine. It'll be fine." *Fine, walking around the school all year as Invisible Girl. I've done it the last ten years—what's one more?* "Or maybe I could look into homeschool?"

"Do you really want to spend every day cooped up inside with me? Wouldn't you rather be with your peers?"

My peers, most of whom ignore me and the rest of whom smirk at my dorky socks and old-school literature picks? "I dunno. What do you think?"

"I know it sounds frightening, starting over so far from home, but I think you need to jump in with both feet. After the kind of year we've all had, sometimes what we need is a fresh start."

"I guess. But what about—"

Gramma's gaze hardens, and I shut my mouth, teeth clicking together. Better not push my luck. "Public school is fine."

"Thank you." Gramma sighs as we pull in front of the church pavilion. "For being so understanding, I mean. You've grown a lot these last few months." Her eyes are so tender, her smile so soft and sweet, that I almost squirm under her gaze. If she could only know what kind of woe-is-me thoughts I'm thinking half the time, she wouldn't be smiling like that.

And, as I hop out of the car and mount the steps to the church, I'm not smiling either. Because there's no way I'm going to survive a year spent swimming through the halls of the Lahaina public high school by myself. There has to be a better option—one that doesn't involve paying an arm and a leg to enroll in Brander's ritzy prep school.

Lucky Jazz—her doctor didn't love the idea of her hobbling all over the high school so soon after getting her prosthesis, so she's doing homeschool this year.

She doesn't know how good she has it, doing school online. It'll let her take it easy while she rebuilds her strength and immune system. She can catch up from when she fell behind last year, after finding the tumor.

But, knowing Jazz, she'll be stir-crazy within a week.

And besides...I do a mental walk-through of Ruby's house and shudder. That place isn't exactly ideal. If only Jazz and I could do school together—at my place.

And...why can't we?

Hope blooms in my chest as I step into the crowd of kids at youth group. If Jazz and I do school together, Gramma won't be able to say I'm not spending any time with my peers. And I *know* homeschooling can't cost any more than public school. In Massachusetts, at least, there are online programs that work with the state. They must have those here on Maui, right?

And if so—it's perfect.

With homeschool, I won't have to be the new girl, Jazz won't have to spend every day locked up at Aunt Ruby's, and I can help her catch up on the stuff she missed last year.

Now all I have to do is get Gramma on board.

"There you are!" Jazz grabs my arm and pulls me into the buffet line next to her after worship. "Where were you?"

"Sorry, I came in late and got stuck with the beach babes." I jerk my thumb over my shoulder at a group of girls with blinding-white smiles and airbrushed tan complexions.

Jazz snickers, and we shuffle forward in line. I lift my head and sniff the air, which is tinged with the tang of barbecue sauce. *Yum.*

In Hawaii, churches seem to think their parishioners need to get fed with more than just the Good News. At youth group, there's always a dinner break between worship and the teaching. Even though the local-style food is usually kind of wacky, it's actually pretty decent. "What's on the menu tonight?"

"Plate lunch. With ribs." Jazz's eyes light as we reach the head of the line. "One of my favorites."

"Everything's your favorite."

"That's because it's all delicious." She reaches for a plate and piles it with macaroni salad, two scoops of sticky white rice, *and* a sweet Hawaiian roll. "I'd better start carbo-loading now, if I want to be in tip-top shape for tryouts."

"Tryouts?" Someone snorts behind me. "You're going out for the team *again*? We tanked last year, and that's when you had both legs."

I turn to face the speaker—a girl about my age, with skin like rich caramel and dark chocolate-colored hair that cascades over her shoulders in perfect waves. She lifts one thick, manicured eyebrow and juts her chin out toward me. "Who are you?"

"I'm Olive. Jazz's friend." I straighten my spine and meet the girl's gaze, all while becoming more and more aware of my rumpled, maple-colored mane and pale, pasty skin. Everything about me—right down to my tightly laced high-tops—screams *I'm not a local!*

"Jazz's friend?" The girl turns her eyes on Jazz. "Funny, I hung around Jazz at swim team all last year, but she never mentioned you."

"That's because she's a *new* friend." Jazz's prosthesis clunks against the pavilion floor as she takes a step closer to me, juggling her plateful of carbs in one hand. "And she's helping me train for tryouts. Don't worry. I'm sure I won't be captain again this year."

The girl snorts. "Like I thought you had a chance?" She glances at Jazz's prosthesis like it's made of odds and ends from the junkyard. "See you around."

Jazz lifts her free hand, and I do the same as the girl spins on one heel and flip-flops away, hips swishing, hair blowing in the breeze like she's doing a shoot for a Hawaiian teen queen magazine.

"Who was *that*?" Keeping my voice low, I turn to the buffet line with Jazz and hold out my plate for a rack of ribs. "The Queen of Lahaina?"

"Not hardly." Jazz rolls her eyes. "*That* was Malia. I think she's still irked that I beat her out for team captain last year. And even more so that we missed going to state."

"So irked she doesn't have enough decency to be sensitive about your...you know?" I motion to Jazz's leg.

"It's okay. Say it—it's not a bad word." Jazz shakes her head. "Everyone acts so weird about it. Like now that I have a peg leg I'm not *me* anymore."

I focus on my plate, as though my sticky white rice is the most fascinating thing in the room. Jazz stays quiet as we weave through the rest of the line before settling at an empty table by the water. Her face is contorted into a puckered frown, her silvery eyes flicker with something—anger? Sadness?

I take a few bites in silence, but the food is flavorless in my mouth. This is *not* how things are supposed to be going.

"I'm sorry." A clod of rice sticks in my throat, and I swallow again to force it down. "I didn't mean to make things weird. And I shouldn't have—"

"Stop." Jazz holds up a hand and I freeze, one sticky, barbecue-coated rib halfway to my mouth. "It's not you. It's me." She hangs her head, as though the admission is too much to bear. "I'm so—" She stops, breathes out one shuddering breath. When she looks at me, her gaze is watery.

"You don't have to explain." I reach across the table and rest my hand on hers.

Jazz shakes her head, her white-blonde braid slicing the

air with whiplike precision. "No. Hear me out. I'm...I don't know. Everything is so different. And it's *weird*. I'm, like, a freak of nature or something. I was always the odd one out since my mom—" Jazz rolls her lips together, almost as though she's said too much. "But whatever. I want to be *me*. Like—pre-amputation me. Not peg-leg me."

What does she mean, odd one out? Jazz is the life of the party. Everything in me wants to ask, but something in Jazz's wide-eyed expression makes me stop.

She leans across the table and locks her eyes with mine. "You're the only girl that treats me like *me*." Something flickers to life in Jazz's gaze. "Don't ever stop doing that, okay?"

Before I can reassure her, Brander appears and plops into an empty chair between Jazz and me. "Hey, what's up?" He barely waits a millisecond before plowing ahead. "Jazz, did you see? Malia's here."

I snort. "I'm guessing she's not a regular?"

Brander shakes his head, eyes wide. "No. And I've been praying for her ever since I met her at Jazz's swim meet last year."

Of course. Brander makes it his personal mission to pray for every lost person's soul—and he must have a direct line to God, because his prayers always seem to get answered in a fraction of the time mine do.

"I can't believe she actually came. Maybe one of the guys invited her." Jazz plays with the tail of her braid as a peal of laughter from across the room splits the air.

I zero in on Malia, surrounded by not one or two but *five* male admirers. "I think you're on to something, Jazz." I jerk my chin in Malia's direction.

"Figures." A smile tugs at Jazz's mouth. "But at least she's here. I hope Jonah has a good message tonight."

I lower my gaze and pick at my food. Leave it to Jazz and Brander to be praying for Malia. And here I am, wishing she'd hightail it out of here and never return. How does someone get that kind of love? I glance from Jazz to Brander.

I have no idea.

But maybe I should try and find out.

Lucky for Jazz and Brander, Jonah's sermon doesn't disappoint. The youth leader bounds around the speaking platform like it's a basketball court, jumping from one end to the other as he delivers a message of hope, repentance, and forgiveness.

Unfortunately, if the way Malia is making eyes at some surfer guy across the room is anything to go by, she isn't hearing a word.

Jazz sits, notebook out, pen running races across the pages, taking notes like a madwoman. Brander keeps his eyes glued to his Bible. And I...am spying. On Malia. Really, someone could look at me and get the same conclusion—that I'm not paying one lick of attention.

And am I?

I shake myself and sit up straighter in the seat. Why, after all God's done for me—for Jazz—can I not manage to keep my mind on Him long enough to listen to a half-hour sermon?

Bowing my head lower over my Bible, I close my eyes and let Jonah's words wash over me. "God didn't make man to be alone. He created us to crave human interaction—the fellowship we share with other believers." Jonah gestures to the room. "And it's great that we can all come together and study. But sometimes we need something more than that. Maybe some of us here are going through a rough patch. The hardest time of our life.

"That's why we're starting a support group." Jonah stops and spreads his arms wide, as though announcing that he's giving us all coupons for free shave ice.

"Maybe you have a friend that's going through a difficult time—or maybe it's you who could use the extra encouragement. Either way, everyone's welcome. Or..." Jonah lifts a clipboard in the air. "If you'd like to help with the ministry, you can sign up tonight. We'll be meeting on the south end of Ka'anapali Beach from ten to noon every Saturday, starting next month."

Brander perks up immediately and leans over to whisper something to Jazz—probably about how they can drag Malia or another lost soul there.

"Wait—one more thing." Jonah holds up a hand before a wave of chatter can completely wash away his words. "It can be hard to get people to come to something like this. People tend to shy away from a group support system. Which is why we have an incentive for them. Free food."

Jazz giggles, and Jonah goes on to describe plans for a weekly picnic. "We'll also need volunteers to help with that. Come talk to me or sign up if you're interested," he adds before officially closing his sermon.

We all stand as he leads us in a prayer, then he dismisses us, and the crowd begins to thin.

"Shave ice?" Brander raises his brows at Jazz and me, and I can't keep from bouncing on the balls of my feet.

"You bet." Shave ice after youth group was Jazz and Brander's Wednesday-night tradition since way before I came on the scene. And since Brander works at the Shave Ice Shack, that means we all get a discount.

As we file out of the pavilion, Brander leans over, his breath tickling my ear. "What do you think about the support group thing?"

"It's cool, I guess." An image of a tall, pinch-faced lady who worked at Mom's hospital flashes through my mind. She was the grief counselor, the one who was supposed to give me a warm shoulder to cry on. Except, the only time I tried to talk to her, she started in on a lecture on the five stages of grief. Like I needed to hear *that* when my mom was slipping away.

But maybe the support group here will be different. "I hope it helps a lot of people."

"So you don't want to..." Brander wets his lips with his tongue and shrugs his shoulders.

"Volunteer? Nah." I offer Jazz an arm for support as we descend the pavilion steps.

"Are you sure? I'm—"

"You and Jazz can go right ahead. You're great at that stuff, but it's not my thing. I'm a behind-the-scenes person." But put me in a support group, in the middle of a group of miserable teens?

No. Way.

Brander nods. Though I doubt my answer was what he was hoping for, he doesn't press the issue. Instead, he leads the way to his spiffy red Porsche convertible and opens the door. I crawl over the passenger seat and plop into the back as Brander helps Jazz into the front seat.

She turns to face me the second she gets settled. "I need to get in the water. Tryouts are coming up soon and right now, I feel like a lazy old sea urchin. You game for helping me?"

"I'm ready when you are."

"Maybe we can go next Wednesday? We could do a few laps during the day, when it won't be so crowded."

"Sure, I'll..." The rest of my answer dies on my tongue. *I'll be in school.* I make a fist and press it against my leg. "I'll check with Gramma."

Jazz's face brightens a million watts, and she punches a fist in the air as Brander zooms out of the parking lot and pulls onto the main road. "Thanks, Olive." She's nearly yelling, but I can barely hear her over the sound of the wind—and the Porsche's motor. "I knew I could count on you."

Jazz is counting on me? I bite my lip. I'd better be able to talk Gramma into this homeschooling thing. And fast.

Chapter Five

GRAMMA AND MACIE ARE FAST asleep the next morning when I slip onto the front porch. The promise of sunrise is no more than a faint whisper on the horizon, and I settle myself on the swing, tucking my bare feet up beside me.

I've got a chest filled with determination, a handful of #2 pencils, and a notebook—the one that's supposed to be for my AP chemistry class.

Except...

There's no way I'm going off to school next week. Not only would I be a fish out of water, I'd be letting Jazz down. Big time. In all reality, homeschool is the perfect—the only—option.

Unfortunately, if what I learned this summer is anything to go by, Gramma won't let me ditch school unless I have a very good reason. Which is why I'm up at the crack of dawn.

I need a solid argument—cold, hard facts—if I want to have any chance of doing school online. If that doesn't work, *then* I'll play the sympathy card. Surely Gramma hates the idea of Jazz spending the year cooped up in Ruby's house five days a week as much as I do.

The next hour passes in a whirl of studies and statistics. By the time I'm done, I have more than enough evidence to argue my case. Especially since I hardly have any more credits to earn, thanks to Dad's high expectations and my old school's slew of double-credit courses and honors classes.

By the time Gramma calls me in to breakfast, I'm ready.

"Look what Grammy made us." Macie lifts her plate as I

step into the kitchen. A stack of pancakes, smothered in syrup, nearly slides onto the floor, but Macie steadies her mess in the nick of time.

"Looks good, Grams." I hop onto a stool at the breakfast bar and send off a quick prayer—with an extra plea for my persuasive efforts—before digging in to my own stack of pancakes.

"Is this coconut syrup? It's great." I point to the plate with my fork after a few bites of fluffy, sugary deliciousness. A few compliments never hurt anything. Before I can dive into my prepared oration, Macie lets out a sniffle and a whine. "What's up, squirt?"

Her lip is pooched out, her eyes downcast. "I don't look right." She snuffs again and pushes away her half-empty plate. Yikes. If Macie is refusing perfectly good food—pancakes, no less—then her pity party has the potential to turn into an untamable temper tantrum.

"What do you mean?" Gramma wrinkles her brow and steps around the breakfast bar to give Macie a hug. "You're my big, bold, and *beautiful* granddaughter. How could you not look right?"

"I'm not tan. And I don't have cool *slippas* like the other girls." Macie ducks her head and glares at her sparkly light-up sneakers. "And they'll probably bring Spam for lunch, and I'll only have sweets."

Before I can interject and assure Macie that ninety-nine percent of the population would *way* rather eat sweets than canned ham, Gramma jumps into action, swiping her keys from the counter and motioning toward the door. "Then hurry up and finish your breakfast. We'll get you *slippas*. And Spam. And anything else you need. Olive, you should tag along. We can double-check to make sure you've got everything on that school supply list. You still have it?"

I have it all right, buried deep in Gramma's garbage can. But maybe—this could be the perfect time to plead my case. Convince Gramma that it's my year to become a homeschooler. "I know what I need." *And it's not anything for that public high school.*

"Grams?" I lean over and whisper to her as Macie tries on her fifth pair of flip-flops at a tacky boutique-wannabe stuck in a corner of the Lahaina Cannery Mall.

Gramma barely looks up from sorting through her hodgepodge of coupons. "Don't you want to try anything on? I have a coupon for *slippas* right here—buy one, get the other shoe free." Her goofy grin reveals she's joking.

I have to close my eyes to keep them from rolling around like a wayward beach ball.

"Seriously, though. I'd love to get you something."

"I'm good. All I need is some time to talk."

"Oh?" Gramma raises a brow.

My stomach twists, but I swallow hard against my nerves. "Listen, I know I can't go to private school with Brander, but maybe I could—"

"Look at me!" Macie prances up, modeling a pair of sequined pink flip-flops with garishly giant flowers stuck to the straps. I guess finding haute couture in a renovated pineapple cannery *would* be too much to expect. "I want these."

"Beautiful, sweetie." Gramma motions for Macie to take them off and stand at the counter with us. "Are you sure you don't want a new pair?" She turns to me as we wait in line. "Come on, let me spoil my granddaughters."

"Actually, I'd rather—" before I can get a word out about homeschooling with Jazz, Gramma plucks a pair of gray striped flip-flops—size seven—from a nearby rack and holds them up. I reach out to finger the knotted rope straps. "They *are* my size..."

"Done." Gramma's lips quirk up, and she plops the shoes

onto the counter next to Macie's plunder.

I choke out a thank-you and tighten my grip on my notebook. There's got to be a way to get Grams to listen, but not while Macie's running around like a turbo-powered grasshopper.

Usually she wears herself out at some point, but today she runs us ragged, spending the better part of an hour picking out notebooks, binders, and pencils. And it takes half an hour for her to finally find the right lunchbox—one that looks like a giant can of Spam, of all things.

Then, in the true manner of *Give a Mouse a Cookie*, she decides that she doesn't want to stop there. Instead, she begs Gramma to drop her off for a play date with Leilani, one of her friends from church camp.

Grams must be in a good mood, because she agrees. Even though it means going out of our way, it works in our favor. Leilani's mom offers to drop Macie at Gramma's place after dinner, and Gramma decides to run another quick errand.

By the time we pull in front of Foodland, Hawaii's favorite grocery store, I finally have the perfect opportunity to plead my case to Grams without Macie around.

Inside the store, Gramma grabs a cart and strides toward the produce department like an army general. "What do we need?" She hands me a rumpled piece of paper, covered front and back with her loopy script.

"Pineapple." I read a few more items off the list, then shove it in my pocket and hold up my notebook. "Can we talk now?"

"Certainly." Gramma blazes through the aisles, grabbing everything on the list and half a dozen other items, including a loaf of...

I blink and squint at the bread. "It's purple."

"Yep." Gramma laughs. "Taro bread is a favorite here. You'll fit right in."

"I don't need to fit in."

"Really?" Gramma turns down another aisle.

"I want to do school at home. With Jazz." I trot after her. "I'm helping her get in shape to try out for the swim team, and she's going to be training during the day. Besides, think of how lonely she must be, doing school alone at Ruby's all day. And then—" I stop short of mentioning whatever weirdness was going on when I stopped by Jazz's house last week. Even without that part, Gramma's expression is nearly putty by the time I'm done explaining. I grab a can of macadamia nuts and twine my necklace around one finger as I wait for her response.

"No."

Say what? I drop the macadamia nuts into the cart with a *clang*. "But Grams—"

She holds up a hand, and I screech to a halt in the middle of the canned food aisle. "It's impractical. I'm far too busy to teach you two, and I doubt you'd be able to handle it on your own. Especially considering Jazz's situation."

"Situation? What do you mean?" I grab a trio of Spam cans and toss them in the cart.

Gramma cocks her head to the side. "I shouldn't say."

"Seriously? After everything Jazz and I have been through together, you won't tell me?" I shake my head. "Come on Grams."

She frowns and opens her mouth. Probably to scold me for my tone of voice which, I'll admit, is a little harsh.

"Sorry," I say before she can start in on me. "I just want to know. She's my best friend, and it kills me to not know what's up with her."

Gramma stares at me, her gaze boring into my own. "Okay. But remember I'm telling you this because I know how much you care about Jazz. *Not* because she'd want you to hear it."

I mime zipping my lips and nod for her to continue, but

something niggles at the far corner of my brain. Does Gramma know something I don't? Could the cancer have returned?

No.

I close my fist around my necklace and follow after Gramma as we start moving again. There's no way Jazz would hide something like that from me. Her best friend.

"Jazz..." Gramma lowers her voice as we pass by the seafood counter, as though the live lobsters will eavesdrop and tattle to Jazz. "She's been struggling for a while now—since before the cancer."

Struggling? Jazz? I shake my head. There's no way that ball of sunshine could have any more problems—at least, she *shouldn't*. It's not fair.

Unfortunately, if I've learned one thing in the last year, it's this—life is often far from fair.

And that, in itself, is totally not fair.

I shake my head and tune back in to Gramma. "Toward the middle of last year, Jazz's grades fell so low she got suspended from the swim team until she worked up to a B average. She was barely scraping by, and even that was far from easy for her."

Ouch. I wince out of embarrassment for Jazz. I bet Malia gets straight A's.

"By the time Jazz discovered the lump, it was almost time for finals..."

"But instead of studying, she was stuck in a doctor's office." I finish for Grams, concern for Jazz pulling at my heart as we make our way to the front of the store.

"I'd hate to see Jazz struggle, especially without competent help around to give her individualized attention. If the gallery wasn't so busy this time of year, I'd be more than happy to step in and tutor her, but..." Gramma pulls a chopstick from her tangled bun and her gray hair spills around her shoulders.

"I get all that." I lean in closer as we wait in line. "Jazz *would* have individualized attention." At least, kind of.

Gramma raises a brow. "From whom?"

I jab a thumb toward my chest. "I finished last year with a four-point GPA. I could have graduated early if—" my voice falters. I gulp down my tears before they can escape. Even after all these months, I can't think about Mom without—a stray tear pricks my eye—crying.

Mercifully Gramma ignores the tear and instead lays a hand on my shoulder. "I admire what you're trying to do, sweetie. And I know Jazz would be honored. But I don't think it's the wisest decision. Not right now."

With those words, my eyes flood all the more. I force my chin up and down, then turn and stare at the tabloid rack, as though I care which celebrity is headed for rehab next. Why doesn't Grams get it? Jazz would be so much better off with me than she would be at Ruby's place. And so would I.

"Don't pout." Gramma's words are low as she steps up to the checkout stand and places her groceries on the conveyer belt.

"Fine." The word is wooden and brittle as it comes out of my mouth, and I'm sure Gramma knows as well as I do that I have no intention of keeping my word.

Because, even if this whole arrangement *is* the best choice for Jazz—and I highly doubt that—I know one thing.

It's definitely not the best choice for *me*.

Later that afternoon, I'm curled up in Gramma's oversized, plumeria-slipcovered armchair, texting with Dad while Macie takes inventory of her new school supplies. She's got enough pairs of *slippas* to start a shoe store, and half as many island-style dresses, plus that tacky Spam lunchbox and a bunch of other, more conventional, back-to-school items.

"I can't wait for Monday, can you?" Macie turns to me, chocolatey eyes wide, cockeyed curls flying every which way. "Everyone is going to be so excited to meet us!"

I snort at Macie's farfetched optimism, then turn to the phone. Maybe I can get Dad to talk some sense into Gramma.

Gramma wants me to go to public high school. There's no way. Can you talk to her?

Dad's reply is quick:

No.

My thumbs start working overtime as I tap out a rebuttal, but Dad is faster:

Your schooling is your grandmother's decision. Respect her wishes.

I sigh and roll my eyes at the ceiling, but he's right. Like it or not, I'm stuck. And if I'm not careful, I'm going to turn into a brat about it. I tell Dad as much—save for the brat part—and we exchange a few more messages before saying goodbye.

As soon as we do, Gramma walks into the room, almost as if on cue. And then, before she can even say anything, the words—words I didn't even know I had the guts to say—are spilling out of my mouth.

"I'm sorry, Grams." My voice is smooth and steady, even though everything inside of me is cowering in embarrassment. "For being snarky earlier. It's...I'm sad for Jazz." *And for me.* Thankfully, those words stay tucked inside my brain where they belong.

Gramma's brows shoot up and a smile plumps her rosy

cheeks. "I understand." Her words are heavy with conviction. "It's hard to be unable to help a friend in need. But sometimes we have to trust—and let God work out the details."

Before Gramma can say any more, her clunky landline in the kitchen rings. Macie nearly jumps out of her skin and shoves her fingers in her ears. "It's too *loud*." Her voice is tighter than an overfilled water balloon, and Gramma hurries to answer the call.

"Hello?" She presses the earpiece against her face, eyes wide, for a few seconds before lowering her voice and stepping into the hall. The kinky phone cable stretches around the wall until it looks like an overextended rubber band, but the reception must be okay—Grams stays tucked away in the hall for what feels like forever, her hushed words drowned out by the waves crashing beyond the front window.

By the time she returns, the sun is hanging low in the sky, and Macie has organized both boxes of crayons in reverse rainbow order. Curiosity tickles the nape of my neck, but I chomp on my tongue to keep from asking who was running their mouth on the other line. After all, I know that Gramma will only explain if she wants to, and no amount of begging or coercing will convince her otherwise.

"That was Jazz." Gramma's words are simple, but the glint in her eye reveals otherwise. "Olive, what do you think about tutoring?"

Before I can explain that, up until last year, I spent my afternoons tucked away in a corner of the public library, helping half a dozen struggling grade-schoolers, Gramma continues. "If what you told me about your GPA is true, and the school allows it, I might be willing to let you and Jazz give this homeschooling thing a chance. As long as you're sure this tutoring business won't get in the way of your own schoolwork."

"Are you serious?" My eyes must widen to the size of

sand dollars—or bigger—because Macie marches right over and waves a hand in front of my face.

"Are you okay?" Macie blinks at me. "Can you still see?"

"I'm fine. But...." I let my eyes fall shut a moment before I lift my head to look at Gramma. "What changed your mind?"

"You teenagers can be awfully persuasive, did you know that?"

I shake my head, excitement fizzing inside of me. "Homeschool? You're serious?"

Gramma nods. "I suppose there's no harm in it, as long as you're sure helping Jazz play catch-up won't interfere with your own work."

"You mean Olive gets to stay home all year? With *Jazzie*?" Macie gapes at Grams like a discombobulated sea turtle, then her gaze falls upon her pile of new school supplies, and she snaps her mouth shut. "Won't she miss school?"

Leaving Gramma alone to answer Macie's questions, I race up the stairs to my room, taking the steps two at a time and sending off a silent thank-you to God.

Thank you, Lord, for making this work. Now, if you could help me hold up my end of the bargain, that would be great.

There's no way I'll let Jazz wither away at Ruby's house. There's no way I'll admit defeat and start classes at the public high school mid-term. I'll do whatever it takes to make this thing work—for all of us.

I have to.

Chapter Six

"I DON'T KNOW HOW YOU DID it but *thank you*." Jazz drops her backpack on the coffee table and nearly collapses onto Gramma's couch next Monday morning. "I was going to go crazy if I had to spend one more week stuck at Auntie's place all day."

"Me? No way. It was all you." I turn to the window and wave goodbye to Brander as he pulls away from the curb. He was our missing puzzle piece—the perfect chauffeur for Jazz while Ruby is working swing shift—and, thankfully, he's happy to help out. "Grams was convinced it was a bad idea until she got on the phone with you."

"Whatever." A shadow flits across Jazz's face, beneath her wide-eyed smile. "I'm glad it worked."

"Same here." I plop onto the couch next to Jazz, and we get started.

Unfortunately, it's a bit of a slow start. By the time Gramma leaves to walk Macie to the bus stop an hour later, Jazz has barely made it through the first chapter of her biology textbook.

"You doing okay?" I lay aside my literature book—*Pride and Prejudice*, which I've already read half a dozen times—and peer at a simple diagram of a cell.

"Sure." Jazz nods, but her chin hitches, and she shakes her head. "No. This dumb cell is making me see spots."

I glance again at the drawing—looks simple enough to me—and frown. "What's the problem?"

"It's bo-oring." Jazz sticks out her tongue at the book. "I'd way rather read about swimming. Or talk about it." She clasps her hands over her heart and stares at me. "Ready for a break?"

My gaze wanders to my dog-eared copy of *Pride and Prejudice*. "Why don't we both finish our chapters first?"

"Fine." Jazz crinkles her nose, but she softens the expression with a smile before turning to her work. Even so, by the time she finally finishes reading and fills out the corresponding worksheet, it's nearly noon.

Maybe this is going to be harder than I'd thought.

I don't voice my concern to Jazz, though. Instead, I head to the kitchen and grab the veggie wraps Grams made for us this morning. As we eat, Jazz keeps up a running conversation about all things swimming. Before we start work again, we already have plans made to go to the community pool after we finish our work tomorrow.

"Thanks again for helping me." Jazz slings an arm around my shoulders and hugs tight before pulling away. "With school, swimming—everything."

"That's what friends are for. And besides, we're more than friends now. We're *ohana*." I smile, hearing the Hawaiian word coming from my own mouth. "Family. And family always helps each other out."

"Yeah." There's a catch in her voice, but she flips her braid over one shoulder and reaches for her math book like all is right in the world. Within minutes, her nose is buried deep somewhere between a parallelogram and an isosceles triangle. Still, even under the guise of concentration, she looks different—off, somehow. Her forehead is scrunched up like an old-fashioned washboard, and she nibbles on her lip like she's a nervous hamster. I keep one eye fixed on her as I reach for my own book.

Maybe it's school that's giving her grief, or maybe it's something else. My mind flits back through everything that's happened since I came back to Maui. Jazz's attitude could be a simple case of nerves—over the loss of her leg, the impending swim team tryouts, her unsteady GPA—or it could be something...else.

It's up to me to figure it out.

Even with half my efforts devoted to observing Jazz's mood swings and helping her decipher the more perplexing mathematical jargon, I manage to finish my afternoon's worth of work first.

"Let me know if you need any more help." I snuggle against the pillows, a warm breeze blowing in from an open window, and flip to the next chapter in *Pride and Prejudice*. Might as well start chipping away on tomorrow's workload. Besides, this is my favorite book—one that Mom and I read together more times than I can count.

As I lose myself among the crinkled pages, the familiar words wash over me. I fall so deeply into the story that I can almost hear Mom's voice, swooping high for the flighty young ladies, then pitching low for Mr. Darcy's condescending tone.

And then...

I turn a page, and something flutters to the ground from between the pages of my book. Buried up to her eyeballs in research for a civics essay, Jazz barely stirs as I bend to retrieve the fallen paper. My fingers skim against the ground, brushing first the dusty floors, then the glossy surface of—I grab hold of it—a photo?

The couch creaks as I lean back and study the picture. It's from a year or two ago, when Mom and I tried our hand at English country dancing, complete with full Regency dress and goofy, old-fashioned hairstyles. We're standing in front of the camera, arms slung around each other, smiles nearly about to split our faces. We were awful at the dancing, but we had a lot of fun. We had even planned on going again.

Until...

A pang grows in my chest until my heart is completely cloaked in the burning agony of unshed tears. I mutter a half-excuse about going to the bathroom before running into the powder room at the end of the hall.

My knees wobble as I sink onto the toilet seat, a tear slipping out despite my best efforts to keep it contained. Another comes, then another. I clench my jaw and swipe at my eyes, but Mom's voice keeps ringing in my ears, torturing me with its deceptive nearness. I clamp my eyes shut and stroke the shell on my necklace with one finger. If only Mom was—

"You okay in there?" Jazz's voice floats under the crack between the door and the scuffed tile floor.

"Yep." My voice is taut with the strain of a thousand more unshed tears, but I grab a tissue and blot at my face before squaring my jaw and stepping back into the hall.

"Are you sure?" Jazz squints at me and scrunches her nose as she limps after me.

"Positive."

"What? Is it a sad book?"

"You've never read it?" I sit on the couch and wait for Jazz to join me. Maybe Jazz's lack of scholarly skills will work to my advantage this time around.

"*Pride and Prejudice?*" She flops onto the couch and nudges her stack of textbooks aside. "No way. Don't plan on it, either, if it's *that* sad."

"Yeah, it's sad. Depressing, actually." I slip the photo into my pocket—hopefully before Jazz can see—and nod at her stack of work. "All done?"

"Finally." Jazz sags against the pillows right as a horn honks from outside. A peek out the window reveals Brander's Porsche idling by the sidewalk. "Wanna see if Brander can help us snag a free shave ice?"

I lift a shoulder, the picture in my pocket practically burning through the fabric of my shorts. "Maybe another day." I should say yes. It would be better for me to get out of here, do something other than mourn over a crumpled photo, but I can't. Not now, when this gray cloud of sadness has rolled in and stolen all of the day's fun.

Instead, after I help Jazz down the front steps, I crawl upstairs to my room, sag onto my bed, and pull out the picture of me and Mom. Light pours from the window, glinting off of the shave ice necklace—the one Brander gave me before I left for Boston—that hangs from my bedside lamp.

Why would *this* picture—of all things—make me morph into a sniveling baby?

Except it's not *this picture*. It's anything. Or, more accurately, *everything*. Every memory, every picture, every time I'm forced to examine the Mom-shaped hole in my heart, sends me right back to that horrible day in the hospital room.

The Day We Said Goodbye.

And right now it's too hard—too painful—to deal with any of it.

So I won't.

Giving the picture one last glance, I let my finger trace Mom's face, curl around her halo of cropped golden waves, before I shove it underneath my pillow.

And then—only then—do I let the tears fall.

Because, whether I'm willing to admit it to myself or not, I really, really miss my mom.

By the time Gramma's station wagon growls into the driveway later that afternoon, I've cried myself dry, and the only thing I got out of the experience is one whale of a headache. I'm about to drag myself downstairs when Macie barges into the bedroom, a stormy scowl etched on her face.

"What's wrong?" I wait for her answer—but, if her blotchy, tear-stained cheeks are anything to go by, she didn't do much better on her first day of school than I did.

"Everything." She throws her princess-kitty backpack onto the floor and gives it a swift, square kick.

"Whoa." I jump off the bed and move to stop Macie before she can do anything more violent. No one should get away with kicking a cat, even if it's not a real one. "Want to talk about it?"

Macie shakes her head and manages to stay silent a whole twelve seconds before the words start spilling out. "We're learning how to talk Hawaiian, but I don't know how to say anything but *aloha,* and the rest of the kids talk like pigeons."

Pigeons? I raise an eyebrow, but Macie keeps going.

"The boys all tried to kick my lunchbox. Most of the girls already have friends, and"—Macie's lip quivers— "everyone keeps talking about their *ohana,* and *I don't have one!*" Macie's voice creeps up until it's louder than a tsunami warning signal.

"Girls?" The front door slams, and Gramma's slow, measured footfalls pad up the stairs. "What on earth is going on up there?"

"Don't ask me." The words come out in a squeak, Macie's hysterics about her lack of *ohana* reverberating in my ears. "*I* was trying to relax."

"What about you, Macie?" Gramma steps into the room and squats in front of my sister. "You seemed fine in the car. What's the problem now?"

Macie repeats her mini-rant, except this time, the emphasis is placed on the kids that talk like pigeons.

"Actually, honey, it's called *pidgin.*" Gramma places a hand on Macie's shoulder and guides her toward the door. I follow a few steps behind, casting one final glance over my shoulder at the shave ice necklace. "Some of the locals use it here."

"Like a secret language?" Macie cocks her head at Gramma as they descend the stairs. I follow behind, Macie's words about *ohana* hanging heavy on my heart, and I tune out as Gramma explains the origins of Hawaii's pidgin language.

By the time Gramma's done talking, Macie is marching around the house talking about *brah*s and *grind*s and who-knows-what else, and Gramma has dinner all ready to go. After we sit and say grace, Gramma turns her attention on me.

"How was your day?"

I take an extra-big forkful of pineapple and chew as I form a proper answer. "It was good. But we're reading this book in Literature and it—"

"Is it about a dog? My teacher read us a dog story today." Macie reaches for a sweet roll.

"No, thank goodness." *But it might as well be.* I don't say as much out loud, but Gramma seems to pick up on my meaning anyway. She casts a syrupy, pitying gaze my way and nudges my foot under the table.

After dinner, as soon as Macie has gone to play in the hibiscus grove out back, Gramma touches my arm. "You okay?"

I lift a shoulder. "Tired."

"Other than that?"

I look up to meet Gramma's gaze. Her eyes—the same shade of clear, deep blue as Mom's—are wide and caring. If I could trust myself to explain without bursting into tears again, I would. But if the events of this afternoon are anything to go by, there's no point in fooling around with something as messy as emotions when my faucet of tears is already leaky. "I'll be okay."

"Remember, I'm here to talk if you need me." Gramma casts me a look, mouth crimped into a frown, eyebrows scrunched together, before motioning toward the sink. "Help me with the dishes?"

I pick up a plate and plunge it into the dishwater. A trio of bubbles float up from the sudsy water, and they catch the early-evening light pouring in from the window, turning into swirling rainbows. I let my eyes wander, tracing the paths of the bubbles until the glistening globes burst, one by one, vanishing into the golden light.

"Did you hear about the support group at church?" Gramma's words split through the shimmering quiet like a chainsaw, and I nearly drop the plate I've been scrubbing. Why does everyone keep bringing it up? It's not like I'm emotionally stable enough to be a volunteer at something like that, and I'm sure not going for myself.

"They talked about it at youth group. Why? Are you helping with the food?"

"No..." Gramma shakes her head. "Just wondering. Pastor Dave's excited about it."

I nod, and we lapse into silence, the only noise coming from the swishing dishwater and chattering birds beyond the open window, until Gramma speaks again. "Have you thought about it?"

"Thought about what?" I rinse suds off my hands and cross my arms. There's no way on this island I'm actually going to consider going to that support group, if that's what she's asking.

"Support group."

I almost scoff, but I catch myself. Right now, my best line of defense is to play dumb. Don't let Grams see my heart, shattered like a thousand pieces of sea glass. "Not my thing. I'm better helping with stuff behind the scenes. I mean, who knows what kind of kids might show up?" A roomful of tattooed, ex-juvenile-delinquents and half-stoned teenagers floods my imagination, and I shake the image away. Even though I'm having a hard time getting used to everyday life without Mom, that doesn't mean I'm one of *them*. Does it?

"Ah." Gramma nods sagely. "I know putting yourself out there like that can sound unnerving. But remember, sometimes God calls us to do things that are outside of our comfort zone."

"Don't you think I've been pushed out of my comfort zone enough lately?" I rinse a dish and scrub at it with Gramma's ratty old dishtowel before putting it away.

"Maybe." Gramma hands me another plate to dry, her gaze deep with something I can't quite decipher. "But some things aren't up to us. They're up to God."

Chapter Seven

I PLUNGE INTO THE POOL and nearly scream as the cool water sucks me down to its icy depths. Clearly the good people of Maui are tired of the warm, temperate ocean waters, because the community pool is *freezing.*

"What on earth?" My words come out as a shriek when I resurface a few seconds later. "Why didn't you tell me I'd be taking an ice bath today?"

"Don't be a baby." Jazz softens her snicker with a smile and dog-paddles to my side. Her stroke is uneven, thanks to her one-legged state, and her breath comes out in wheezy little puffs, but she's actually *swimming.* With one leg. How does this girl do it? "Come on—the others are here." She swims over to the side of the pool and waves at a group of kids, some of whom I recognize from youth group—Malia included. They instantly strike up a conversation about training schedules, kickboards, and swim caps, but Malia stays quiet. And, if her snide smirk is anything to go by, she's already plotting her next verbal attack.

Rolling my eyes, I flip onto my back and stare up at the sky above the pool. It's bright blue and clear as a diamond, but a few clouds hover over the craggy West Maui Mountains.

Dear God, please keep those clouds over there. Jazz's training session can't get rained out—not today. And help me to be able to—

Splash.

"Hey!" I flip over and rub chlorine water out of my eyes before shooting a mock glare at Jazz. "There *are* better ways to get my attention, you know."

"It worked didn't it? Ready to race?" Jazz's voice goes low, and she juts an elbow toward the crowd gathered at the side of the pool. "Everyone's supposedly here to work, but I think they're here for the Jazz show."

Great. That's *what we need.*

A frown flicks over Jazz's face. "I guess I shouldn't have told anyone."

"What's the big deal? Might as well show them what they have to compete against."

"That's the spirit." Jazz gives my shoulder a teasing punch before dogpaddling to the wall.

I follow, my cheeks already burning. It's not that I'm a *bad* swimmer necessarily, but I'm certainly not up to swim-team standards. Helping Jazz is one thing, but doing it in front of an audience? It's enough to make me want to dunk back into the water. And stay there for a long, long time.

Instead, I grab hold of the wall, arm and leg muscles tensing as I wait for one of Jazz's swim team friends to give the signal.

A scrawny guy with an uneven crew cut holds one hand high in the air and starts the countdown, his voice cracking as he yells. I laugh as he whistles in place of an air horn, and I end up with a nose full of water on the first stroke.

Lifting my head above the water, I suck in a gasp of air, but my throat burns like someone poured a whole bottle of chlorine down my nose. Why couldn't Jazz have wanted to try out for the chess team?

My teeth ache as I grit them together against the burning in my nose, but I keep pushing forward against a symphony of cheers from Jazz's swim team friends. I keep my eyes closed tight against the water, kick as hard as I can with my legs, until—

Ouch.

My elbow conks against the pool wall. I wince and rub

my arm as I surface to an eerie hush. When I open my eyes, they fill with tears brought on by the harsh glare of sunshine, but more tears come as I watch Jazz struggle to propel herself across the last few yards.

"You won." She grabs onto the edge of the wall and faces me, a tight smile denying any feelings of disappointment. She's breathing in ragged little gasps, but the spark in her eyes reveals the truth—Jazz *loves* being in the water. "Want to go again? This time I won't go easy on you."

Her words must carry across the pool, because a resounding cheer rises up from her old teammates. Their enthusiasm is contagious. It sparks a fire in my heart that fuels me as we push off again. Thankfully, the burning in my nose has subsided, and I'm able to concentrate on my stroke.

Each time my arm slices through the water, I'm pierced by an icy knife. But as I reach the middle of the pool, the sensation begins to fade. I turn my attention to my breathing. Every other stroke, I lift my head above the water to suck in a quick breath. Every time, Jazz is right on my tail.

Until...

She's not.

My stroke falters. Jazz is a few feet away, treading water as though her life depends on it. Her silvery gaze has turned to flint, her face seems to have buckled under the weight of a stony scowl.

"Jazz?" I reach her in a couple of strokes. "What are you doing?"

She doesn't answer, but something radiates from her eyes, and it hits me straight in the heart. "Are you okay?"

Jazz jerks her head back and forth, then shuts her eyes. I reach for her hand, and my stomach turns over as I half-drag her to the edge of the pool. *What's wrong?* I want to scream the words that are burning within me, but I don't. If the contorted mask of pain on Jazz's face is anything to go by, she wouldn't be able to answer me anyway.

Jazz stays silent, eyes shut tight as I help her up the pool ladder. One of the swim team kids from youth group tosses me a towel, and I catch it before wrapping it snugly around Jazz's shoulders. She blinks at me, gaze wide and frightened, and I give her my arm for support as she sits.

The rest of the team hovers a safe distance away, and I bend low to whisper in Jazz's ear. "Do you need me to get more help?"

She shakes her head. "Phantom pain." The words are choked. Her eyes flash a million shades of gray, and pain churns in her gaze.

"Hey, is she okay?" The pimple-faced crew cut guy's voice cracks as he hollers.

I turn toward the group. "Give us a few minutes?" I don't bother waiting for a response before turning to Jazz.

"Would aspirin help? I might have a bottle in my purse."

Jazz scoffs out a weak, wavering laugh. "I'd need a lot more than aspirin."

"Oh." I shuffle my feet before bending to sit next to Jazz.

"Do you mind? I need space." Each syllable is short, clipped—like someone hacked each one off with a razor—and she rocks on the bench, face twisted.

Oh. My heart crunches in my chest, but I nod and step away.

"Is she okay?" The speaker's voice is soft, halting.

I turn and face one of the girls from youth group. "She said it's phantom pain."

"Oh." The girl nods, as though this explains everything. And maybe it does. Only a few minutes later, Jazz hops over as though nothing happened.

"Sorry." She addresses the crowd before turning to me. "Sometimes the ghost of my leg likes to show up and make me think it's still attached. And boy, does it hurt." Jazz smiles but, despite her jovial tone, there's a blade of steel hiding between her words as she collapses onto a nearby bench.

"And you still expect to make the team?" Malia pushes to the front of the group and stares at Jazz, arms crossed tightly over her rather abundant chest. "What happens if we make it to Nationals and *that* happens?"

"I dunno." Jazz runs a hand over her stump.

"You don't know? So we'll wait until then and see?" Malia scoffs, her deep brown eyes darkening until they turn almost black. "We already lost last year." *Because of you*, her tone implies. I wince. Her admonition, though silent, is as piercing as if she'd said it aloud.

"Is this what swim team's all about?" I step closer to Malia, meeting her hawkish gaze. "Winning?"

Malia fixes her eyes on me, *duh* painted over every part of her expression. "Maybe things are different where you come from, but here—"

"Whoa, Malia." One of the other girls tugs at Malia's arm. "Give it a break, she's—"

"I didn't ask for your opinion." Malia schools her features into a scowl that sends the other girl scurrying to the safety of the gathered crowd.

"Listen." I take a step closer to Malia. "Where I come from, we actually care about people other than ourselves. Unless things are *way* different here on Maui, I'd say you're out of line."

A growl rumbles up from Malia's throat, but, before she can say anything, Jazz jumps to her feet—er, foot—and throws herself between me and Malia. "Give it a rest, okay guys? I'm not worth it."

"No way." My chest flames with the injustice of the whole situation.

And then, in a second, Jazz discards her mask of a smile. Her eyes are watery, and her lips tremble as she wobbles on her one and only leg. "Please?" She mouths the word, the defeat in her gaze enough to make me shut up.

"Fine. Sorry, Malia." I force the words out, though I'm apologizing to Malia's flip-flops more than I am to the rest of her. At least, that's what it must look like.

But there's no way I'm looking *her* in the eye anytime soon—not when one glance at her venomous gaze will get me riled up all over again.

Before Malia can accept—or, more likely, *reject*—my apology, a gust of wind blows through the pool complex. It's so strong I nearly lose my balance. I automatically reach to steady Jazz, and she holds onto my arm with a white-knuckle grip.

"Come on." I work with Jazz and help her hobble to the bench where she stashed her stuff. She stays silent as she struggles with her prosthesis, and I hover nearby like a nervous lump.

By the time Jazz has her prosthesis on and I've pulled on a cover-up, the clouds covering the mountains have stretched out like a blanket over the entire sky. The wind continues to whip across the pool area, and the rustling of the palm trees lends an eerie quality to the afternoon.

The rest of the swim team kids have dispersed. Half of them are in the pool, swimming laps like a pod of dolphins, while the rest of them are...gone. Must've come for the show after all. My chest constricts at the thought, and I'm hit with a pang of sympathy for Jazz as we walk out to the parking lot.

"Don't be sorry." Jazz turns to me. Even now, in the middle of this awful afternoon, it's like she can read my mind. "It's not your fault I'm a failure."

"You shouldn't say that."

"Right." Jazz tosses her head, and the sky brews black and gray behind her. "I know, God has a plan for all of this. He's going to work it all for His good. I'm perfect the way I am, even though I feel like a broken wreck." Jazz rattles off the words—the same words she used to speak with such confidence—like they're nothing more than a fairy tale.

"But—"

"*Look at me.*" Jazz's eyes cloud with tears. The wind whips her damp blonde hair into her face. "I'm a wreck. Useless. What you saw—"

"It was your first time!" The wind howls over my words.

"What you saw was my dream dying." Jazz makes a fist and punches the air. And I'm not talking a punch of victory, either.

"Stop!" I stamp my foot on the ground so hard pain shoots up from my heel, but I ignore it. "This isn't like you."

"Yeah?" Jazz squares her shoulders as Ruby's van pulls into the parking lot, and she gestures to her prothesis. "*This* isn't like me, either." Her expression cracks. A tear leaks from her eye as she starts across the parking lot toward her aunt's car.

Another gust of wind nearly knocks her off balance as she walks, and my breath hitches. A gasp escapes me as she stumbles.

I start after her, but a hand closes around my arm and pulls me back. "Let her go." Malia's gaze is dark, her full lips are compressed into a thin frown. "She needs space."

"Like you'd know."

"I *do.*"

"Sure you do." Raindrops prick against my face. I lift my arm to wrench away, but Malia tightens her grasp, fingernails digging into my skin. "Hey, that hurts."

She eases her grip—enough for me to pull away. Raindrops spatter my face as I race toward Jazz, but I'm too late.

Instead of catching her, comforting her, I stand at the edge of the parking lot, rain pouring down on me, and watch as Ruby's van pulls away.

Chapter Eight

GRAMMA'S CLUNKY LANDLINE WAKES ME from my sleep before dawn the next day, and I stumble downstairs in my pajamas to find Gramma in the kitchen, already up and dressed, a frown on her face.

"Who called?" I slide onto a stool at the counter.

"Jazz won't be coming over to do school today," is all Gramma says. She hefts a cookbook from the top shelf and flips through it before turning to the fridge and pulling out a bag of fresh limes.

"Why not?" My stomach twists. After all the drama yesterday, there's no point in letting Jazz spend the day sitting around like a mopey mess. I've done that enough times to know it's the epitome of misery.

Gramma sighs. "Sometimes things are better left unsaid."

"*Grams.*" My voice is so squeaky—okay, whiny—that I sound almost exactly like Macie. Gramma must agree, if the look she shoots me is anything to go by. I clear my throat and try again. "How can I be a good friend to Jazz if I don't even know what's wrong?"

Gramma dips into a canister and returns with a cupful of sugar. "We all have our secrets."

"It's obviously not much of a secret if you know about it."

Gramma lifts a shoulder. "I don't know because Jazz *wanted* to tell me."

"What's that supposed to mean?"

Gramma regards me for a moment, her gaze warm and heavy. "Sometimes, when we learn things about others, it changes the way we see them. Even if it doesn't have to do with them at all. We can't help our circumstances."

I blink at Gramma. "I know *that.*"

"Then it's settled." Gramma brushes her hands together and reaches for a block of cream cheese on the counter. "Jazz'll tell you when she's ready. And I can only hope that you'll be ready too."

I'm Brander's last customer at the Shave Ice Shack that afternoon, and he hands me a mango-coconut shave ice—my favorite—before hanging up his apron and handing things over to the next shift. A pang of nostalgia hits my chest, and I'm swept back to the hours I spent inside the quirky little shack this past summer.

"It's weird working without you." Brander takes a bite of his own pineapple shave ice as we kick off our shoes and head for the shoreline.

"It's weird for me too. But Grams is kind of edgy about this whole homeschool-slash-tutor thing. I doubt she'd be crazy about me taking time to work. In her opinion, I have *way too much piled on my plate.* Tutoring is easy, and I hardly have any work to do, but I think it's going to take the first semester's report card to convince her."

"I can see her point. I mean, you *are* spending extra time helping Jazz get caught up."

A groan escapes me at the mention of Jazz's name, and Brander quirks an eyebrow. "What's that about?"

I take a bite of shave ice, as though that could sweeten my mood, before relating yesterday's failed swimming attempt. "She left in a huff. I've never seen her like that before. Then she skipped out on school today."

"She did?"

"Yep. Plus, Grams is making all these weird comments

about how Jazz can't help her circumstances and I need to be understanding. I mean, obviously she didn't want to get her leg hacked off."

Brander bobs his head up and down at a turtle-like pace. "Yeah, but maybe..."

"What? Do you know?"

Brander winces, as though caught. "Know what?"

I kick at the remains of someone's washed-away sand castle and sigh. "Never mind. Obviously, Jazz has a secret. And she's not going to tell me until the time is right." I sure hope that time is soon. "But there's got to be something I can do to cheer her up."

"Shave ice?" Brander lifts his half-melted cone, but I shake my head.

"Something bigger than that. Like a trip to Disneyworld."

Brander knocks his shoulder against mine. "Not realistic. But I get what you mean. What about a day trip? Somewhere cool on the island. Maybe it would take her mind off stuff."

I lift my head to look at him. "That might work. Could you take us around?"

"No problem. I have this Saturday off, if that works for you."

A ray of sun splashes onto my face as Brander's eager willingness to help warms my heart. I skip across the sand as the frothy waves sweep forward and wash over my bare feet. "Where can we take her?"

"Anywhere. Except Hana."

"Hana?"

"Cool place. Gnarly road to get there." A flush of pink sweeps across Brander's cheeks. "And, um, I don't want to chance scratching my car."

"Ah, right." Of course he wouldn't want to risk damaging his precious rig—not that I'd blame him. That Porsche could put me through all four years of undergrad school, with money left over.

"What else could we do?" I stop and stand at the shoreline before pointing at one of the islands across the channel. "What about that place? Anything cool over there?"

Brander stares out at the island, the aqua blue waters reflecting in his glossy brown eyes. "An old leper colony." There's a smile in his voice. "What about the upcountry?"

"What about it? I've never been anywhere other than here and Kahului."

"That's right." Brander tilts his head to the side for a moment before launching into a description of foggy mountain hills, family-run farms, and fields full of flowers.

"And you're talking about the upcountry?" I cross my arms and stare at him when he's finished. "Like, here. On Maui?" I close my eyes and attempt to conjure an image of a part of the island filled with vegetable gardens and dairy farms, but the picture eludes me. I open my eyes to a sandy beach, dotted with tourists and flanked by a grove of palms—the only Maui I could ever envision.

"Yep." Brander shoves his hands in his pockets and leans on his heels. "What do you think?"

"I'm game." We hammer out the details—I'll invite Jazz for a sleepover on Friday night, and Brander will show up early Saturday to kidnap both of us—as we stroll toward the Shave Ice Shack.

"Want a ride?" He jerks a thumb toward his shiny silver moped.

"Thanks." I clamber aboard with much more confidence than I did the first time Brander offered to take me back to Gramma's. Still, I can't deny that it *is* pretty awkward putting my arms around his waist, especially since our relationship is in that something-more-than-friends-but-not-actually-*together* category.

Thankfully Brander knows how to keep things light. He spends the ride regaling me with stories about that bozo dog of his. I snicker as he describes the way Rosco cowered and tried to hide under the Delacroix's suede leather couch during the windstorm yesterday, but I can't ignore the tremor in my chest.

Rosco isn't even around, and I'm still half-trapped in a mini panic attack. Good thing Brander pulls up in front of Gramma's and walks me to the door before I can start shaking, crying, or doing anything else that will make me look like more of a baby than I actually am.

"Thanks for the ride." I manage to get the words out, along with a brief wave, before ducking into Gramma's cool, dog-free house.

I sag against the front door, shoot off a quick, desperate prayer, and wait for the image of a growling, howling maniac dog to fade from my imagination. When it does, I push away from the door before heading toward the kitchen.

What is *wrong* with me? Why am I so determined to let every pooch on planet earth turn me into a quivery mess? All because of that one day...

No.

I shake my shoulders, as though I can magically shake off the terrible memories of that long-ago day—the race down the street, trying to catch the pit bull. The screams, the sobs. A few deep breaths later, I'm as settled as I'll ever be.

I could think of a thousand things right now—about Rosco, about *that day*. About Mom. It would be oh-so easy to fall into the mush pot and stay there, sniveling about things I'll never be able to fix. But I can't. I have to snap out of it, get my brain back on track.

I send up a prayer, more of an SOS signal, really, before flopping onto the couch and pulling out my phone. Might as well get Jazz on board for this kidnapping thing.

Who knows? Maybe it'll help me too.

"Jazzie! Olive!" Macie dashes into the kitchen early Saturday morning. Jazz and I are still chowing down on breakfast, but Macie was done ages ago. "Brander's here. And he brought his fancy car."

Jazz raises her eyebrows and shoves another bite of Gramma's buttery macadamia-nut pancakes into her mouth. "What's he doing up so early?" A light flickers in her eyes—the first I've seen since her aunt dropped her off yesterday. She hasn't said that anything's wrong, necessarily, but that's just it. She hasn't said much of anything.

Hopefully my plan will get that sparkle back in Jazz's eyes for good.

I wipe my mouth with a napkin and jump to the ground. "Guess we'd better go see. Thanks for the pancakes, Grams."

Gramma steps over to help Jazz slide off the stool, but she manages to shoot me a smile over her shoulder. As soon as I got Jazz onboard for a sleepover, I ran Brander's plan by Gramma. Thankfully, she was more than happy to help me keep the surprise a secret.

Thank goodness for grammas.

Even though Jazz seemed a bit reserved last night, her step seems springier today, her eyes brighter. Hope flickers to life in my chest as I move to answer the door.

Nothing can cure cancer or give Jazz a real leg. Nothing can take away a dying dream...but surely this will help.

It has to.

"Aloha." Brander raises a hand in a *shaka.* "You two ready?"

"Ready?" Jazz turns and shoots me a look somewhere between a grin and the famous Hawaiian stink eye. "For what? I thought we were going to have a Hawaii-5-0 marathon."

"Not today." Brander waves an arm to indicate his Porsche, top down, parked in front of Gramma's house. "You're getting kidnapped."

"Kidnapped? Like, for how long?"

"Only a few hours." I give her a light push out the front door before following suit. "Come on, it'll be fun."

"Okay." Jazz shrugs, and Brander and I help her navigate the front steps. I scramble into the Porsche's back seat, leaving Jazz to ride shotgun since that's easier on her leg.

The cool morning air brushes my shoulders, but the sun is hot on my head as Brander jumps into the driver's seat and starts the car. We pull away from the curb, and I tug on Jazz's long, white-sand-colored braid. She turns around in her seat and pushes a pair of chipped sunglasses onto her nose.

"Are you excited?" I press my lips into a smile, but it feels funky—I can't see Jazz's expression beneath her reflective shades. She could be giving me the meanest stink eye this island's ever seen, for all I know.

"Yeah. Sure. But you and Brander didn't have to do all this for me, you know." Jazz's words are nearly drowned out by Brander's V8 engine as he pulls onto the highway. But from what I can hear, her tone is cool. Too cool. Completely unlike Jazz. Or at least, the Jazz I know.

"Since when shouldn't we do something nice for you? Besides, we wanted to surprise you. Take your mind off...stuff." I close my eyes to keep them from rolling far, far back in my head. *How do you take a person's mind off something? Tell them, point blank, that's what you're trying to do.*

Oh. Brother.

"Thanks. I guess." Jazz fiddles with the tail of her braid, her words nearly lost in a rush of wind. When she lifts her head again, her cheeks flush pink, almost as though she's embarrassed—but how can she be?

Brander and I bought her a whole *leg* after all. Surely a day trip to see some gardens and a goat farm isn't all that extraordinary.

Before I can give the matter any more thought, Brander leans over and turns on his radio—full blast—then gives Jazz control over the station. She picks one that sounds like a strange cross between vintage rock and contemporary Christian. The style's kind of quirky but before long, we're all singing along to a new artist's breakout single.

Jazz howls like an injured pussycat, I'm singing under my breath to avoid complete humiliation, and Brander...well, with a voice like his, there's no wonder he's belting out every word at the top of his lungs.

Maybe *he* should be the one with the breakout single.

After a while, the station gets staticky, and Jazz switches it off. Brander pulls off the main highway and turns onto a road that must lead to the upcountry. When we pass a sign for the Kula Botanical Garden, Jazz finally relaxes against her seat.

"This is fun." A smile sneaks onto her face as Brander pulls into a sloped parking lot. "Thanks for thinking of me."

"Of course." Brander turns off the ignition and jumps to help Jazz out while I scramble from the backseat with the grace and agility of a wobbly hedgehog.

By the time I finally tumble out onto the pavement, Jazz has laughed more than I've heard all week, and even Brander isn't hiding his amusement.

"So glad I can provide your entertainment for the day." I dip into an exaggerated bow, which gets another giggle out of Jazz.

Unfortunately, Jazz's smile is the only sunny thing up here. The garden, though filled with a million different kinds of tropical blossoms, is enveloped in a thin veil of mist that reminds me more of San Francisco than Hawaii.

"Guess we didn't pick a very good day for this, huh?" I lean close to whisper to Brander as we start down a winding path.

"Nah." Brander runs a hand over his cowlick. "It's always like this—a nice break from the heat."

"I guess." A breeze rustles the leaves of a nearby palm, and I run my hands over my bare arms.

Maybe, if you're used to roasting on the beach every day, something like this could be considered a treat. Jazz certainly doesn't seem to mind the chill. When she stops in front of a large wire cage, she gawks for a second before turning and waving us closer, arms flailing in the air. "Come see their chameleon."

I draw near to find a googly-eyed, reptilian creature inside of the cage. Brander joins me, and we hover over the critter for a few minutes before I wander off to snap a picture of a giant hibiscus plant. I would totally post this on Instagram.

If more than five people ever liked my posts.

Whatever. I meander along a cobbled walkway for a while, snapping a few more pictures to show Gramma and Macie if nothing else.

After a while, I turn toward the others and start to pocket my phone. But before I do, something about the way Jazz is standing alone in front of the chameleon's cage—eyes wide, mouth half-open, face filled with obvious delight at God's creation—strikes me. Suddenly, the sun pierces through the thick veil of mist, the light glinting from the metal of Jazz's prosthesis. I stop walking a few feet from Jazz and tighten my grip on the phone. This would make a great picture.

Footsteps crunch behind me. "What are you—"

"Shh..." I turn and press a finger to Brander's lips, then jerk my hand away as soon as I realize what I'm doing. Brander doesn't move away, but his stance seems to shift somewhat.

My finger grows warm, as does my face. "Sorry, I didn't mean anything by that. I..." I nod toward Jazz and turn to snap her picture, but the moment is gone. Instead of being painted with innocent, childlike wonder, Jazz's face is drawn tight. The sun slips behind a cloud, and a shadow falls across the bridge of her nose as she digs her own phone out of her pocket.

My breathing seems to intensify a thousand decibels as Jazz scrolls through something on her phone and grimaces, then takes a few shaky steps in our direction.

"Sorry, guys." She shoves the phone in her pocket as she walks, eyes narrowed, shoulders drooping. "But I'm gonna have to cut this short."

"Short?" My voice comes out as a near-squeak as we start for the parking lot. "You mean you don't want to look around anymore? There's a koi pond around the corner."

Jazz dips her head. "I've got stuff to take care of at home."

"Oh." A pang echoes in my stomach. What kind of *stuff* does Jazz have that needs taking care of? Probably something to do with that secret of hers, if the way her face is scrunched up like a wad of gum is anything to go by.

She stays quiet during the entire ride to Lahaina and, taking my cue from her, I do the same. Brander makes a few attempts at conversation, but even he seems to give up after a while.

The air between us is ripe with my unasked questions, and I end up spending the ride staring out at the passing scenery. I twiddle my necklace and let a whispered prayer slip into the rushing wind every now and then, but I barely know what I'm praying for. All I know is I've got to pray—for Jazz, for her secret, for everything.

And I'm glad I do, because, when Brander pulls up in front of Ruby's crackerbox—really, *house* is too positive a word—Jazz jumps onto the sidewalk before he can even stop the engine.

"Good grief. Be careful." I shake my head at Jazz. "We've barely got you walking again. No sense in you overdoing it now."

Jazz doesn't even blink, simply lifts a shoulder halfway in the air and offers a wave before clunking up the path. She stumbles halfway to the front steps, and my heart nearly ricochets out of my chest as she flails her arms and wobbles on her good leg.

"Need any help?" I attempt to crawl over the front seat to escape Brander's Porsche, but I'm too slow. Before I can get out of the car, Jazz has thrown herself inside the house. Not even a goodbye.

"This isn't right." I shake my head. "I'm going to check on her." Without waiting for a response, I spin on my heel and start up the overgrown front path.

"Wait." Footsteps pound against the pavement before a hand grabs my own, pulling me to a halt.

"Hey." I yank my arm away and rub my wrist. "What's the big deal?"

Brander shakes his head, cowlick standing straight at attention. "I've known Jazz since our first year of Sunday school. If she wants to be left alone, she has a good reason."

"Oh, *really*. Bet you won't tell me what it is, either." Why is everyone determined to keep me out of the loop all of a sudden?

Brander tugs at his shirt collar. I stand there a moment before mentally replaying my words. Maybe I came off a bit too harsh.

"Trust me. Jazz *does* have a reason. But I wouldn't feel right telling you."

"But—" my voice crackles. I swallow hard before continuing. "Aren't we all friends? If something's bugging Jazz, I'd like to know. To help."

"I know. You just want to help—same as me." Brander shuffles his polished Oxford shoes. "But sometimes people are walking through things that only God can fix."

Chapter Nine

"So." I STAND IN THE KITCHEN in front of Gramma, arms crossed.

"So what? Scoot, honey. I've got to get this cake in the oven." Gramma pushes past me and slides a cake into the oven before turning and eyeballing me.

"*So*, I need to know what's up with Jazz. Brander won't spill, and it's driving me nuts."

Gramma stares at me, her eyes boring into my own for several long seconds before she turns to the sink and starts on a load of dishes. "We've already talked about this. She'll tell you—"

"When she's ready, I know. But whatever it is, it's eating her alive. She bailed on us before we even got to the goat cheese farm."

"Hmm." Gramma picks up a batter-coated spoon and rinses it in the sudsy water.

"*Hmm*? That's it?" I step closer to Grams and plunge a whisk into the dishwater. "Aren't you worried about her?"

Gramma sighs. "I love Jazz, and I know that she's in the Lord's hands. He'll take care of her."

"Like He took care of Mom?" The words leave my mouth before I can consider their impact. Gramma turns to face me, dishwater dripping from her hands onto the squeaky-clean tile floors.

I cringe inside, for my lack of faith as much as my icy tone. "Sorry, Grams. I know God's got this, but I don't...I don't know." I lean against the counter. "I need something to *do*." Other than watching. Because watching Jazz struggle is like watching Mom die. Wanting to help—and knowing there's no way I can.

"You can pray." For once, Grams doesn't address my attitude, just dries her hands on a towel and pats my shoulder.

"But I want to do more. I didn't do anything but pray for Mom when she was struggling. Look how that worked out."

"I know it's tough. But Jazz is already making a fantastic recovery. God always has a plan."

"I know."

And the thing is, I *do* know. But it's impossible for me to rest in that fact with the certainty Grams seems to have. "I think I'd feel better if I knew Jazz was getting help. Like if she went to that support group or something."

Gramma looks past me to the kumquat tree beyond her kitchen window. "Maybe that's a good idea."

I pick up a bowl and swish it around in the clouded dishwater. "I sure think so."

"You two are both in a place where you *know* what God's Word says, but you could benefit from seeing it working in the lives of others."

"Wait a minute. *Two*?" I nearly drop the bowl I'm washing. "Like, Jazz and me? I don't need to go to any psycho counseling sessions."

"I didn't say anything about psychos. Or counseling. But God does tell us we should share each other's burdens." Gramma takes the bowl from me and dries it with a holey, aqua-blue dishtowel. "I was talking to Pastor Dave earlier this week. He said the group is having its first meeting next Saturday."

I let out a grunt that makes me sound like an especially perturbed pig—not exactly attractive, but necessary in this situation. "No way. It might be good for Jazz, but I don't need it. I'm fine." I square my shoulders.

Gramma returns to her dishes. "I'd pray about it if I were

you, before I made any rash decisions. And maybe mention it to Jazz. See what she thinks."

"Fine." I shove my hands in my pockets, duck my head, and back out of the kitchen. Somehow, Gramma has that magic quality. One that helps her convince people to get up-close and personal with everything they'd rather run from.

Sometimes that's a good thing.

And then, during times like this...it's not.

I lie awake, moonlight filtering in through the window and glinting off the necklace hanging from my lamp, the smell of plumeria floating up from the yard. In the other bed, Macie is conked out, her soft snores rustling the air. I close my eyes, but something keeps me from falling asleep.

Rolling over in bed, I reach for my phone on the nightstand. I texted Jazz earlier to check up on her, but she never replied. An image of her—alone in her room at Ruby's—blooms in my mind, and I bite my lip.

Whatever's eating her up is about to start devouring me too.

Well, staring at an unread, unanswered text message certainly won't do me—or Jazz—any good. So I swipe over to my photo app and review the shots I got today. I send one of the chameleon to Dad before flicking to one of my own personal favorites—a large, white orchid. Maybe this one should go on Instagram...

Without warning, Macie lets out a Gramma-sized snore. I sit bolt upright in bed, and my thumb slips, sending the pictures from today scattering across the screen in reverse. Macie returns to her normal snoring, and I tap the screen to stop the speed-cycle slide show.

The pictures slow, then stop altogether. Right on an image I'd rather forget about. The first day of school.

Sophomore year.

It's only me and Mom in the frame, and the sight sends both a pang to my stomach and a tear to my eye. We're huddled together in a tiny booth at our favorite place—Tokyo Tom's—feasting on plates loaded with General Tso's chicken and fried rice.

Our smiles are so wide, so vibrant—so *alive*—that I bite back a sob.

The cafeteria drama at school was sickening, so I put my open campus privilege to good use and escaped for lunch out as often as I could. Usually I went on my own, or with a group from my literature club, but that day...

My chest grows warm. Closing my eyes, I can see the conspiratorial glint in Mom's eyes when she met me at the restaurant. But the fuzzy feeling fades all too quickly, the warmth replaced by the icy fact that I'll never share a meal—share *anything*—with Mom again.

Now, with the heaviness in my chest even worse than it was before, I lay my phone on the nightstand. Mom's face flashes in my mind again, and I give my pillow a few hard punches before rolling over in bed, clamping my eyes shut against a well of tears, and willing myself to sleep.

I'm fine. I don't need a shrink. Or a psycho support group. I'm fine.

I stare at myself—bloodshot eyes, tumbleweed hair—in the bathroom mirror Monday morning. My silent chanting isn't doing much good. Even if I don't need a shrink, I sure look like I do.

I throw my hairbrush on the counter after only a few halfhearted strokes at my mop and storm into the hall, nearly swatting Macie with the door on my way out.

"Olive!" She narrows her eyes and knots her arms over

her chest. "It's bad enough Gramma's making me go to school with the pidgin kids. Now you're trying to kill me too."

"Sorry, Mace." I ruffle her curls and thud downstairs to the living room. Jazz should be here any minute, and it would be nice to get a head start on my own stuff before she shows up.

Only...

She never does.

I'm already done with my science work for the day by the time Macie leaves for school, and still no Jazz. She seemed fine at church yesterday, so what gives?

When I'm done with my math worksheet and she hasn't shown up, I pull out my phone. No messages, no missed calls. What, did she decide to drop off the face of the island or something?

"Gramma?" I wander upstairs to where she's bent over a narrow table in her makeshift crafting closet, stringing iridescent beads onto a long, thin length of jeweler's wire. "Jazz didn't call you, did she?"

Gramma shakes her head, and I groan. "I should go check on her. Whatever it is that's going on, I don't like it. And she can't keep skipping out on school like this. If she does, her grades—"

That's it.

"Is this about her grades?" My brain picks up speed and starts whirling, faster and faster. All the secrecy, the embarrassed glances...could it be? Of *course* it could be her grades—and after what happened at the pool last week, maybe she's embarrassed to keep messing up in front of me. "She should know that I don't care about stuff like that. I want to help her with her grades, not—whatever."

"Well..." Gramma shakes her head, as though hesitant to say anything that will affirm my guess at Jazz's secret. "Don't get too nosy."

"I won't. But I've got to help." I spin on my heel and get

out the door as fast as I can, barely stopping in the living room to gather my books. I slide them into one of Gramma's reusable shopping bags, since my backpack is still in Boston, and then I'm gone.

Outside, the sun-warmed air welcomes me. A spring sneaks into my step as I start toward Ruby's place.

Jazz should know better than to mope around over something as silly as her grades. Like I would care. Even though I'm determined to pass the year with a perfect 4.0, that doesn't mean I'm bothered by the fact that Jazz is further behind.

It stinks that she can't swim like she used to, that she fell so far behind, but does she think that would make me see her differently?

But maybe...my own stomach flickers with a twinge of guilt. Maybe I haven't been doing enough to help. I thought I'd made myself clear—that she could ask for help whenever she needed it. But knowing Jazz...

She wouldn't. She's too independent.

Now that I know what's going on, though, I can take extra time to help her figure things out.

And maybe, if I put all that extra brainpower to use helping Jazz, I'll be able to keep from thinking about Mom *all the time.* Maybe this will work out good for both of us.

"Olive?" The door to Ruby's place creaks open half an inch, and Jazz sticks her snip of a nose out onto the porch. "What are you doing?"

"Good morning to you too. You know you can't play hooky without the attendance monitor tracking you down. Good grief." I blow out a puff of air, then wink to confirm that I'm messing with her.

Her expression remains unreadable as she opens the

door another half inch. The midmorning light glints in her silvery eyes. "So what? Can't I take a sick day?"

"You're sick? Then why didn't you call?"

"I didn't say I was *sick* exactly." Jazz purses her lips, and the crack between the door and the wall grows an inch or so wider, revealing her dingy gray nightshirt and rickety pair of crutches. No prosthesis in sight. "But I did need a day off."

"No way. That's called slacking." I lift my bagful of books and step closer to the door. "I know it must be rough trying to get your grades up, but I'm here to help. You don't have to be embarrassed. I used to stink at math until Mom started helping me with my homework." My lips twist over that last sentence, and a pang echoes in my stomach. Who will help me when I get into trig this year? Somehow, I doubt Google has the same gentle patience as Mom did.

Whatever.

Can't think about that now.

"Come on, Jazz. Open up."

Jazz sighs and swings the door wide. Good thing, or I would've had to resort to other, more forceful methods. Like using my algebra textbook to break down the door. At least it would have put both objects out of their collective misery.

"Are you sure you're feeling okay?" I ask once we're settled on Ruby's saggy loveseat, circa 1999. It's one thing for Jazz to be discouraged by her grades—it's another to see her, still in her pajamas, at ten o'clock on a weekday morning. A few months ago, Jazz was the one getting me out of *my* PJs. At eight a.m. on a weekend, to boot.

"I'm fine. Can you get my stuff?" Jazz gestures to where her backpack is dangling precariously from a wimpy-looking hook in the wall, and I hurry to retrieve it for her.

"Are you're sure you're okay?" I lay her pack on the coffee table. Somehow the rickety piece of furniture manages to stay upright, despite the weight of Jazz's textbooks.

"Sure. Having a rough morning is all." Jazz gnaws on a

hangnail, as though debating whether or not to elaborate. She stays quiet so I plunge ahead.

"I know you had a rough go of it Wednesday, but it was what? Your first time in the water in how many months? Even if you can't make the team now, there's always senior year. But you can't expect to get on the team unless you've got good grades." I lean forward and unzip Jazz's bag. "I'm going to make sure you're up to speed by then."

"Forget it." Jazz's voice fades into the dim bleakness of the cluttered living room.

"What do you mean?"

Jazz's bottom lip quivers. "Swim team was a crazy fantasy—something to keep me from croaking the first time I saw my stump without its bandage. I'd get on YouTube and find those dumb inspirational videos of one-legged athletes and dancers and stuff." She snorts. "It was all a farce. It'd be better for me to take up ballet than try out for the team again."

"That's not—"

Jazz shakes her head. "Malia's right. Even if I *could* make the team—this year, next year, doesn't matter. If my leg went bad during relays, we'd tank."

"But it was your dream."

"Not anymore. Like I said, it was a nice thought. Enough to keep me from going crazy cooped up in the hospital. But now I see it was a fairy tale. This is real life." Jazz leans forward and digs out her math textbook. "It's late. Can you help me with these triangle theorems?"

My shoulders tense, and the ticking of a wall clock echoes in the living room. Jazz threw away her dream—because of what? Malia? My chest warms, and not in a good way.

Sure, if Jazz's performance at the pool last week was anything to go by, she wouldn't have made the cut this year.

But for her to not even *try*, not even fight for next year...

"Olive." Jazz snaps her fingers in front of my face. "Triangles?"

"Oh. Right." I blink, clearing away the fog of a million unasked questions, and scoot close to Jazz as she flips through the pages of her math book. "Let's get to work."

And, while Jazz is busy cracking the codes behind the Pythagorean Theorem, I'm going to be watching her. There must be more to all this than grades after all. If Jazz is giving up on swim team—forever—then things are even worse than I'd thought.

Chapter Ten

"*I AM THE HAPPIEST CREATURE IN the world. Perhaps other people have said so before, but not one with such justice.*"

Mom's quote.

Her sweet, low-pitched voice resonates in my head, singsonging the words like she did every time she was really, truly happy. And today, with sunshine filtering through Ruby's tattered drapes and Jazz's presence beside me, the words are surprisingly accurate.

This is why I came to Maui. *This* is why I'm not in Boston. I'm here because—

Mom's dead.

That is why I'm here. Because Mom *isn't*. I sigh and swallow a groan. Why is everything—even Mom's favorite quote—determined to remind me that Mom is gone. That, no matter how much I miss her, I'll never hear her quote *Pride and Prejudice*, never see her smile, again.

My vision clouds, and—oh, no. I'm *not* crying every time I read this stupid book. I'm *not*.

So instead, I slam the cover of *Pride and Prejudice* shut with such force that Jazz nearly leaps off the couch.

"What are you doing?" She clutches her chest and stares at me through wide, unblinking eyes, as though she really is afraid.

"Sorry. Didn't know you were such a scaredy-cat." I huff out a laugh, as though my heart *isn't* breaking into a thousand pieces inside. "Need any help with your math?"

Jazz hesitates a second more than I can stand. The silence stretches on a moment too long, so I reach out, grab her worksheet, and—what?

Save for a handful of scribbled-out chicken scratches near the top, the sheet is empty. "What's wrong?"

"You were so into your book I didn't want to bug you. But now maybe you could..."

"Yeah. Sorry." I grab a pencil and walk Jazz through the first equation, then the next. Anything to get Mom's voice out of my head. Even as we work, though, the silly mnemonics Mom used when she tutored me keep swirling in my brain. In an effort to get them out of there, I share a few with Jazz.

Maybe they work, because, by the time we've gone through the whole sheet, Jazz is working at twice the speed she was earlier.

And it's also over an hour past lunchtime.

"You hungry?" I stand from the couch and cross the room to a tight, cramped kitchen that's more the size of a pantry. It would be hard enough for me to prepare a meal in a five-star chef's gourmet kitchen, but this gut-job? I shudder.

It'll have to do though. Hopefully Ruby has a pack or two of lunch meat. I'm about to peek in the fridge and start digging through what will no doubt be a month's worth of moldering leftovers when a heavy *thud* sends me whirling around to face the living room.

Without her prosthesis or her crutches, Jazz hops toward me like a deranged kangaroo, her face twisted with concentration—or is it pain?

"Hey, take it easy." I hesitate, one hand on the refrigerator door.

Jazz leaps halfway across the living room, landing so that her good leg nearly buckles under the impact. "Don't get in there." Another hop.

"What? The fridge?"

"Don't."

Hop.

"Get."

Hop.

"In there." Jazz lands in front of me and plants one hand on the door. "Trust me, Ruby is *not* a good housekeeper. It's super gross."

I nudge Jazz out of the way. "It's not worth going hungry over." I open the fridge a crack, only to get hit with a sour, acrid smell that can only come from—I blink at a river of amber liquid spilled from an overturned bottle on the shelf—beer? "What's this?"

"I *told* you." Jazz throws herself against the door, slamming it shut. I wince and yank my hand away before my fingers can get flattened into fish sticks. "Stay. Out." Jazz's eyes spit sparks. Her teeth are clenched together so hard I'm afraid she's going to break one.

"Whoa, sorry." Raising my hands in the air, I slink away, the sour stench of beer now stuck in my nose. "But Jazz, what's with the bottle?" It must be Ruby's. Jazz wouldn't have started drinking—right? I peer into my friend's bloodshot eyes.

"None of your business." Jazz leans against the refrigerator, chest heaving.

"It is too my business." I shake my head at this girl—the girl I thought I knew so well.

Jazz and I stand in the kitchen, trapped in some kind of unofficial stare-off, until a sound floats out from the hall. It's half sob, half groan, and it makes my heart take off like a racehorse. "What is *that*?"

Jazz stands, leaning against the fridge, face a tableau of pain and words left unspoken. "You should go."

"You're kicking me out?"

"Trust me. It's best for both of us."

"What? What's best? The fact that you're moping around in here, not even getting dressed and—" *drinking beer.* I choke on the unasked question. *Not Jazz. She wouldn't.*

"It's not what you think."

"Then what *is* it?" I search Jazz's face, but her steely gaze is a shield, keeping me from seeing what lies beyond the surface.

"I'll explain later. Right now, you need to *go*."

"No." I cross my arms and stand straight and tall like a palm. If I could, I'd grow roots right here. And I wouldn't leave until Jazz spilled the beans.

Another groan comes from the hall, and Jazz snaps to attention, nearly losing her balance. "Olive!" Her yelp is so shrill it nearly pierces through the residual stench of that beer. The agitation in her voice rings in the silence.

"Please." Jazz's voice cracks. Her eyes fill with tears, and she drops her chin. "*Go.*"

I reach out to put a hand on her sagging shoulders, but she pulls away and stares up at me. Her gaze is pitiful, so pained that it pierces right through my resolve. "Are you sure you're okay?" I edge out of the kitchen, toward the front door.

Jazz shakes her head, and her uncombed blonde rat's nest flops in her eyes. "I'm okay." But, if the wooden tone of her voice and the hesitancy in her words are anything to go by, she's *not*.

The front door creaks shut behind me as I leave. A tremor wracks my entire body. I've speed-dialed Grams before I can even reach the sidewalk, but she doesn't pick up. The answering machine recording rattles in my ear. I'd leave a message, but I also don't want to freak her out. Instead, I hang up and head toward Gramma's, my book bag a thousand times heavier than it was a few hours ago.

The afternoon sun is a weight on my shoulders as I trudge along the main road. A half-dozen cars whiz by in either direction, but it's the honking of one particular cherry-colored Porsche that catches my attention. I lift my head as Brander drives by. Not a second later, my phone buzzes.

"What's up?" Brander's voice is a soothing balm to my

ears. "Playing hooky?"

"I wish." I choke out something between a groan and a growl. "You don't think Jazz would start drinking, do you?"

"Drinking?" Brander's exclamation nearly cracks the screen of my phone, and I flinch as his car swerves into the other lane.

"Sorry." I wince as a chorus of car horns blare. If there's one thing I've learned in my short time on the island, it's that one honking horn is Hawaiian-style road rage at its finest. "Maybe you'd better get off the phone."

"No. I mean, yes. Stay there. I'll come grab you."

"But aren't you—"

"Just give me a second." Brander hangs up, and I stand, the soles of my high-tops glued to the sidewalk. A gaggle of passing tourists elbow me aside as Brander makes a U-turn and speeds toward me.

When he reaches my part of the sidewalk, he flashes his emergency lights and pulls up to the curb to let me in. I do, and he barely waits for me to close the door before he guns the gas and pulls onto the road.

"What's going on?" Brander keeps his eyes fixed on the road, hands clenched around his custom teakwood steering wheel.

My heart pounds as I give him a rundown of the morning—Jazz's absence, her rumpled PJ's-and-bedhead look, and the half-empty bottle of beer in the fridge. "And then she kicked me out."

"Hmm." Brander runs a hand over his cowlick. His shoulders relax a bit as he pulls into a parking space on Front Street, Maui's favorite shopping hub-slash-tourist trap. "Was Ruby there?"

"I think she's sick. At least, I heard her in the hall, and she sure sounded sick. But Jazz didn't say."

Brander doesn't respond, just jumps out of the car and moves to open my door.

"What are you doing?" I squint at him in the bright light as he ushers me out onto the sidewalk.

"Taking you to lunch." He points to an imposing two-story building, complete with a tiny cabana in front of it. A woman sits inside the luxury hut, taking dinner reservations from wide-eyed tourists.

"Aren't you in school today?"

"Lunch break." Brander rests two fingers lightly on my arm as we step into the lobby. "We'll have to make it quick, but there's no sense dealing with this on an empty stomach."

A flight of stairs, two oversized menus, and a prayer for wisdom later, Brander and I are sitting across from each other, digging into plates loaded with Ahi tuna BLTs—which bear no resemblance to the canned tuna sandwiches I'm used to choking down.

"Good, huh?" Brander wipes a smear of basil aioli from his hand before knitting his fingers together and staring across the table at me. "Now. What about Jazz?"

"I don't know." I take another bite of sandwich, as though it can magically soothe my sorrows. And maybe it can. Whoever owns this restaurant—an ancient rock legend, says Brander—really knows their food. "What can we do? If Jazz is drinking, it's not like we can hold another fundraiser and buy her an easy fix."

"And if she *isn't* drinking?"

"How would we ever know whether she is or not? Unless we ask her. And even then, would we know if she's telling the truth?" The food in my stomach turns to lead. I push away my plate. "How can we be having this conversation about Jazz, of all people? I could see it with the others—Malia, maybe. But Jazz?"

The same Jazz who has it on her heart to save every lost soul, the same Jazz who goes to youth group every Wednesday, no matter what? The same Jazz who couldn't bring herself to say a tart word about anyone—even me, even

Malia?

And speaking of Malia... "What about the support group? Isn't it for kids like that?"

"Kids like what?"

"You know." I shrug. "Addictions. And other...stuff."

"No." Brander shakes his head. His cowlick droops, like even his shock of ebony hair is disappointed in my answer. "It's for people who need Jesus's help."

"Exactly. Druggies and—"

"Stop." Brander reaches out and lays a hand over mine. "We *all* need Jesus. Some of us more than others. Maybe Jazz is in a place where she could use the extra support."

"Maybe." Gramma's words from Saturday replay in my mind. Even if the support group isn't exactly my scene, maybe it *could* help Jazz. "It's worth a try. I'll call tonight and ask her."

"Good." Brander gives my hand a tap, then withdraws to grab a handful of fries. "It could be a great choice. For her and the others."

I nod and reach for my sandwich. A cool breeze wafts over the open-air dining deck, bringing with it the whisper of answers—of hope.

"Are you going to tell me what this morning was all about, or do you want me to think you're a drunk?" My voice toes the line between teasing and condemning when I call Jazz later that night. I'm tucked up on the porch swing, a nubby blanket shielding me from the evening chill. But nothing can calm the tremor in my heart.

It's dark out, a moonless night. The only light comes from a covey of boats anchored in the bay. Jazz's breathing is heavy on the other end of the phone, and I have to chomp on my tongue to keep from pressing her for an answer.

Finally, she sighs. "It's complicated. Will you believe me when I say I'm not drinking?"

I take just as long—maybe even longer—to answer. "I want to. But when I come over and find you bloodshot and bleary in your pajamas on a school morning, it's hard to not think you look—"

"Hungover?" Jazz scoffs. "Trust me, I know what hungover looks like."

"And how would you know that?"

"Trust me. I *know.*"

"How?" The word echoes in the resulting silence. A dove coos somewhere in the distant blackness, and the waves lap against the shore, but that's it.

"Fine," I say after a while. "If you're not going to tell me, maybe you'd rather talk to someone else. Like, the people in the support group."

"The support group?" Her words are ragged. "Why would I want to tell—"

"Brander has a saying." I cast about in my brain for the phrase he tossed at me early this summer. "'Better to talk to a friend than keep it all inside.' Even if you don't want to talk to me, you should talk to *someone.*"

"Maybe. Will you go with me?"

"Only if you want the company."

"Nu-uh. I mean you need to *go.* Like, be a part of the group."

My stomach curdles at the thought of sitting around with a group of nutcases, all of us answering "discussion questions" about our mental well-being and whatnot. But the thought of Jazz falling into a pit of drunkenness or depression—or both...

"I'll do it. For you."

And maybe, though I'd never admit it to anyone, it's not only for Jazz. Maybe there's a tiny part of me that wants to do it for *me* too. So I can read *Pride and Prejudice* without having a breakdown, look at pictures of Mom without wanting to pitch them into the trash, think of her without getting all sappy and teary-eyed.

But like I said, no one else needs to know about *that*.

"It worked."

"The support group thing? Really?" Brander's voice swoops up on the other end of the phone just minutes after my chat with Jazz. "That's great. How hard was it?"

"Not too bad." I cross my fingers, as though that can somehow excuse the little fib I'm about to tell. "All I had to do was promise I'd go with her—for support."

I cringe as the words leave my mouth, but they're far, far better than the alternative. There's no way on this earth I'll admit that Jazz thinks I need group therapy. And besides, it's not a complete lie. Jazz does want me there for support—among other things.

Even so, as Brander and I keep talking, a creepy, crawly feeling blooms in the pit of my stomach. Maybe it's nerves about what those *other things* will entail. Or, more likely, it's no small measure of guilt.

We say our goodbyes, and I hang up, the creepiness spreading to the tips of my fingers and toes. I shove the phone in my pocket, wrap the blanket around my shoulders, and pace the front porch. The rickety floorboards creak beneath my bare feet in rhythm with the churning in my gut.

But why?

I didn't do anything wrong. Really, I didn't—and Brander will never know if I don't tell him.

I'll have to keep my Saturday-morning shenanigans buried deep in the sand at Ka'anapali Beach.

It'll all be fine. Jazz will get better. Maybe I will too. And this way, no one will know that I'm quite as much of a wreck as I actually am.

Chapter Eleven

THE TRADE WINDS WHIP ACROSS THE seaside path leading to Ka'anapali Beach on Saturday. I rub my hands over my arms as a few misplaced raindrops—pineapple mist, Gramma calls it—spatter on my shoulders.

Every step makes me feel more and more like a lazy slug, but I've got to stick with Jazz, who is trudging along at an even slower pace than normal. It's not that long a walk to the south end of Ka'anapali—especially since Gramma dropped us off at the main entrance on her way to work—but Jazz is making it last an eternity. At this rate, we'll miss the entire session.

Which, come to think of it, wouldn't be *such* a bad thing.

We continue along the path, neither one of us offering a word other than an occasional "aloha" to a passing jogger. The air is thick with—not tension exactly, but something else. A kind of reluctant determination that makes the skin at the back of my neck prick.

Jazz kept to herself all week. I can't even imagine how much—or how little—schoolwork she got done.

I, on the other hand, kept busy all day every day. Not that I was particularly excited about doubling up on my chemistry work or solving half a textbook's worth of math equations, but at least it kept my mind off the impending weekend and the drama at Ruby's place. Hopefully the support group won't be as bad as I'm imagining and the old Jazz will reappear soon. Otherwise there won't be any schoolwork left for me to do after Christmas break.

When we make it to the south end of Ka'anapali Beach, there's already a decent crowd gathered around a cluster of picnic tables by the shore, and Jonah is presiding over a table laden with food. My shoulders climb halfway to my ears as I walk closer, and I catch Jazz squaring her jaw as she follows a half-step behind. Her gaze is set in steel, her fists clenched at her sides. And then, right before we come within earshot of the group, she stops walking and yanks me behind a scrawny palm.

"What are you doing?" I lift my arm to show my watch. "We're going to be late. If I'm stuck going to this thing with you, we might as well be on time."

"Come on. Hear me out." Jazz lifts her eyes to meet mine, her gaze wavering. "I'm not drinking."

Everything in me begs to breathe a giant sigh of relief, but something stops me. "Really? You promise you're not drinking? Because I know—"

"I'm *not.*" Jazz sets her jaw and squares her shoulders. "Aunt Ruby likes to have a beer every now and then. Sometimes too many in one sitting. She can get a little tipsy, and..." Jazz's cheeks redden.

"Hold it." I reach out and rest a hand on Jazz's shoulder. "You don't have to be embarrassed."

"But you don't—" Jazz hums under her breath. "I've tried so long to talk to them about Jesus, but they don't—I mean, *Aunt Ruby* doesn't get it."

It's right on the tip of my tongue to ask who *them* is— does Ruby have a creepy boyfriend I don't know about?—but, before I can get the words out, a shrill whistle splits the air.

"Come on, everyone. Let's get started." Jonah's voice rolls over the park, and I shrug toward Jazz.

"Guess we'd better go."

"Right." Jazz sets her jaw, and I take her hand as we march into the first meeting of the support group. Together. Sun shining, birds chirping, waves crashing—this moment could be perfect.

Though I believe Jazz's words, something tugs at the edge of my mind. Warning me, *don't get too comfortable.* There's more to this than I know.

But now's not the time to get nosy. Instead, Jazz and I lock fingers and cross the park, flashing *shakas* to Jonah as we go.

"Hey, girls." He pauses in handing out little booklets and lifts his hand in a *shaka* of his own. "One more?" He waves a hand in my direction, and my cheeks flame red. Sure he wouldn't expect Jazz to need a support group, but do I look like *that* much of a mess?

"Two, actually." Jazz lets go of my hand and steps forward to receive a booklet. Jonah raises both bushy brows, then motions to the others, who are dispersed among a quartet of weathered picnic tables. "Go ahead and grab a seat, we're about to start."

I take another step forward to collect my workbook and peer at the kids in the group. I don't know what I was expecting—an army of juvenile delinquents, maybe—but the actual assemblage of kids is far from that. I recognize a few from youth group, and everyone looks like they're pleasant enough.

My cheeks burn. I might not look like a maverick like some of the others, but I probably need help more than any of them. Except I hide it really well. At least, I *hope* I don't walk around all day looking like a grief-crazed lunatic.

Jonah makes a few announcements, mainly introducing himself and explaining the day's schedule, then he motions to a rickety canoe club boathouse. "I arranged for a treat to kick things off. One of our own, Brander Delacroix, is going to lead us in a few songs."

My heart leaps into my throat as Brander appears from around the side of the boathouse, fancy koa wood guitar clutched firmly in one hand. He ambles to the front of the group and perches atop a picnic table before strumming a chord to begin the first song.

I open my mouth to sing, but no words come out. Of all the times for me to be publicly humiliated, Brander had to pick this one, didn't he? Then again, if I hadn't lied in the first place...

Whatever. He knew I was going to be here. If I play it cool, maybe he'll never—

Yeah, right. My cheeks are already flaming. I must be flushing redder than a cone of raspberry shave ice. Plus, I'm clutching that workbook Jonah handed me—*God's Got This, Now Go Get 'Em: Your Guide to Surviving Tidal Waves of Change.* Pretty much a dead giveaway.

Has he noticed yet? I glance at him, but his eyes are clamped shut, his head bowed low as he sings about amazing grace, amazing love, and all of those other amazing God-things.

Taking my cue from Brander, I bow my head and close my own eyes. At least that way I don't have to stare at him the whole time.

Maybe he'll scoot out of here after worship, before things get too vulnerable. Maybe I can even tell him I somehow "happened" to get roped into the discussion—but that would be twice as bad.

Besides, it's not fair to him—to keep fibbing about why I'm here.

Embarrassing as it is, I'm here for more than moral support. And the sooner I'm willing to admit that to Brander and to myself, the sooner I can start to relax.

My short-lived jig is up. And now I'm stuck dealing with the consequences.

"Okay, gang." Jonah claps his hands and flips through his notebook as soon as Brander's finished. "Let's get started. We'll eat in a bit, but I thought we'd introduce ourselves, maybe do an icebreaker, first. Brander?"

"Need something?" Brander glances up from where he's

tucking his guitar into its case.

"Why don't you help us kick things off with an icebreaker?" Jonah scooches aside to make room for Brander, who plops next to a guy with the size and countenance of a sumo wrestler like it's the most natural thing in the world.

"Okay." Brander claps his hands together and casts a look over the group, somehow seeming to make eye contact with every single one of us. His gaze passes over me, and I wince. Something deep in his eyes flickers to life. *He knows.*

"Why don't we say our name, why we're here, and one fun fact about ourselves? I'll start." Brander laces his fingers together and rests his elbows on his knees. "I'm Brander, I'm here to make music and help out, and I have a scaredy-cat of a guard dog named Rosco."

He *had* to mention that dog of his, didn't he?

A sense of unease pricks at my skin, so I push away the thought of Rosco's gleaming canine teeth and focus on the others. As everyone in the circle takes a turn sharing about themselves, it becomes clear that Brander and Grams were right. The kids here aren't psycho. Or, if they are, they hide it well.

Mostly, it's a group of beaten-down misfits. Finally—a place where I fit in. "Hi." I twirl my shell necklace around my fingers when it's my turn to introduce myself. "I'm Olive. I'm here because..."

I stop. Tug at the strap of my tank top. I could fib again—say I'm here to support Jazz—but one glance at her reveals that she's already one step ahead of me.

Say it, she mouths, a challenge in her eyes. I give a deep internal groan and then a sigh. "A bunch of stuff happened to my family this summer, and my dad kind of went off the deep end. He's okay, now, but I'd rather stay with my Gramma than him."

Brander's eyes are wide, and his chocolatey brown pupils

swim in a sea of white. He gapes at me like he's a hungry tuna fish, so I narrow my gaze at him. Maybe I'm taking things a little too far, because he flinches and scoots back on the bench.

But I can't leave the rest of the group hanging. "A fun fact about me is that I really, really hate Spam."

Suddenly, Brander isn't the only one looking shocked enough to pass out. Half the kids in the group trade glances and murmured comments. I lift a shoulder. "I'm from the mainland." Like *that* needed any explanation.

Thankfully, Jazz whisks away the pressure by lapsing into a chipper monologue, her somber attitude from this morning nowhere to be found. "I'm Jazz." She shakes her wrist, thumb and pinky extended, at the group before reaching to tap on the metal pole of her prosthesis. "And I'm here to get a bit of a *leg up* on life, if you know what I mean." Half-muffled laughter ripples through the group, and I shake my head.

How can Jazz do it? I'm sitting here, tiptoeing around the fact that I'm still sad that Mom died, and Jazz is...Jazz.

I lean my chin on my hand and watch Jazz out of the corner of my eye as a few other people in the group introduce themselves. She's actually smiling. Like she's at a party or something.

I roll my eyes, though even I'm able to relax a bit. By the time everyone's introduced themselves, I can look at Brander without feeling as though I'm about to break out in hives. My pulse is almost back to normal.

Now, if only I can keep from further mortifying myself in front of him for the entire session...

Thankfully, Brander makes that easy. After handing out a packet of worksheets, he plops onto a bench on the other end of the circle and lets Jonah takes over. "Okay, gang. Now that we've gotten to know each other better, let's dig deeper. This is a safe place where you can talk about what you're struggling with. And we absolutely want to pray with you—about everything. In fact, let's do that right now."

Jonah bows his head and leads us in a prayer that is at once heartwarming and heartbreaking. My stomach twists as he prays that God will take away our fear, anger, sadness, and shame—in other words, everything I'm feeling right this very minute. "Tear down the walls around our hearts, Lord. Let us not be afraid of the truth but help us share our struggles with one another. Give us strength to comfort one another and grace to understand what each person is going through. Amen."

My eyes meet Brander's for a second as I raise my head. The corner of his mouth quirks up, and he waves in my direction, but I jerk my gaze away. Best to deal with one mess at a time. And, right now, that *mess* is the first page in my workbook, a piece of paper filled with exactly the kind of questions I hate dwelling on.

1. Do you feel emotionally stable?

Jonah passes around a cup of pencils, and I take one before scribbling in the book:

Do I feel emotionally stable? Yeah, right. I'm about to blow my cork, and it's all my fault. Can't Jazz do something wrong one of these times? But no, it's always my fault. And good grief, now I have to apologize.

2. Do you ever feel depressed?
No comment.

3. Have you experienced a significant loss recently?
No duh.

Why can't I get it out that I miss Mom? That I'm sad she died? It's not like it's unusual. But nooo...I have to tiptoe around every answer. Act like a big baby about it when Jazz is sitting right next to me, making a comedy act out of her prosthesis.

My pencil presses against the paper so hard I nearly rip through the page, but I keep writing. I used to keep a journal on my nightstand. Wrote in it every night. Somehow—during that chaotic week between Mom's death and my first move to Maui—it must have been pushed aside. Where is it now?

A shiver crawls along my spine, but I shake it off and keep writing. The words wash over me in synchrony with the gentle pounding of the waves. I catch a whiff of plumeria, and my shoulders unknot as the sun inches over my neck.

When Jonah finally whistles for our attention, I've filled all of the allotted space in the book, plus a few extra pages in the back. "Okay, guys." Jonah stretches out his legs and wiggles his bare toes. "How did that feel?"

Um...it felt like writing. I widen my eyes and fake-smile at Jazz, but her face is drawn, her eyes glued to the page in her book. "It felt weird. Like I was putting down parts of myself I didn't even know existed. Except, I guess they do." She peers up at the group and clutches the book to her chest.

Half of the others murmur their agreement, and Jonah gives the closest member a fist bump. "Awesome. That exercise was designed to help you take things past the surface of your pain. As we keep going, we'll dig deeper and deeper, and we'll take a look at what the Bible has to say about everything you guys are feeling. It's about time to eat but first, would anyone like to read part of what they've written?"

Nope. Nu-hu. I scrunch my shoulders and slam my book

shut tight, gripping it in both hands. I'm never going to read what I wrote today in front of anyone. I wouldn't even read it in front of Brander's nutzo guard dog—not that he would understand a single word.

No, these words are mine alone.

Jazz pokes me in the arm as we start home after the session. "What's the rush? I'm dying here." She stops in the middle of the path and pants.

"Sorry." I slow my pace, taking a long look over my shoulder. There's Brander—edging away from a group of stragglers. He isn't looking our way, but I hate to take the chance. I know I have to apologize to him, but can't it at least be on my time frame?

I lift a foot, ready to continue my half-jog toward Gramma's place. But then I look over at Jazz again. Her hair hangs limp, her good leg wobbles as she struggles along after me.

Anything for a friend. I slow my pace, chanting those words over and over again in my mind as Jazz lags behind.

We're almost around the first bend in the path when Jazz squeaks and stops walking again. "See them? Look!" She jabs her finger at a pair of lumpy, leathery blobs floating in the water. "Turtles!"

"Uh-huh." I slide a pair of sunglasses out of my purse as Jazz continues to coo over the turtles—*honus*, I've heard the locals call them. Slipping the glasses onto my nose, I take a casual glance over my shoulder.

There's Brander, making a beeline toward us.

He's not going to let me escape, is he? My knees twitch, my calves tense. Everything in me begs to burst into action and carry me far, far away from what is sure to turn into a disaster in five seconds flat.

"Hey, guys." Brander screeches to a halt in front of us, hair mussed, chest heaving. "Wait up." He offers a smile that, at this moment, seems anything but reassuring.

Still under the magical spell of those turtles, Jazz barely bothers to give Brander a *shaka* before turning to the ocean and pulling out her phone.

I, on the other hand, stand there like a lump of coral. I'm sure Brander and I both know what's coming, but I also know I'm not going to be the one to bring it up.

"So..." Brander hooks a thumb in the pocket of his tailored linen shorts and raises an eyebrow. "You okay?"

"Nope." I cross my arms and level my gaze at him. "Listen, I know what I did was wrong." Even those words, though they're barely more than a whisper, make my cheeks flame with remorse.

Brander stays quiet, head cocked. Everything in his gaze—or maybe it's my own brain—screams *you already said you're in the wrong. Now apologize.*

But...

"But I'm not going to say I'm sorry." I cross my arms and stick out my chin. Brander's eyebrows shoot up, and he stares at me like I've lost my mind. Maybe I have.

"What do you mean?" The words sputter as they leave his mouth.

"I'm not going to apologize until I'm ready to. And I'm not ready." I'm half-joking, but my every word sounds like it's snipped in two by a pair of extra-sharp scissors. Way more hostile than I'd intended.

Brander's mouth twitches upward, but the expression only lasts a second before his gaze hardens. "When *will* you be ready?"

"What are you guys talking about?" Jazz shoves her phone into her pocket before looking from me to Brander. Guilt must show on my face, because she's quick to laugh in my direction. "What'd you do?"

"Why is it always me?" The words burst out of my mouth before I can stop them. I clench my fist, bite my tongue. Anything to keep from speaking again. But the words press against my lips, beg to be released. "I'm always slipping up and making mistakes and *mortifying* myself because— whatever. Never mind." I stare at my flip-flops, glancing at Jazz, who squints at me like I'm crazier than I really am. Everything in her expression asks *what is going on?*

Brander holds his palms up in the air, brows scrunched together like he's as baffled as Jazz is. Which, of course, he's not. No, he knows exactly what kind of a mess I've gotten myself into this time.

"Sorry, guys." Those words—the ones I've wanted to say all along—are the hardest to choke out. I hang my head and sigh. "I need some time alone. Brander, can you take Jazz to her place?"

He shuffles his feet for one long moment. "Are you sure you're—"

"I'm fine." The words come out in a half-groan. "Mad at myself."

Brander and Jazz exchange a glance that makes me feel like I'm participating in some sort of interrogation, but neither of them questions me further. Instead, they both offer a *shaka* before turning toward the parking lot.

And me?

I stand there. Watching them.

Two friends. Trusting each other so earnestly—so wholly—that they aren't afraid to share their deepest, darkest secrets. I thought I could finally learn to be that kind of friend.

But instead, I lied. About something that wasn't even that big of a deal. I had to go make a mess of my relationship with Brander—for one reason or another. Maybe this is why I never had any close friends in Boston.

I start toward home, the disappointment in Brander's

eyes burned into my memory. The intensity of his gaze pierces me with every step.

Why am I such a disappointment to everybody? Even when I try to do the right thing, I mess it up. And the worst part?

No matter how upset Brander is, there's someone else even more disappointed in me.

I'm sorry, God...

Chapter Twelve

"OLIVE?" GRAMMA TAPS ON THE BATHROOM door as I'm finishing my paltry hair-and-make-up routine before church the next morning.

"Yeah, Grams?" I set my hairbrush on the counter and peek into the hall.

"There's someone downstairs who wants to speak with you." Gramma waggles her brows, sending a whisper of dread creeping into my stomach.

"*Who* wants to talk to me?"

"A certain young man with a cowlick." Gramma's lips twitch up. "And he said that if you're not ready to apologize yet, it doesn't matter. He wants to talk no matter what."

I groan. "What's he going to do? Blackmail me?"

"Yes." A voice floats up from below, and the stairs creak. "Talk to me now, or I'll make you doggy-sit Rosco next time my parents and I go to Hana for the weekend."

"Very funny." I fake-smirk at him and step into the hall. "What gives? You here to steal a piece of Gramma's Sunday-morning breakfast strudel?"

"Maybe."

The three of us laugh, though my giggle feels a bit rusty, before Gramma gracefully disentangles herself from the conversation with an excuse about making sure there are enough eggs left in the fridge.

The second she's gone, Brander leans against the wall and smiles at me with all the patience of a saint. "What gives?"

I sigh and sag against the same wall. "I'm sorry. Honest.

I was too embarrassed to tell you that Jazz asked me to, like, *go* to the group. Needing to go to therapy is…weird. Not that I *need* to or anything, but since Jazz—"

"Whoa, take a breath." Brander plants one hand on my shoulder. "It's okay. I don't think there's anything wrong with participating in the group. I think it'll be a great experience—for everyone. But I *am* disappointed you lied."

"Me too." I stare through him, waiting for the right words to come. When they do, they're nearly impossible to get out. "I'm sorry. Will you forgive me?"

"I already have." But, despite his kind words, there's something in his gaze that strikes a tremor in my heart. His hot-chocolate eyes have grown lukewarm. Something in the set of his jaw is more defined—more tense—than ever before. He's forgiving me, but the chill in his gaze says more than his words ever could.

Brander is forgiving me because that's what he's called to do. Not because he necessarily *wants* to.

And now, even though I'm forgiven…

I've lost his trust.

The realization blooms inside my heart, eclipsing every bit of shame within me until all I feel is *sad*. There's no other way to describe it. A chill runs through me, like someone turned on the air conditioning. Full blast.

Brander and I stay standing in the hall—together yet so, so alone—until Macie patters up the stairs and races toward us. "Grammy says breakfast's ready. Are you staying, Brander?" Macie gazes upon him with rapturous eyes.

"Nah." Brander shakes himself—barely more than a twitch, but I catch it—and pushes off from the wall. "I've got to get going. Will you be at church today?"

I nod. Even if I had words to answer him with, there'd be no way they could make it out past the thick, sticky lump in my throat. I barely choke out a goodbye as he turns toward the stairs, his stride lacking its usual energy.

Brander and I have had little tiffs before, but they've never been like this. Usually we patch things up with an apology and move on.

But this time it's different. I've driven us straight past the Point of No Return. And I don't like it one bit.

"Why's Olive grumpy?" Macie's voice splits the silence as we rattle our way to church in Gramma's station wagon.

"I'm not grumpy." The words leave me in a growl, and I'm almost sure I hear a chuckle escape from Gramma in the seat beside me.

"If you're not grumpy, then why are you frowning?" Macie kicks my seat. "I frown when I'm grumpy."

"I'm not frowning." I press my lips into a pseudo-smile. "Am I frowning, Gramma?"

Gramma stops at a red light and turns to study my face. Her own mouth twitches, and she taps her fingers against the steering wheel for a moment before answering. "No, you're not frowning. I would call that an all-out grimace."

Great.

I scrunch down in my seat and pull out my phone to text Jazz.

Help! Brander hates me.

My thumb hovers over the SEND button, but I can't quite make myself push it. I'm being overdramatic, and I know it.

Besides, Jazz has enough of her own problems to deal with. Instead of bugging her, I turn to look out the open car window and spend the rest of the ride working up my courage.

Right before we start up the stairs to the church pavilion, I pull Grams aside. "Can I talk to you after church? I've got a mess on my hands, and I hate to bug Jazz with it right now." I whisper in her ear so Macie doesn't hear.

Gramma nods. "Why don't we take a walk after lunch? You and me."

The growing weight in my chest sheds a few pounds, and I nearly sag against the staircase railing in relief. "Thanks, Grams."

She doesn't offer an answer, just a gentle squeeze of my arm as we start up the stairs, but I'm filled with hope all the same. Gramma will know how to fix things. She always does.

After lunch, I help Gramma clean up as Macie busies herself clicking through the channels of Gramma's boxy TV set, presumably in search of her favorite cartoon show.

She must find it, because suddenly the room is filled with the cheesy, chirpy theme song to the bane of my existence—also known as *Lucky the Unicorn and the Fiery Dragon*. In five minutes flat, my ears are burning and my head is pounding. "How 'bout that walk on the beach now, huh, Grams?" The words must be a decibel too loud, because Macie springs from her spot in front of the television and bounds over toward us.

"We're going for a walk on the beach? Ooh, can I put on my swimsuit first?" She skids across the tile floor into the kitchen and hops up and down like a mini pogo stick. "I want to find a mermaid!"

I bite my lip against the groan begging to slip out and squat so I'm eye level with Macie. "What about your show? I don't want you to miss out on that."

"It's a rerun." She shrugs, sending her crop of brown curls quivering. "It's always a rerun on Sundays. Hey, if we're going to the beach, can we take a picnic?"

"I've barely finished washing the lunch dishes, sweetie." Grams reaches out a hand to smooth Macie's hair. "So no picnic this time. But hurry up and put on your suit if you want to come with us, okay?"

Macie is gone practically before I can blink, scrambling up the stairs to get ready for an afternoon spent crashing my plans. I frown and knot my arms over my chest.

"Don't pout." Gramma lifts my chin with a finger so that our gazes lock.

"Who says I'm pouting? I need to talk with you. Alone."

"Don't worry." Gramma pats my shoulder. "I'll work it out." She winks, then turns to call up the stairs. "Hurry up, kiddo!"

"I wanna build a sand castle." Macie plops onto the sand and grabs a shovel from the beach bag Gramma brought. "That way my mermaid can live in it after I catch her."

Before I can explain the flaw in Macie's logic—that, even if mermaids *do* happen to exist, they shouldn't be captured and forced to live in sandy castles—Gramma steps in. "Can I help, Macie?" My stomach sinks, and I swallow a groan as Gramma digs a plastic pail out of the beach bag. What is she doing? If Macie thinks we're willing to help, we'll get stuck shoveling sand all afternoon.

Gramma scoops up a bucketful of sand, but Macie harrumphs and shakes her head, her curls standing on end in the humidity. "*No.* I'm a big girl. I can do it all by myself."

Gramma holds up both hands and inches away from Macie's sand castle construction yard. "If you're such a big girl, does that mean I can trust you to stay right here while Olive and I take a walk?"

Macie bobs her head and sticks her shovel into the sand again. Knowing my little sister, I can bet she'll be happy to sit there and dig for hours.

Without another word, Gramma motions for us to start down the shoreline. The beach across from Gramma's place isn't huge, but it's long enough for us to take a nice stroll—and, more importantly, get out of earshot of Macie.

We scuff through the sand for a while, the waves occasionally sweeping forward to tickle our toes. The water is cool on my feet, and the sun wraps around my shoulders like a comforting blanket. A light breeze plays with tendrils of my hair as laughter echoes from one end of the shoreline.

"I don't know how long Macie will be happy, building that mermaid castle by herself." Gramma's words split the peaceful quiet, sending my thoughts spiraling toward planet earth. "We should probably get talking. If you still want to, that is."

"Oh, I want to." I scuff at the sand as I spill about Brander's visit this morning. Gramma walks with one ear cocked toward me, her face stretching into a frown as I weave my twisted tale.

I take a gulp of salted air when I'm done and stare up at a blue, cloudless sky. "I shouldn't have lied, and I'm not proud that I did. Even after Brander forgave me, something was...*different*. Wrong. I think I broke his trust."

Gramma nods, the loose skin beneath her chin quivering. She lends me a sage expression, one that must come from years and years of time spent alone with God. Finally, she stops walking and lays a hand on my arm. "Trust is a precious thing, Olive. When someone chooses to give us their trust, it's a special gift. One we shouldn't play with. We should treat it gently, with care. We should honor it."

I snort. "Guess I blew that."

A bird cackles at me from somewhere deep in the nearby grove of palms. The waves roll back only to rush forward, crashing over my feet.

"Olive, trust is more than something we're given. It's something we can earn. Even though you've broken Brander's trust, that doesn't mean it can't be rebuilt."

I squint at Gramma in the sunlight. Before I can ask *how*, she's squeezing my hand.

"You earn his trust little by little, day by day. It's not a quick fix, but it's a solid one." Gramma peers into my eyes, her gaze so much like Mom's it hurts. "Stop lying. Be honest. Vulnerable. Share your heart with Brander—with everyone. Show people that they can trust you."

"But—"

"Gramma!" Macie's voice splits through the midday calm, and I peek over my shoulder as a wave crashes over Macie's sand castle-in-progress.

"Uh-oh." Gramma chuckles, and we both splash through the froth of the waves, heading toward Macie's decimated castle. A charter boat chugs across the crystalline blue water as Gramma's words echo in my ears in rhythm with the pounding waves.

Be honest. Vulnerable.

"You realize—everything we talked about—it's all easier said than done, right?" I turn to look at Gramma when we're but a few steps from Macie.

"Oh, I know. But I also know you can do it."

Chapter Thirteen

"WHAT'S WRONG?" JAZZ CRINKLES HER NOSE and peers at me when I open the front door Monday morning. "You look like someone died or—" Her cheeks grow red, and she slaps both hands over her mouth. "Oops. You know I didn't mean anything by that. Right?"

Ruby's van backfires as it pulls away from the curb, and I wave a hand in the air. "Don't apologize. It's a colloquialism."

"What's a colloquialism?" Jazz's cheeks are bright pink, but at least she doesn't have that sickly-sweet glaze over her eyes like other people get. "And I'm serious. Are you okay?"

"I've been a major idiot."

"Oh, is that all?" The once-omnipresent twinkle in Jazz's eye sparks. "Should be an easy fix then." She stamps into the living room and plops onto the couch before resting her good leg on Gramma's scarred wooden coffee table.

"You don't get it." I flop into the armchair across from Jazz and bury my face in my hands. "I told Brander I wasn't doing the group thing. That I was going along for moral support."

Jazz knots her eyebrows, but I hold up a hand before she can say anything. "I didn't know what else to say. Going to a support group made it sound like I was a nutcase or something."

Jazz pulls a pillow into her lap. "Is that what you think *I* am? A nutcase?"

I shake my head and snort. "I was worried about you is all. But for me to need the group too, when I didn't get *my* leg sawed off over the summer...it's embarrassing."

"Admitting there are parts of our life that aren't perfect shouldn't be something we're ashamed of. It's okay to need help." Jazz lowers her gaze and picks at a hangnail, like she doesn't want to heed her own advice. But that's ridiculous. Jazz is always spilling her heart to everyone—even perfect strangers.

"Whatever. I know I want to get better. And I'll keep going to the support group. Now it'll be even *more* mortifying, seeing Brander there every week." I slide my science textbook off the end table and flip to the right chapter as Jazz watches me out of the corner of her eye.

"What ever happened with Brander? Did you talk with him? I tried to text you yesterday, but my phone's on the fritz."

"We're okay. I guess." I tug at my necklace.

"What does that mean? Did something happen?"

My shoulders slump as I try to string together an answer, every creak and groan of the settling house amplified a million times in the silence. "Kind of." The words creep out of my mouth. "I'm going to have to regain his trust."

"Oh. Gotcha." Jazz's gaze flickers, and she unzips her backpack and pulls out a stack of books. "Guess we need to get to work now, yeah?"

"Sure." But even as I read through the next chapter in my science book, I keep one eye fixed on Jazz. The twinkle has returned to her eye, but her step is still missing its usual spring. Maybe that's because of her prosthesis...maybe not.

But if the heavy black bags under her eyes are anything to go by, I'm banking on *not*.

I don't go to youth group on Wednesday.

Neither does Jazz.

It's kind of an unspoken agreement that we'll take this week off—me, because my cheeks spontaneously combust every time I think about facing Brander again, and Jazz because...well...I don't know why she doesn't go.

All I know is that, instead of wolfing down dinner and listening to Jonah teach, we spend the evening out on Gramma's porch swing, taking turns reading aloud from *Pride and Prejudice*. Jazz has never read it before, and she launches into it with reckless abandon, her tongue tripping over the Regency-era vernacular. Every time she butchers one of Mom's favorite quotes, she laughs out loud and, though I join in, I can't keep from cringing inside.

A cool, quiet breeze sweeps over the porch, bringing with it the sweet scent of plumeria mingled with a hint of char from a neighbor's barbecue. Jazz keeps reading, stumbling here and there over dialogue that Mom could have recited in her sleep. My stomach knots itself around my heart, and my skin pricks at the thought that this isn't right.

Pride and Prejudice is Mom's book. Hearing the familiar phrases coming out of Jazz is...not wrong exactly, just different. And different can hurt. Bad.

I stare past the street, past the bay, all the way to the neighboring islands, but my vision clouds nonetheless. I blink half a dozen times—until the tears are safely tucked away.

"Olive?" Jazz pokes my shoulder and shoves the book in my lap. "Your turn."

"Thanks." I clutch the book and read, my throat cracking as I recite the old, familiar words. The knot inside of me grows tighter and tighter, until it feels like it's about to cut off my air supply.

God, are you listening? Because I need help.

I scrub at my eyes to keep the tears from leaking out, and Jazz casts a shifty-eyed glance my way.

"You okay?"

"Yeah. Sure." I sniff. So much for that transparency thing Gramma mentioned. How can it be so hard to open up—share my heart? Other than the fact that it's totally mortifying to be crying over some dumb Regency romance novel. "Why do you ask?"

Jazz doesn't answer, but she picks up the book and turns to the next chapter. Mom never liked this part—when Mr. Wickham first shows up—so I'm able to relax a bit. But even now I can't chase away the flailing, drowning sensation in my chest. The one that, if I'm not careful, will take me and pull me under, into an ocean teeming with grief.

Guess it *is* a good thing I'm in that support group.

Then again, now that things are so awkward between me and Brander...maybe not.

On Saturday morning, the same knot that started growing on Wednesday has multiplied until every inch of my body is coiled tighter than a steel cable. My heart pounds, and I barely taste Gramma's cinnamon bun breakfast.

The thought of going to the support group and having to deal with those questions, the ones that plague me, haunt me—the ones I've gotten so good at ignoring—is enough on its own. And knowing that I have to face Brander while I'm at it?

A chill runs over me, and nothing, not even the balmy breeze, can wash it away. I grow colder by the minute. When Grams drops Jazz and me at Ka'anapali Beach a few hours later, I'm almost shivering.

"What's wrong?" Jazz shakes her head at me.

"Nervous." The word escapes from behind clenched teeth.

"Why? I thought you liked scribbling in your workbook."

I hold the book up to the light and cringe once again at the corny title. "It's okay. But—"

"This is about Brander, isn't it?" Jazz hooks her arm through mine and gives me a tug toward the group. Brander's perched on top of the picnic table, guitar in hand. He strums a chord and looks out over the group as Jazz yanks on my arm again. "Come *on*."

"Geesh, why couldn't they have amputated some of your muscle?" I wink at Jazz as she pulls me closer, and she returns the gesture with a decidedly cheerful glare.

"They had to leave me with *something*." She smiles so wide her entire face scrunches up, then she lowers herself onto a bench.

I slide onto the bench next to Jazz, the knot within me slackening a tiny bit, as Brander leads us in the first song. I join in on the chorus, the words rolling off my tongue and into my heart, loosening the knot a bit more.

Beside me, Jazz sings at the top of her lungs, arms high in the air. Her eyes are shut tight, her expression washed clean from whatever it is that's been bothering her. She's in her own little world—no one there but her and God. Maybe I should try doing that.

I close my eyes, but in what feels like only seconds, something jabs my side and a voice hisses in my ear. "Scoot. Over."

Cracking open one eye, I find Malia seated next to me on the bench. Her gaze is even narrower than usual, her full lips compressed into a scowl—or is it a sneer? "What are you doing here?" My gaze flits to Jazz, oblivious to it all. *Lucky Jazz.*

Malia scoffs. "Either I come to this dumb group, or I'm off the swim team. Dad says. And you'd better know by now. *Nothing* keeps me from swim team." Her scowl deepens, and she pulls out a shiny pink smartphone. In a matter of seconds, she's in a little world of her own—somewhere a whole lot different than the perfect place Jazz is in right now.

Speaking of Jazz...I elbow her, and her eyes fly open.

"What?" She mouths the word, shaking her head at me.

I motion toward Malia in response, and Jazz's eyes grow wide. After a few seconds she trains her attention back on the music, which is where it stays for the entire rest of the worship session.

The second Brander puts his guitar away, Jazz leans over me and flashes Malia a *shaka*. "Hey. How're you?"

"Alive." Malia pockets her phone. "How long does this thing go for?"

"Until we're done." Jazz laughs, but her chuckle falters when Malia's expression sours. "Usually that's around noon."

Malia opens her mouth, as if to say more, but Jonah gives a shrill whistle before she can respond.

"Welcome everybody, and congratulations. You've made it to week two." Jonah lets his gaze pass over the group gathered around him, then he shoots Malia a second glance. "*Aloha.* You weren't here last week, were you?"

Malia shakes her head. Her long ebony mane swats me in the face, and I get a nose full of something that smells like a cross between chlorine and wet dog. *Yuck.*

Jonah gives her a quick rundown of the schedule and presents her with her own copy of *God's Got This, Now Go Get 'Em.* "Why don't you introduce yourself? Share your name, why you're here, and one fun fact about yourself."

Malia rolls her eyes so far back in her head she might as well be giving herself a brain exam. "I'm Malia Akina. I'm here to convince my parents I can stay on the swim team. And...I hate Spam."

This final admission is met with the same wide eyes and gaping mouths as mine was last week. Before I can process what I'm doing, I reach out and slap Malia a high-five. Her eyebrows bend, and she cocks her head at me. "Excuse me?"

"I hate it too. Nice to see that not *everyone* on Maui loves the stuff."

A teaspoon of sweetness sneaks into Malia's sour-grapes

expression, but it disappears as Jonah takes control of the floor again. "All right guys, listen up. Before we pull out our journals, I have an exciting announcement.

"One of the best ways to help ourselves is to help others. Whether we're angry, hurt, grieving—whatever. Doing good for someone else takes our mind off of our own problems and puts our focus on God's work. Who's with me?"

I find myself nodding along with about half of the others. No surprise—Malia stays stock still. In fact...I sneak a peek out of the corner of my eye. She's on her phone again.

"I thought of a couple of different projects we could do, but then I heard about something I think you guys'll love. Brander?" Jonah whistles and motions to where Brander is standing, holding a leash attached to—*no*.

Everything seems to stop for a moment, and it's like I'm floating high above the clouds, hovering over what is sure to become a disaster. There's Brander, clutching a leash attached to a tubby, toffee-colored puppy. There are the others—expressions varying, but with some degree of a smile on their face. Even Malia's lips are quirked up.

And then there's me.

Whiter than the sand on Ka'anapali Beach. Blood frozen like one of those giant blocks of ice at the Shave Ice Shack. Sitting there like a sea monster or something equally frightening had crawled out of the ocean.

And then everything starts up again.

Brander unclips the leash, and the puppy darts through the crowd of kids—right toward *me*. Every nerve ending in my body coils like a sail ready to unfurl, and I grab Jazz's arm so hard she whimpers. "What are you doing?"

"Sorry." I can't make myself let go of Jazz, but I do manage to keep from screaming. Out loud, anyway.

"You okay?" Jazz looks from me to the puppy.

With my lip clamped tightly between my teeth, there's no way I can answer. Especially when any answer I'm capable of right now is something akin to a horror-film scream.

And then—the puppy bounds over someone's discarded backpack and lands in front of me. The harsh morning sunlight glints off his beady little eyes, and his tongue hangs out in a pant, revealing two rows of gleaming white teeth.

The puppy and I stare at each other for what feels like an eternity before it takes one more step closer, teeth bared, and—licks me?

His warm, wet tongue makes contact with my bare leg, and a shriek splits the air—*my shriek*. All eyes fix on me, and my cheeks erupt into flames as Brander trots over and tugs at the mutt's collar. "Come on, buddy." He gives another tug, but the dog stays put, wagging its tail and staring at me like I'm the last steak left in a butcher shop.

The mutt comes in for another slurp, and I cringe. "Can you—please?—get him off me?" My words come out in a strangled whisper, but Brander simply scoops the pup into his arms with a disturbing amount of nonchalance. Does he have any idea what that mutt could do to him? Brander could get his eyes gouged out in two seconds flat. Or...worse.

"What's your problem?" Malia rolls her eyes again—at me, this time.

"Sorry. I don't like dogs."

"Are you serious? Not even puppies? I mean, look at that guy." Jazz's eyes have practically turned into goofy cartoon hearts, and she stares at the pup like he's the cutest thing in the world. Which, even I'll admit, wouldn't be *that* much of an overstatement.

"Can I pet him?" One of the others asks.

"Of course." Brander sets the mutt back on the ground, resulting in a puppy-petting-zoo that lasts until Jonah whistles for attention.

"Come on, guys. Take it easy. You'll have plenty of time to play with Koa after we talk." Jonah corrals the puppy and reattaches the leash. "If you haven't already figured it out, this little rascal is the newest member of our support group. He's fresh out of the Maui Humane Society, and he needs a lot of love."

"You mean he's gonna be hanging with us at the meetings?" A thick Hawaiian dude's face softens as he watches the puppy chew on the end of its leash. "That's dope."

"He'll be doing more than that, actually." Jonah hands a piece of paper—a photo, maybe—to the girl closest to him. "Pass that around."

The paper makes its way around the group, then to Jazz. When I get it, I take an extra moment to study the picture of a small boy with buzzed black hair and a vacant expression spread across his face. I pass the photo on to Malia and focus in on Jonah.

"The little boy in the picture is Lio, and he has autism. His family has been praying for an emotional support animal for years, but they haven't been able to afford one. My neighbor volunteers at the humane society, and when she told me about Koa here, I knew he'd be the perfect candidate for the job." Jonah scratches the puppy—Koa—beneath his caramel-colored chin.

Jazz waves her hand in the air. "How'd he get the name Koa?"

"That's what they were calling him at the shelter, and I thought it fit. It means brave and fearless. I figure we could all use a dose of bravery in our lives."

Seriously?

Here I am, face-to-face with my biggest nightmare, and his name means *fearless*?

"Lio and his family don't know about Koa yet." Jonah strokes the pup's floppy golden ears. "And we're going to keep it that way for a while. Koa's still a puppy, and he hasn't been trained yet."

Uh-ho. My stomach twists as I anticipate Jonah's next

words. I lean close to whisper in Jazz's ear. "You don't think we'll have to—"

"We're going to spend part of each Saturday session teaching Koa a few basic commands." A wave of chatter builds, but Jonah pushes on. "But that doesn't cover his care during the weekdays, which is why I'm giving you the opportunity to take him home. Only a week at a time—we want everyone to get a turn if they want—but you'll be amazed at how much joy this little guy can bring to your life."

"I always wanted a puppy when I was little." Jazz gazes at Koa before digging out her phone and shooting off a text. "Aunt Ruby'd better be on board with this. There's no way I'm giving up a chance to have a sleepover with this guy every night."

"Maybe you can take my week." I shudder at the thought of Koa lurking around in Gramma's house. Who knows what kind of damage he's capable of doing with those pointy baby teeth?

Jonah passes around a sign-up sheet, or "Koa's Custody Form," as he's unofficially named it. Unfortunately, though most of the others can't keep their hands off of Koa, they can't commit to taking him home, either.

"I'll have to check with my stepmom." One of the girls frowns. "She has a thing about shedding."

By the time the sheet makes its way to us, it's about halfway filled, but the first few weeks are empty. Jazz's eyebrows squeeze together, and she checks her phone. Not a single new message. "He's a puppy. How mad can Aunt Ruby get?"

Jazz picks up the pen and hesitates, hand hovering over the line. The pen quivers in the air for a moment before she swoops in to sign her name.

"Might as well take my spot." I point to the empty line below Jazz's name.

"You're sure you don't want to take him? He's a teeny little puppy. I'm sure *Tutu* and Macie would be thrilled to have him. What's the big deal?"

I fold my arms over my chest. "Teeny little puppies grow up to be big, bad dogs."

"Your loss." Jazz scribbles her name on the next line, then hands the sheet off to Malia. I'm ready for Malia to put up a fuss—about poop-scooping, dog-walking, or anything else that requires a miniscule amount of effort, but she doesn't. Instead, she picks up the pen and puts her name in the slot beneath Jazz's.

"What are *you* looking at?" She narrows her eyes at me. "I don't want that guy to get stranded without a place to go. Everyone should have a home."

Jazz's expression shifts into a mask of—something. Like she's not here anymore, but in her room at Ruby's. Or maybe on the boat she used to live on with her mom.

Her mom.

I nearly topple off the bench. All this time, I've been missing *my* mom—but where is *Jazz's* mom? I rifle through the wealth of information I've filed away since I came to Maui—*slippas* are flip-flops, waving is out and *shakas* are in—but what I know about Jazz's mom amounts to pretty much nothing.

According to Brander, Jazz's mom has always been a little south of normal, and Jazz's dad has been out of the picture since before he can remember. Still—Jazz must think about her mom *sometimes*. Right?

"Olive." Something jabs into my side, and I glance up to find Jazz half-glaring at me. "Are you paying attention?"

"Sure?"

"Yeah, right." Jazz shakes her head. "If you were paying attention, you'd already be halfway done with the journaling assignment."

"Assignment?" Maybe I'd let my mind wander farther

than I'd thought.

"Pages five and six." Malia shakes her head, swatting me again with her glossy mane. "You'd better hurry up. Jonah said we could start working with Koa as soon as we're all done."

"In that case, I'll *try* to finish before the next millennium." My stomach curdles as I flip through my notebook. We seriously have to train that mutt today? My pulse thrums in my temples as I read today's first question:

1. What are you most afraid of?

Ha. I bring my mechanical pencil to the page with so much force that the lead snaps. I close my eyes for a moment, then pump the eraser until another lead appears.

Dogs. I'm scared of dogs. They're big, ugly, slobbery, and they're bred to hunt and kill and destroy. Like cancer. And tsunamis. Plane wrecks. Maybe it's not the dogs I'm afraid of. Maybe it's everything that can turn a life upside-down.

That's it.

I'm afraid of everything.

Chapter Fourteen

"WHAT WERE YOU WRITING TODAY?" JAZZ twines Koa's leash around her hand as we walk along an empty stretch of beach. Gramma's late to pick me up, and Jazz's Aunt Ruby is nowhere to be seen or heard from, so we're killing time by doing what we do best—hanging out on the beach.

Except, now our cozy little twosome has become a threesome. And, to be perfectly honest, I'd rather hang out with Malia than our new, four-legged tagalong.

"Hey. Earth to Olive." Jazz waves her free hand in front of my face. "What's up? You keep zoning out, and you acted like you were writing the constitution during that journaling thing." Jazz furrows her brow and mimes scribbling in a notebook like she's a frenzied politician.

I cast a wary glance at Koa as he lifts his leg near the remains of someone's washed-away sand castle. "It's—ugh, dogs. They're all out to maim and destroy, and now I have to worry about you sleeping with one every night? What if he bites off your other leg?"

"You know that's impossible, right?" Jazz rolls her eyes at me.

I roll my eyes right back. "Impossible? Says who?"

"Me." Jazz purses her lips and whistles. Koa's fluffy golden ears perk up, and he trots over to Jazz before sliming her with that extra-large tongue of his.

"Gross." I wrinkle my nose. "Why do people like dogs, anyway?"

"Because." Jazz sighs. "They're cute. And sweet. And fluffy."

"No. Cats are cute and sweet and fluffy. Dogs are evil."

Jazz opens her mouth, like she's about to come up with another flimsy counterargument, but her pocket chirps before she can get a single word out. She shifts Koa's leash to her other hand and pulls out her ancient-looking flip phone.

"Aloha, Aunt Ruby." She cocks her head, a frown stretching across her face. "Right now? Okay. But you should probably—" Jazz stops talking, almost like she got cut off, and holds the phone away from her face.

"Did your aunt hang up on you?"

"Must have been a bad connection. She's waiting in the parking lot. See ya." Jazz turns to go, her face one giant storm cloud.

"Hey, wait." I trot after her, staying far enough behind that Koa won't get any ideas about running over and harassing me. "Is everything okay?"

"Fine." Jazz tosses the word over her shoulder in a way that makes her sound anything *but* fine. I pick up my pace but even with a gimpy prosthesis, Jazz manages to beat me to Ruby's van in the parking lot.

I draw up short and stand there, watching as Jazz clambers into the passengers' seat, Koa close behind. The door slams shut, and Ruby pulls away, heavy-metal music pouring from the open windows. Hand held in a half-wave, I stand on the sidewalk until the van has disappeared down the long stretch of highway.

I pull out my phone, already composing a text in my head. Jazz can't possibly get offended if I send her an I'm-worried-about-you text, can she?

Before I can decide whether or not to text her, a familiar rich, rough voice calls out my name. "Need a ride?"

I whirl around to find Brander standing behind me, hands shoved in his pockets, head bowed. A cold bucket of realization douses me. Brander wants to take me home and—could he want to be friends again?

Or, maybe we never stopped.

But I'll never know if I don't stop staring and *say something.*

"Hi." The word stretches as it leaves my mouth until it has about ten syllables. I take in a quick breath and try again. "I mean, sure. Thanks. How are you?"

"I miss you." Brander motions toward his Porsche. "Working the Shave Ice Shack alone gets old."

"Yeah." The word rasps in my throat, and I wipe my palms against my shorts before stepping aside and calling Grams to let her know I got a ride.

She doesn't answer, so I leave a message before turning back to Brander. "Sorry, again, about last weekend."

"Don't keep apologizing." Brander jumps off the curb to open my door before ambling around to the driver's side. "If you've asked God for forgiveness, that means everything is in the past now."

"But—"

"That's all there is to it." Brander sinks into his buttery leather driver's seat. "Come on. Jump in."

I do as I'm told, but I can't help feeling out of place as Brander peels out of the parking lot. Not that the ritzy rig makes me uncomfortable—I've ridden in it enough times that it's no more intimidating than Dad's sedan or Mom's old SUV. It's more the vibe in the air, the one that says: No Sinners Allowed.

I tell Brander as much, and he throws back his head and laughs so hard he almost swerves into the other lane. "Sorry." He tightens his grip on the steering wheel and glances in the rearview mirror. "Come on, Olive. If no sinners were allowed in this car, it would *never* get used. We're all sinners. You know that."

"Except some of us are a whole lot worse than others."

Brander shakes his head, and his cowlick flaps in the

breeze as we pick up speed. "God doesn't see it like that. If we've sinned—even once—it's as bad as if we sin a thousand times a day. We're all guilty, but none of us can say we're the worst sinner. That's like saying we're a first-place loser."

"Huh?"

"Exactly." Brander pulls off the highway, but he's going the wrong direction. A few turns later, we're at the Shave Ice Shack. "Want a treat?"

My stomach answers for me, letting out a growl more ferocious than anything Rosco or Koa could muster.

Brander's eyes widen. "That's a yes?"

"For sure."

"Didn't you get anything to eat during group?" Brander sticks close to my side as we walk up to the line winding away from the scrubby little shack on the beach.

"Nope. Too nervous." I crane my neck to read the menu, though I know I won't be able to resist the lure of a large coconut-mango ice with sweetened condensed milk.

"Nervous?" Brander's hand flutters above my shoulder before coming to rest there for a moment. "About the group?"

I shake my head. "The dog."

"Oh. Can I—"

"Don't bother."

"What?" He lifts his hand. "You didn't even let me finish."

"I know what you're going to say. You're going to ask me why on earth I'm afraid of a sweet, cute, innocent little puppy. You're going to tell me I'm crazy. You're going to—"

"Whoa." Brander holds a hand in front of my face, as though he's about to muzzle me. "Instead of telling me what I'm *going* to say, why don't you let me talk?"

"Fair enough, I guess." I wrap the chain of my necklace around my fingers, and we shuffle forward in line.

"I don't fault you for being afraid of dogs. We're all afraid of something. I just want to know why." His cheeks redden. "So I can, um, help you through it."

"I can tell you the story, but I want you to know—there's nothing you can do to change my mind about dogs. I hate them. Always will."

Brander raises his eyebrows as he steps up to the window to place our orders. The white parts of his eyes glint like whitecaps. *Uh-oh.* If that look is anything to go by, I've offered him a challenge on a silver platter. Namely, the Make Olive Like Dogs challenge.

And he's accepted.

We wait in silence for our cones, then take a seat on a bench by the beach. While Brander has his mouth full of shave ice and ice cream, I hurry to speak. "You said you want to hear the story?"

He nods, then wipes a drop of blue syrup from his chin.

"Okay." I set my shave ice on the bench and shake out my hands. This is eerily familiar—too familiar. Why do I always end up spilling my guts to Brander? Why not Jazz, or even Gramma?

Or why can't I learn to keep it all inside?

"Here goes." I wrap my necklace chain around my thumb and slip back in time to that summer day so many years ago.

"When I was little, I had a kitten. Her name was Peaches." Even all these years later, my voice still cracks on the orange-spotted feline's name. My fingers twitch. For a moment, it's like I can feel her fluffy ears and the ticklish roughness of her raspberry-pink tongue.

Brander cocks his head at me, clearly confused—what does a kitten have to do with my fear of dogs?

"A pit bull got her." I close my eyes as the frantic mewls of my kitten, the panting of that pit bull, and my terrified screams echo in my head. "We were outside one morning, and he came out of nowhere. Snatched Peaches in his jaws and wouldn't let her go."

The waves sweep the coastline, their rhythmic crashing onshore acting as a sort of balm to my aching chest. This story is a wound that has been left untreated for so many years I can almost ignore it. Until I start picking at the scab.

That's when I remember it's still as tender as it was the day it happened. I'll never forget the life taken away from me. "I chased after that dog, screaming, crying. Begging him to stop. When he did..." My hand flutters to my chest. How can the memories hurt after all these years?

"Peaches was already gone?" Brander reaches out and rests his hand over mine. It's warm and solid, something comforting to hang onto amid the sea of painful memories.

I shake my head. "She was still alive. I don't know how—she was barely three months old." The pounding surf, the scratchy sand beneath my feet, even Brander's presence beside me all fade away as I'm swept through the vortex of time.

Peaches' frantic meows ring in my ears. I can almost feel her cradled against my chest, her blood soaking through my shirt. "I screamed all the way home. Mom must have heard me, because she was already outside by the time I made it in the door.

"We rushed to the vet's office, and Peaches managed to hang on." Tears blur my vision, but I blink them away. No use crying over a decade-old death now. In front of Brander.

"But the animal hospital was packed. She died"—the words trip over my tongue, and I wince—"in the waiting room."

Brander is silent. Not in a weird way or an uncomfortable one, but in a way that says he gets it. He understands.

"You're probably wondering why I never got another cat, huh?"

"And risk saying goodbye again? Besides, you probably couldn't stand the thought of replacing Peaches."

I squint at Brander. Is he secretly some sort of junior prophet, like in the Bible? Nah. More likely, he's *way* more intuitive than 99.9% of the population. "Now I bet you understand why I hate dogs."

"Yeah, but..." Brander studies his clasped hands. "You know not all dogs are like that, right?"

"If dogs weren't that vicious, policemen would have certified attack gorillas instead. Come on, have you ever looked at Rosco? That mouthful of teeth could destroy a person." My squint narrows until I'm almost glaring, though why I should take my grief out on Brander, is beyond me.

"Whoa, okay." Brander holds up his hands and motions to my shave ice. "Sorry. Why don't we forget about it? Enjoy our food?"

"Fine." I blow out a breath through pursed lips as the scene from long ago fades from my mind. I'm hit with a gust of warm air as the trade winds pick up, and the sweet scent of plumeria floats on the breeze. "Sorry. I don't know what got into me. It's the same as it is with Mom—I guess it still hurts...too much."

"But sometimes we have to hurt before we can truly heal."

I shove a heaping, slushy spoonful of ice into my mouth to avoid giving an answer. Maybe hurting *does* lead to healing. But, if it does, I'm sure not about to find out. Better to let the memories scab over, get crusty and hazy. Forget about them.

Because, if I don't, they'll haunt me.

Awake.

In my dreams.

It won't matter—they'll always be there.

Chapter Fifteen

MONDAY MORNING, I'M UP AND OUTSIDE early, before the first wild rooster can make a sound. The sun has yet to begin chasing away the shadows, but I'm wide awake, heart drumming in my chest at the memory of a not-too-distant nightmare.

Ever since I told Brander about that pit bull, I can't get myself together. It's like opening up that part of my life, allowing one crack to form in my pain-proof armor, has signaled the beginning of my emotional downfall.

Pit bulls and helpless kittens, cancer wards and whirring oxygen tanks—they all come rushing into my mind, bringing with them tears to cloud my vision. But that's better than what I've faced in bed the last two nights—a constant battle between sleeplessness and nightmares.

Which is why I'm awake now, the snarling of an imaginary pit bull ringing in my ears as I sink onto the front porch steps. A car swishes by in a rush of silver, stirring the early-morning air. I watch its taillights, glowing red in the dark, as it slows to a stop at the end of the street. In a moment, a single flash of the blinker, it's gone.

Like Mom.

Peaches.

One moment—here, hanging on for life.

The next—gone. Vanished.

His eye is on the sparrow—that's what Grams would say. Or maybe she'd quote one of her other favorite Bible-isms about God's plan. And I get it. I really do.

But also...well...there's a part of me that *wonders*.

What's Mom doing right now? Can she see me? Hear me? Or is she trapped in a heavenly holding cell, waiting for the rest of us to bite the dust and float on up to join her?

A dog barks as he peels around the corner, a hodgepodge of white splotches on his back illuminated by the streetlight.

My stomach grows cold, like I swallowed an entire block of ice, and I jump to my feet, ready to dive inside and lock the door behind me. But then someone—must be the mutt's owner—joins the dog under the light. The person laughs, her voice floating above the rough crashing of the waves, and stoops to snap a leash to the beast's collar.

I force myself to hold my breath an extra second—then two. The mutt isn't going to attack me now, and he wasn't going to. Even without the leash attached to his collar.

I'm an idiot.

But though I can tell myself that, will fully admit it, I can't make myself change.

I sit back down and stew a while longer, letting my thoughts come and go like the tide, until my pocket buzzes. Jazz's name appears on the cracked screen as I pull out my phone. I frown. What's Jazz doing calling me at—I squint at my watch in the half-darkness—not even six in the morning?

"Is everything okay?"

"Happy Monday to you too." Jazz's voice is different—scratchier—than usual. Did she just wake up, or is something else going on? "Maybe I should ask you the same thing. Why're you up so early?"

"Couldn't sleep." I shrug. Hopefully my tone of voice is as nonchalant as my body language.

"Nice try. What's wrong?"

"Nu-hu. You first."

The line crackles with static for a few seconds, then Jazz speaks again. "I wanted to tell you that, you know—my aunt?"

"What about her?" I can think of half a dozen thing

about Ruby, but nothing worth talking about. Unless Jazz is planning on trying to save Ruby's soul, something I would heartily endorse. And the sooner the better.

"Never mind. Want to come here to do school today? We can play with Koa after we're done." All of a sudden, Jazz's tone is light and snappy. Chipper. *Too* chipper.

"For one, I highly doubt you woke up before six to talk about school. For two...no. How many times do I have to tell you? I hate dogs."

"No, you don't." Jazz's voice is so plain, so matter-of-fact, that I almost believe her.

"I do too hate dogs."

"No, you're afraid of them. There's a difference." I can practically see Jazz's smug, Cheshire-cat grin from here. It's like the sun creeping up from behind Gramma's house, lighting the entire street.

"Fine. I'm afraid of them. I don't want to come over."

"But..." Jazz sighs on the other end. "I can't leave him here."

"Why not?"

"Long story. You come over, or I'm bringing Koa with me to Tutu Bonnie's."

"No way!" My voice splits the morning calm, and a stray chicken glares at me from across the street. "I mean," I soften my tone. "Gramma probably wouldn't like the mess."

"Good excuse." Jazz laughs. "Except Tutu loves puppies, and I bet Macie will have a blast hanging out with Koa after school."

"Sorry, but no. Maybe if we put him outside—"

"No!" Jazz's voice blares like a foghorn in my ear. "I mean, I don't want him to be lonely. Plus, Jonah expects us to keep an eye on him. Come on. Please?"

For a second, one single, glistening moment, I almost cave. Tell Jazz I'll be at her place by eight. But, before I do, she says, "Maybe we should do school on our own today. We

can work something out for the rest of the week, but—"

"This is the weirdest conversation ever. You called to talk to me about your aunt, then decided you didn't want to. And now you want me to come over, except you don't, and...what is going on with you?"

"Nothing!"

"*Sure.*"

"I'm serious."

"And I seriously don't believe you. You can tell me anything. You know that, right?"

Jazz huffs on the other line. "I don't have to tell you *everything* if I don't want to."

"Then don't." I stamp my foot against the porch step. My grip tightens around the phone.

Jazz lets out a mighty sigh. My shoulders droop and my heart sags. "You know, if you do want to talk, I'll be here."

"Thanks." Her voice is shrunken, shriveled. Like she's turning into a shell of the Jazz I used to know, the girl who was fearless. Shameless. Bold. Now, she's cagy. Edgy. Afraid to share her secrets with anyone—even me.

We hang up, and I slide the phone into my pocket, its cool smoothness a comforting weight amid a tsunami of confusion. I bring my hand to my necklace and roll the smooth shell between my fingers.

What is wrong with Jazz that she won't *talk* like she used to? Is it because of her leg? Her aunt? Is it because of me?

Shaking my head, I lean against the top step and sigh. This is as much my fault as it is Jazz's. After all, if I'd been able to face my fears and go over to Jazz's in the first place, things wouldn't have ended the way they did.

*Maybe...*the thought sneaks into my brain as the first rooster finally crows. Maybe I can't be a true friend until I quit being a coward.

I'm embedded in Gramma's couch later that afternoon, nose-deep in a literary analysis essay about the first fifteen chapters of *Pride and Prejudice*—steering clear from any of those scenes that have been making me tear up—when the front door slams. Something falls to the floor with a great *thud*, right as Gramma's oven timer lets out a blare.

"I hate Hawaii!" Macie's voice echoes in the hall.

"What on earth?" Gramma's voice swoops up seconds before a clatter comes from the kitchen, and Gramma hisses. "There goes my shortbread."

I peek at the kitchen chaos over my shoulder as heavy footfalls sound from the hallway.

"I hate Hawaii." Macie's voice is swollen with tears, and so is her face. She stomps around the corner into the living room, face twisted in a pout. "And Hawaii hates me."

"Whoa, watch your mouth. Don't say *hate*, okay?" I slide my laptop onto the coffee table as she runs toward the couch. "Why don't you tell me what's going on?"

"No." Macie skids to a halt in front of the couch and punches the cushions with one balled-up fist.

"Macie." Gramma crosses over to the living room, dusting flour from her palms. "Try to settle down. Let's talk." Gramma settles onto the couch next to me and motions for Macie to join her.

"No." Lip quivering, Macie stomps her foot. "I hate school. I'm never going there again. Not even when I'm really old. Like, twenty."

A flicker of pity gleams deep in Gramma's gaze, but she hardens her mouth and wags a knobby finger in Macie's face. "If you keep talking like that, there are going to be serious consequences."

Macie folds her arms over her chest. "Like what?"

I almost snicker at the exchange. Attitude must run in the family.

But it's no good laughing at Macie now. Not when she's about to blow like a humpback whale. *I've got this*, I mouth to Gramma, then stand and take a few steps toward Macie. "I know how you feel, squirt. Things here are way different than they were in Boston, but that doesn't mean they're bad."

"Does that mean Boston isn't bad, either?"

"Don't be silly." I reach forward to ruffle Macie's head of curls, but she pulls away. "Why would you think that?"

"The kids at school think it is. They keep calling me a *haole* transplant." Macie's lip quivers again, and a sob slips out.

Haole? I squint at Grams.

A white person, Gramma mouths, pulling at her skin for emphasis.

Got it.

"Why don't we take a walk on the beach?" I lift my head toward the open window, where a gentle breeze ruffles Gramma's filmy curtains.

Macie shrugs, and I take that as answer enough. Before she can object, I grab her hand and lead her down the hall, assuring Grams that we'll be home in time for dinner.

Once we're on the beach, Macie's hand loosens in my grip and her shoulders droop. We walk in silence, letting the waves fill the conversation void.

"Still think you hate Hawaii?" I pop the question after a half hour—probably the longest Macie's ever stayed quiet.

"I thought 'hate' was a bad word." Macie pulls away and crosses her arms triumphantly across her chest.

"Okay, so do you still really, really not like Hawaii?" I quirk an eyebrow and lead her over to sit on a fallen palm.

"I like Hawaii." Macie chews on the end of one of her cockeyed curls. "But not the people. And they don't like me either. They all play the ukulele and do hula and go surfing with their daddies on the weekends."

"You don't want to start *surfing*, do you?" The thought of my little sister balancing on a flimsy board in the water isn't the most comforting idea in the world.

Macie shakes her head. "But I want a ukulele. And friends. And a daddy. And..." She chomps on her hair again. "I want a mommy again."

My breath escapes in a silent whoosh. Any words of comfort I had for Macie are washed away in a wave of confusion—no, make that *horror*. How could Macie want to replace Mom? So soon after we lost her? It's not right.

"Alina's mom is nice. She brought cupcakes for us yesterday. Do you think she'd want to be my mommy?"

The weight of her words presses on my chest, squeezing every molecule of air from my lungs until I can barely breathe. I clutch my necklace. "You mean, you—I don't..."

"I don't love Mommy less, but she's not coming back. And I know she wouldn't want me to be lonely. She'd like Alina's mom anyway."

Tears blur my vision until the turquoise waters and the sky fuse into one big, blue sheet. "But—"

"I don't want to only have a *tutu*. I want to be like the other kids with aunties and uncles and mommies and daddies." Macie's entire face trembles. "I want to be normal. Daddy didn't even remember to call on the first day of school."

Ouch. I wince, and my hand curls into a fist. It takes every bit of restraint to keep from grabbing my phone and sending off an angry text right then and there. But, even though my blood's boiling, it's no use chewing Dad out now.

No, right now is all about Macie.

The sun winks off the water in the bay, and a trio of sand-crusted little girls run by, chasing one another through the sand and surf. Macie's gaze hardens as they frolic in the waves, hands linked together, dark hair blowing in the breeze.

"Do you know those girls?" I slip an arm around Macie's hunched shoulders as a tear dribbles from her eye.

"They sit in front of me in class. The tall one tossing her hair in my face." Macie wrinkles her nose, and I do the same. "I still want to be friends with them, though." Macie lifts a hand and pops her thumb in her mouth.

"Whoa." I grab Macie's arm and tug her hand out of her mouth. Her thumb is red and shriveled, like it's been kept underwater for the last month. "What's this?"

"Don't." Macie squirms and wraps her fingers around the thumb in question.

"How long has that been going on?"

"Since Kanani called me a baby when I cried on the first day." Macie twists her face up and sticks her tongue out in the direction of the three girls on the beach. If the way the tallest girl, the one with an impressive mane of black curls, is strutting around is anything to go by, I know exactly which one of them is Kanani.

"Have you talked to the teacher about any of this?" I peer at Macie, who shakes her head. "And why haven't you told me or Gramma?"

Macie hangs her head and lifts her thumb toward her mouth. "I don't want to get in trouble for tattling." The words creep around the thumb stuck in her mouth.

"Tattling is one thing. Standing up for yourself when you're being bullied is another." I stand and take a step toward the three little girls. "Which one is Kanani?"

"The tall one." Macie's voice comes out in a whisper. "But don't tell her I told you anything."

"Leave it to me." I toss the words over my shoulder as I jog across the beach toward the girl gaggle. "Aloha, girls." I waggle my hand in a *shaka* as I draw closer, and the girls whirl around to face me.

"Mama doesn't like it when I talk to strangers," one of

them whispers to her friend. But the tall one—Kanani—stands with her head held high and returns the *shaka*.

"Aloha." She stares up at me with wide eyes.

"You're Kanani?" The little girl's gaze narrows. "I'm Macie's big sister. You know her from school, right?"

Kanani nods in slo-mo and crosses her arms over her chest.

"I hear you and Macie haven't been getting along very well. Is that true?" I squat in the sand so I'm eye level with the girl.

"I dunno." Kanani scrunches up her face, almost as though she's not sure whose side I'm on. Her little friends back away, whispering to each other, but Kanani stands her ground. "Macie's weird. She thinks breadfruit is made from bread."

I bite my tongue to keep from asking what breadfruit *is* made from and instead shake my head. "Sure, maybe Macie's different. But that doesn't mean she's weird. I hate Spam—do you think I'm weird?"

Kanani shrugs. "My sister hates Spam."

Ha. I knew there had to be more people in the world that hate Spam. "See? We're all different. Maybe you should try and be friends with Macie before you decide whether or not she's weird."

Kanani scratches her nose. "I guess. But it's not fair that she—"

"Kanani!" Someone jogs up behind me, her strident voice splitting the late-afternoon calm. I whirl around to find a bikini-clad Malia, wet hair scraped into a ponytail, frown on her face. "What are you doing talking to a stranger?"

Stranger? My spine arches and I squint at Malia—not because of the bright sunshine, either. "I'm not—"

"She's not a stranger." Kanani kicks at the sand. "She's Macie's sister."

"Whatever. You shouldn't be talking to her. You know the

rules." Malia brushes past me and grabs Kanani's hand. "Time to go."

Kanani's face falls. She pooches out her lip before turning to wave at her friends. "Aloha! Goodbye!"

The little girls respond with a chorus of goodbyes and pleas for Kanani to stay longer, but Malia ignores them and yanks Kanani away from the group. "If you're trying to parent my little sister"—Malia's voice is low, slithery as a snake as she turns to leave—"you'd better cut it out. We don't need help from a transplant."

Frustration lights a fire in my chest, and everything in me is dying to fire off a comeback, but my usual arsenal of arguments has been obliterated. Is this what it's like when someone finally meets their match? Malia marches away, tightening her grip on Kanani as they disappear into the evening light.

After a few minutes, Macie jumps off the log and trots over to my side, concern chiseled into her round face. "Did she call you a *haole* too?"

"It's okay." I ruffle Macie's curls. "I think I was actually getting somewhere before Malia showed up."

"You know Malia?" Macie gapes at me like I told her I have weekly slumber parties with Hitler.

"Sure." I motion for us to start toward Gramma's place. But as we start walking, our backs to the setting sun, something dawns on me. I don't know Malia. Not really. Aside from the few times I've seen her at support group, we've never had a real conversation. At least, not enough of one to give me a read on her personality. We've mostly snarled at each other. It's not like either of us is Miss Congeniality.

Maybe I don't know Malia—don't know her at all.

Chapter Sixteen

"SOMETIMES WE NEED TO TALK. GET things off our chest." Jonah stands above the group at our next Saturday meeting. "Sometimes we don't even *know* we need to talk until we do. You with me?"

The group gives a collective shrug, and I clutch my workbook closer to my chest. Jonah is seriously planning on making us spill our guts to the entire group? Here? Today?

No way.

I scooch closer to Jazz, whose wide-eyed expression must mirror my own, and duck my head. Like my ostrich, head-in-the-sand technique will keep Jonah from calling on me.

"Olive? Why don't you start us off?"

My head shoots up. I stare at Jonah like he crawled out of the belly of a whale. "Me?"

Jonah laughs and stoops to pat Koa. The mutt is curled up under the picnic table, snoring in his sleep, probably dreaming vicious little doggy dreams. "It's nothing to be afraid of. This is a *support* group, remember? In other words, we're all here to, well, *support* each other."

No duh.

I smirk at Jazz, but her own expression is glazed. Her lips move like she's whispering a prayer.

I level my gaze at Jonah, well aware that I'm toeing the line of cordiality. "What do you want me to talk about?" I puff out my cheeks and keep staring at him. Not at Koa, though. No need to put *that* much stress on my blood pressure.

Brander shakes his head at me, almost like I'm a naughty toddler. "There's got to be something you'd like to get off your chest, isn't there?"

"Oh, sure." My hands quiver as I stare at my workbook. The thoughts in there are too personal—too raw—to share. Especially the page I added last night, after I got on Dad for all but dropping out of Macie's life. My blood simmers at the very thought of his one-word answers, his distracted tone. I get it that he's struggling, but does he have to take it out on the only family he has left?

I let my eyes wander over to Jazz, who is still floating off in her own little world.

She's been playing the serious-student card for the last few days, opening her mouth only to ask me about school stuff. Yet her grades aren't improving. Besides, she pretty much refuses to talk about anything other than Koa. And, since dogs are number one on my list of censored subjects...

"I'm having trouble with a friend. They're going through some stuff, and I want to be there for them. But I have a feeling I don't know how much *stuff* is going on, or how to help. I've tried talking to them, but they don't want to talk. I—" A sharp pinch to my arm interrupts me, and I turn my head to find Jazz glaring at me.

I snap my mouth shut and glance away. It's not like anyone would have been able to tell I was talking about Jazz. Unless, of course, they *were* Jazz.

Jonah is either oblivious to Jazz's murderous gaze, or he's an extremely good actor, because he pats Koa's head as though nothing out of the ordinary is going on. "Sometimes watching a friend struggle can be as hard on us as it is on them. Have you been spending time with this friend?"

I nod.

"Talking with them?"

A shrug.

"What about this—have you been praying for them?"

Not as much as I should—another shrug.

"Okay." Jonah claps his hands together and Koa jumps

to attention. I shudder and take a breath of air so big my lungs nearly burst. That dog had better not come near me. "Here's my suggestion. Go hang out with your friend. Don't act nosy or ask a bunch of questions but tell them you're praying for them. And that you'll be there to talk—really talk—whenever they need it."

"But—"

Another kid chimes in, asking for advice on a similar problem, and the rest of my sentence gets lost in the resulting conversation. I tune out and lean against the bench. But even with my head turned toward the beach, I can feel Jazz giving me the stink eye.

Why?

Because I care—want to help?

I refocus on Jonah as he makes his way around the group, beseeching everyone to bare their hearts. Most of them manage to choke out a few sentences, but others—AKA Malia—clamp their lips shut tighter than a clam.

"Come on." I scoot closer to Jazz when it's her turn and whisper in her ear. "It's not easy to talk, but it does help." Not that I'd break down in front of a group this big or anything, but sometimes sharing my thoughts with Grams or Brander helps more than I expect.

Jazz raises her head, shoulders squared, and looks across the circle at Jonah. "I—I'm having a hard time with school." She blows out a breath and picks at an already-ragged nail.

"Aw, dude. That stinks." A tall, tanned girl with a head of dreadlocks offers Jazz a smile and reaches out to pat Koa.

"Yeah, it does." Jazz raises her head a millimeter and makes eye contact with a bench halfway across the park. "And my leg's been killing me. The doc say it's a phantom pain but, real or not, it *hurts*."

I lean closer to Jazz on the bench and nudge her good leg with my own—enough to let her know I care.

And, miracle of miracles, she lifts her head an inch higher and smiles at me. It's weak—wobbly—but it's a *smile*. I return the gesture and reach out to give Jazz's hand a squeeze.

We finish going around the circle, sharing what's on our minds, and Jonah calls for us to bow our heads in prayer. I do, but I don't listen to his words. Instead, I give God some of my own.

I wish I could believe that there's nothing more to Jazz's attitude than an achy leg and a bad report card, but I can't. Please help her. Give her strength to ride out whatever it is that's bothering her and... I lift my head and stare straight across the group at Koa. He's pawing at the dirt, terrorizing an innocent little beetle. How will I survive training Koa to sit and speak and do all of those doggish things on command? I cringe.

Oh, and God? You'd better give me a dose of that strength while you're at it.

A while later, after various kids have helped Koa practice his *sit, stay,* and *come,* Jonah reaches into his backpack and comes up with a tennis ball in each hand. "Koa's future owner, Lio, has been struggling to develop his motor skills. Tossing a ball for Koa could help him loosen up. But we want Koa to be able to drop the ball at Lio's feet—not run halfway across the island with it stuck in his mouth."

Which is why—oh, joy—*we* get to play fetch with Koa now. Jonah beams like he's announced that the entire group is going to Disneyland.

I don't think so.

"You go." I poke Jazz in the side. "Didn't you say the doctor made you play catch to work on your balance? It's a win-win."

"Look at you, being so caring and self-sacrificing." Jazz quirks her brows at me. "You can't hide forever."

Fear rises like the tide, rushing into my chest and nearly drowning me in panic. "But—"

"*But* lucky for you, I love playing catch." Jazz plants her hands on her thighs and rises to her feet before taking a few stiff steps toward Jonah. "Can I go first?"

"Sure." Jonah tosses her a ball. "Then tell your friend to get off her 'ēlemu and help out."

"Say what?" I stand and trail after Jazz, who pitches the ball across the park, then turns to me.

"Jonah wants you to get off your duff and lend a hand. You can't be a part of the group without doing something to help."

"Great." Every part of me turns to cement as Koa tears after the ball, snatches it, and races over to Jazz.

"Good boy." She ruffles his ears, then holds out her hand. "Give it."

Koa lets out a growl and takes a step back, eyes gleaming in typical villain-mutt style. "Careful, Jazz." I jerk away and nearly bump into Brander. "Sorry."

"It's okay." He puts a hand on my shoulder before leaning in, his breath whistling in my ear as he whispers. "Koa's goofing off. All dogs like to play tough."

"So what? That doesn't mean it'll hurt any less when he bites my hand off." I cross my arms and shake my head as a lanky surfer guy chases Koa halfway to the beach. He kneels and wrestles the ball from Koa's toothy grip before jogging over to the group.

"That dude's got some choppers on him." The guy wipes his forehead and puffs out a laugh before holding out the ball, now slimy with dog drool. "Who's next?"

"Her." Jazz jerks her thumb at me and flashes a smile so sunny I don't dare protest. Brander gives my shoulder another squeeze, and I swallow ten years' worth of terror as I take the ball, holding it between my thumb and forefinger.

Before I can even adjust my grip, Koa gallops to my side and launches into the air in an attempt to grab the ball. His jagged white teeth gleam in the fluorescent sunlight, grazing empty air, and a growl bubbles up from his throat.

I've got to get this ball—and this dog—away from me. *Now.*

I pitch the tennis ball with every ounce of oomph I have, but instead of going away from me, the ball shoots straight into the air. Koa tips his head, watching, and I do the same. The others—even Jazz—laugh. I'm about to join in when the ball comes hurtling back to earth—or, more accurately, my skull.

It ricochets off my forehead and lands a few feet away. Koa jumps to his feet and trots after it, and the laughter intensifies.

"Ouch." I grimace and rub my head, though my pride is the only thing that's seriously injured.

"Okay, enough fetch for now." Jonah motions a time-out with his hands, then waves for us to sit. "Let's do a bit of housekeeping before we eat. Koa's a smart little guy. With all of your help, he'll be able to learn his manners in no time. Which means he'll soon be ready to meet his new family."

A few frowns flit around the group, but all I can think is *thank goodness.* The sooner Koa gets out of here, the sooner this thing turns back into a support group, instead of the torture chamber it's become.

"I was thinking we could throw Koa a going-away party. We can have it here or at the church and give people an opportunity to come, hang out, and donate money. Lio's family has been having to scrimp to make ends meet as it is, and dog food isn't cheap."

"That's a great idea." Jazz perks up. "I bet we'd get a ton of donations."

Brander nods, and his cowlick bobs in agreement. "What

if we do it over Thanksgiving weekend? A lot of people will be coming in for the holiday. If we pitch it right—make it a heartwarming local holiday fundraiser—my parents might be able to help us get coverage on the local news."

A collective murmur of appreciation goes up from the group, minus Malia, who's pecking on her phone with the intensity of a hungry woodpecker. Can't she straighten up and at least fake interest for once? After all, we're supposed to be helping this family, and a fundraiser will— "Uh-oh."

"What's wrong?" Jazz turns to look at me.

"A fundraiser—we'll need to get approval from the town council if we want to hold it here."

"Oh. Right." Brander's face falls. "But we don't have to get approved if we want to do it at the church, right?"

"Right." Jonah scribbles in his notebook, and I run my fingers through my hair. Why didn't we think of that—oh, a few months ago, when we were raising money for Jazz's leg?

Whatever. At least we figured it out now. This'd better be the party of the century—for Lio and his family, *and* for me. It'll be a celebration not only of Koa's new home, but of my freedom.

Freedom from Saturday mornings spent hanging out with my biggest nightmare.

Freedom from the fear that said nightmare will ransack my best friend's house.

Freedom from...everything. All of the fear and pain and heartache.

Or at least, some of it.

"You want to come hang out at Gramma's?" I glance at Jazz and shift my workbook from one hand to the other after the group session ends for the day. "When I left, she was taking a loaf of banana bread out of the oven."

"Sure. But I'll have to bring the beast." Jazz tugs on her end of Koa's leash.

I bite my lip and glance from Jazz, her face the picture of hope, to Koa, who is growling—or is it snoring?—as he dozes at her feet.

"Come on, be brave." Jazz makes a fist and punches the air. "If it makes you feel that much better, I guess we could keep him out back. At least for a while."

"Fine." I pull out my phone. "Lemme text Gramma."

"Don't bother." Brander's deep, rich voice reverberates in the air next to my ear. "I'm driving right past Tutu's place—I can drop you off."

"That would be great. Thanks." We start toward the Porsche, Jazz half-dragging a drowsy Koa.

"What are you up to today?" Jazz's words are nearly whipped away in the wind as Brander pulls onto the main road a few minutes later.

"I'm going to the resort, to see if the PR guy's in." Brander adjusts his sunglasses. "He has a lot of contacts, and I bet he could help me find someone to cover Koa's goodbye party."

"That mutt is seriously going to get on the news. Good grief." I shudder as the image of Koa's pointy little teeth flashes through my mind.

"He's not a mutt." Jazz turns and shoots me a half-glare. "He's going to be a miracle for someone like Lio. At least, I know he would be for someone like *me*." Her expression dims.

"Don't tell me you actually wish you had a dog?" I catch myself one millisecond before scoffing, and Brander's gaze meets mine in the rearview mirror.

"I've wanted a puppy ever since I can remember. But now's not the time." She leans forward and flicks the radio to a praise station before turning up the volume.

As we zip along the road to Gramma's, Brander's

subwoofer pounding in my ears, Jazz tossing her head and belting out every song that comes on the radio, something stirs inside of my chest.

What would life be like if I were more like Jazz—completely unbothered, unafraid of the trials of this world? Not trying so hard to hold onto things that no longer *are*. Simply living, breathing, and enjoying the fact that I'm alive.

Even now, amid the secrets she's keeping, the troubles she's facing, whatever they may be, she's calm. Trusting.

What would life be like if I was more like Jazz? I brush my hair out of my face as Brander slows to a halt in front of Gramma's house.

Maybe I'll never know—until I try living that way myself.

"I said, I *want* some." Macie wraps her arms around Gramma's leg and stares up into Grams' crinkled tissue-paper face

Gramma brushes Macie away, like she's no more a nuisance than a pesky fly and screws the lid on her jar of caramel sauce.

"Can I have some, Grammy?" Macie licks her lower lip. "Please?"

"The magic words," Jazz whispers to me, as though she knows from experience. And she's right—Gramma finally goes to work preparing a pint-sized sundae for Macie.

"Want to go outside with this?" I grit my teeth as I say it. We left Koa outside, curled up among the hibiscus bushes right beneath Gramma's porch. The simple thought of being out there with him is enough to give me a heart attack, but the light that blooms on Jazz's face at my suggestion is worth it.

We head out front, Macie trotting at our heels, and I help Jazz ease onto the porch swing before lowering myself next to her. Macie stands in front of us, clutching her bowl and bouncing on the balls of her feet. "Can I sit?" Her eyes widen into great pools of melted chocolate.

Jazz nods and scoots away so there's a gap between us, then motions for Macie to sit. She does, instantly snuggling up next to Jazz despite the almost ninety-degree heat. My ice cream is already half melted out here, so I dip my spoon into the bowl and dig in.

I couldn't make myself stomach much at support group, especially since my hands were covered in Koa-slobber, so I scarf down my snack almost as fast as Macie gobbles hers.

When we're done, I take our bowls inside before rejoining Jazz and Macie on the porch. Unfortunately, the floorboards creak as I cross over to the swing, and Koa's collar jangles as he patters up the steps, ready to destroy the one who dared disturb his slumber.

Chapter Seventeen

WHEN WE STEP INTO THE COOL darkness of Gramma's seaside cottage, Gramma and Macie are putting the last of the lunch dishes away, but that banana bread of Gramma's still sits happily on the counter, begging someone to cut into it.

I hate to let a simple request like that go unanswered, so after washing up, I reach for a knife and slice into the end of the loaf. Sliding the piece onto a plate, I motion for Jazz to do the same, but Grams swoops in and waves her hands in front of the slice.

"Haven't I taught you better than that?" She wags her finger in my face, but there's a smile in her eyes. "You need to experience Tutu-style banana bread. Jazz?"

Jazz obviously knows the drill because she limps to the freezer and pulls out a gallon of ice cream before reaching into the fridge for a jar of caramel and a can of whipped cream. She deposits the ingredients on the counter in front of Gramma, then winks at me and pats her tummy—not so flat, now that she isn't training for swim team. Her expression, already one of rapture, only intensifies a few minutes later, when Gramma hands us each a bowl of banana bread piled high with caramel and ice cream, plus fresh banana slices and whipped cream.

"You two go enjoy." She pats Jazz's arm right as Macie butts in, letting out the most pathetic whine I've ever heard.

"What about me? I want some." She balls her hands into fists and shoves them in her shorts, as though warning that a tantrum is about to occur. Gramma doesn't even bat an eye.

Panic rising in my chest, I scurry the rest of the way to the swing and jump onto my seat before Koa can decide to use me as his next chew toy.

"What's wrong?" Macie reaches to pat Koa, who returns the favor by ramming her knee with his wet, slimy nose. I curl my upper lip, but Macie giggles, the sound a soothing balm to my ears.

I sigh and nudge her off the swing. "Why don't you go run around with that beast?" That way, Jazz and I can have a *real* conversation.

"You honestly don't like Koa, do you?" Jazz turns to me but keeps one eye on the furry little scoundrel as he and Macie tumble down the front steps.

"Honestly? I'm terrified of him. Dogs and I were *not* made to be friends."

"That's sad." Jazz ducks her head. Macie's giggles float up from the yard as Koa covers her in slobber from his wet, slimy tongue. "So you've never had a dog?"

"Nope. What about you?"

Jazz wags her head from side to side. "Mom had a puppy when she was a kid. Always promised she'd get me one, but now..." She presses her lips together, as though afraid to say anything more.

I'm about to dig deeper—to ask why she clams up every time she mentions her past, her mom, but Jonah's words return. Instead, I scoot closer to her on the bench and put an arm around her shoulders. "You know I'm here to talk if you need it."

Jazz's shoulders tense beneath my arm, and she pulls away. "Let me guess. You're going to let me know you're praying for me? Like Jonah told you to do?"

"Of course I'm praying for you." I scoot closer to Jazz, but she scrambles to her feet and inches away.

"I know you were ratting on me to Jonah, and he probably figured it out. Now every time I see him, he'll be badgering me to tell him what's wrong." Jazz crosses her arms over her chest. "I get it that you want to help, and I appreciate it. But next time, don't use me as your scapegoat."

"What are you talking about?" I jump to my feet and step toward Jazz. "I am worried about you. You're a million miles away, and you won't even tell me why. After all we've been through, don't you think I deserve to know?"

Jazz shakes her head and sighs. "Maybe so, but if you expect me to spill my guts to you, why can't you do the same thing?"

"That's different." Hot tears of frustration well in my chest. I push them away. "My mom's *dead*, okay? It's not like talking about her now will bring her back."

"That's not an explanation. That's an excuse." Jazz shakes her head, braid whipping through the sultry afternoon air, and calls for Koa to come.

The little mutt bounds up the porch steps with Macie close behind. Her brow is wrinkled, her bottom lip stuck out like a life preserver. "Why are you and Jazzie yelling?"

"I'm not yelling!" My voice pounds against the wall of humidity in the air, and I puff out a sigh. Maybe I *am*. "Sorry. But seriously." I pull Jazz aside as she turns to leave. "I am worried about you."

"Fine. Be worried." Jazz flips her braid over one shoulder. "But I don't see any reason to come crying to you when you're running off to bawl in the bathroom every time you read that dumb Jane Austen book."

I take a step back, eyes bugging out like I'm a cartoon character.

"Oh, yeah. I'm not dumb." She shakes her head, as though attempting to shake off her frustration, and bends to clip Koa's leash to his collar. Her good leg wobbles, and I reach out to steady her, but she pushes away, face drawn.

I stand like a petrified tiki totem as Jazz straightens,

brushes off her hands, and marches down the porch steps. Her stride is stiff and wooden as she steps onto the sidewalk.

Macie lifts her thumb, as though about to stick it in her mouth again, but I grab her hand and lace her fingers though mine. Macie's lip juts out even farther. "Where are you going, Jazzie?"

"Home. See ya later, squirt." Jazz keeps walking, barely glancing over her shoulder as she heads toward the street corner. Alone. In the midafternoon heat. Isn't she going to at least text Ruby to pick her up?

The front door creaks behind me and Gramma joins us, barefoot, on the porch. "What happened?"

"Don't ask me. One minute, I'm telling Jazz I'm praying for her, the next she's ragging on me for not spilling my soul to the world."

"Huh?" Macie squints at me.

"Never mind." I wave my hand in the air, kick off my high-tops, and march inside.

When will I learn to stop being a brat and *grow up*?

"Olive?" Jazz's voice is low-pitched and soggy the next morning. I press my phone to my ear and swing from my seat at the breakfast bar, more than happy for an excuse to leave behind my half-eaten omelet.

"What's up? Don't tell me you're bagging out on school *again*." I laugh a little, so she'll know I'm teasing, and amble out to the front porch.

"No." Her voice cracks, and I tighten my grip on the phone. "Yes. I don't know. I—it's Koa."

"Is that all? You can bring him if it's that important to you. But make sure he stays away from my stuff." My stomach quivers at the thought of spending more time with that dog, but I shake my head. Jazz is my friend, and friends make sacrifices for each other.

"That's not it." A sob rattles on the other end.

"Then what's wrong? He didn't run off, did he?"

"No." A sniff. "But...you're gonna kill me."

"Try me." I wind a strand of hair around my finger and step onto the front porch.

"You've gotta take him."

"Pardon?" She didn't say what I think she said. She couldn't have. She *knows* better.

Doesn't she?

"I'm sorry." A yell and a yelp—the latter sounding as though it came from Koa—comes through the phone, and Jazz whimpers. "Please," she lowers her voice. "For me? I'll make it up to you, I promise."

"I can't and you know it. There's gotta be someone else. What about Brander?"

"He's not answering. The only other person I can think of is—nu-uh."

"Who?" I press the phone against my face.

"Malia." Jazz groans. "But I'm not calling her. Not today."

Malia. She *did* have the whole goo-goo-eyed-puppy-lover thing going on last Saturday. Figures. "What's her number? I—I'll call her."

"You will?" Jazz gasps. "I thought you two had some sort of mortal enemy-ship thing going."

"Yeah? Well, I have a way worse mortal enemy-ship with dogs. Honestly, Koa makes Malia look like a pussycat."

"If you say so." I can practically see Jazz's eyes rolling around in her head as she rattles off Malia's number and wishes me luck.

"Olive?" Gramma peers outside as I dial Malia. "What's going on?"

The phone rings, and I raise it to my face, holding a finger in the air. *One minute*, I mouth to Grams as someone picks up.

"Who is this?" The voice on the other end is rough, guarded.

"Olive Galloway. From support group?"

"What do you want?"

"Can you take care of Koa? Jazz signed up for two weeks in a row, but something came up."

"And you thought of me? How'd you get my number, anyway?"

"From Jazz. Listen, you seemed to like him. I thought you might be willing to—"

"You thought wrong." Malia huffs on the other end. "I'm not taking him for two weeks. One is already more than enough for my parents. Besides, it's not like he's a rabid pit bull. He's a fluffy little puppy with harmless little baby teeth. Suck it up and deal with it."

"But..."

"Sorry." The line goes dead.

Typical. I bring the phone away from my face and glare at it.

"What's going on?" Gramma pads across the porch and lays a hand on my shoulder. "Is Jazz okay?"

"Like I would know." I kick at the porch railing, then wince. Next time I want to express my emotions using my feet, I'll put shoes on first. "She's being all weird and cryptic. All I know is she can't take care of Koa anymore. For *some* reason."

Gramma runs a hand over her hair. Does she know what's going on? Her gaze is impenetrable—even if she does know more than I do, I wouldn't be able to get her to spill. When someone tells Grams a secret, she keeps it buried ten-thousand leagues under the sea.

Grams wags a finger in my face and clicks her tongue, almost as though she can read my mind. "I don't know what's going on with Jazz, but I can guarantee that, whatever it is, God has Jazz right where He wants her to be."

"Not helping, Grams. What am I going to do? We can't have Koa staying *here* for a week. There's no way."

Gramma lifts one feathery eyebrow. "Who told you that?"

"Well..." I shove my phone in my pocket. "I just..."

"Exactly." Grams gives my shoulder another pat and gestures to my high-tops, lying in a pile by the front door. "Put on your shoes and go get Koa. You can finish your breakfast when you get home."

Cold eggs *and* dogs? "You don't get it. I can't. I hate dogs. I—"

Gramma's gaze hardens, and I gulp down an encyclopedia's worth of arguments. "Don't keep Jazz waiting."

Jazz.

What was it I said earlier—anything for a friend? I hurry to tie my high-tops, the laces tangling in my fingers. My stomach knots up. I don't know whether it's from the rubbery, flubbery eggs in there, the thought of seeing Koa again, or the way Jazz was acting on the phone. Most likely, it's a big, nasty combination of all of the above.

By the time I half-jog to Jazz's place, I'm breathing hard and worrying harder. Jazz has always been my rock, my God's-got-this kind of friend that keeps me steady. Now she's about to erupt like an angry volcano, and I don't know what to do.

But there's no point in putting off the inevitable.

Squaring my shoulders, I march up the overgrown front path and take the rickety steps two at a time before drawing to a halt in front of the saggy screen door.

"Jazz?" I knock on the frame. A putrid odor—beer again?—wafts from inside the darkened crypt.

Clumsy, cumbersome footsteps echo from inside, and Jazz crutches around the corner. Her hair lies limp and lank against her head, and her eyes are heavy. She looks up at me, and a raw sob bursts out from her chest. "I'm sorry."

"Good grief, it smells like a brewery in there." I wrinkle my nose and peer at Jazz. Her gaze, while heavy, doesn't appear glassy. Plus, she promised me the beer was Ruby's problem, not hers. "What's going on?"

"Shh. Not now." She hobbles closer to the door and leans her head against the screen. "Listen, I know how hard this is for you. And I...appreciate it. A lot. So thanks." A tear winks in the corner of her eye.

"You're welcome, but Jazz—seriously. Nothing you tell me will freak me out. Is it Ruby? Does she have a deadbeat boyfriend living here?" I sniff the air again and cringe. "Because, either way, I'd say she needs help."

"Nice idea, but there are people who can't accept help. Even when it's given to them on a silver platter." She turns from the door and whistles softly.

Koa rounds the corner, but he's not scampering like usual. Instead, he's moving at the pace of a sea slug, and his left back leg drags against the ground.

"What's wrong with him?" I crouch to take a closer look. With a screen—albeit a flimsy one—between me and Koa, I can almost imagine that he's kind of...no. I can't go there. Dogs aren't cute. Even little ones. They're all the same.

Right?

Jazz clears her throat. "Ready to get a move on?"

"What's the hurry?" I straighten and cross my arms. "If nothing's wrong like you say, then I don't see why I can't come in and—"

"No!" Jazz's voice finally goes above a single decibel, and she instantly claps a hand over her mouth. The sudden movement must throw her off balance, because she sways on her leg and tightens her grip on her crutches.

"Jaz-zi-mine." A sing-song-y voice that could only belong to an incredibly intoxicated Ruby wobbles down the hall.

"Are you okay by yourself?" I glance at Koa, then again at Jazz, whose wide-eyed expression makes my heart twist. "If your aunt's sloshed, I don't want to leave you alone with her. Why don't you put on your leg and at least take a walk with me? Maybe we can—"

"Jazz?" The voice hiccups.

Jazz's shoulders curl. "I'd better go see what she wants. Call Jonah and see if he has any extra food for Koa. I ran out." Jazz cracks open the door and Koa limps out. She hands me the leash, and I take it between my thumb and forefinger.

Jazz makes a move to close the door, but I leap forward and stick my foot in the doorjamb. "Why don't I call Jonah *now*? Get him to come over and help you out?"

"No." Jazz sags against her crutches as she leans forward to whisper. "That'll make it worse. Trust me. The best thing to do with this kind of thing is to ride it out and—"

"Who're ya talkin' to, Jazz?" The voice still comes from the hall, but it's closer now. Too close. I take a step back and, before I can blink, Jazz slams the screen door shut.

I sputter in protest, but I can't get a real word out before Jazz slams the wood door shut too. Now I'm trapped outside. Alone with my living, panting nightmare.

My heart thuds in my chest, my conscience screams at me to hightail it home to Gramma's, but I suck in a breath and cock my ear toward the door. The words being spoken are muffled, but their tone is crystal clear.

Jazz's voice is steady, strong—almost stilted—but the other person's is...not. It wobbles every which way, growing louder by the syllable. I tighten my grip on Koa's leash, turn around, and sprint down the front steps.

Away from the house.

Away from Jazz.

But not away from the realization that there's something much greater, more drastic, going on than I ever could have imagined. What is it? Who knows.

All I know is, I'm not going to sit around and let my best friend struggle alone.

I need answers, and I'm going to get them. One way or another.

But something tells me time is running out.

Chapter Eighteen

STEP. STEP. *TUG.*

Why didn't Jonah ever suggest that we take time to teach Koa his leash manners? Koa tugs on the grimy blue rope, forcing me to tighten my grip on the handle as I trail as far behind him as I possibly can.

His tiny toenails—pawnails?—click against the sidewalk in a lopsided rhythm, and his hind leg drags against the pavement with every other step.

What happened to him?

Curiosity swells in my chest, threatening to drown my sensibility. Grams can take a look at him when we get home.

Which will be soon, hopefully. Pardon me for being clichéd, but I don't think my nerves can take much more of this.

Did I really never notice how long of a trek it is to Gramma's place? Or maybe having an unwanted canine companion is making it take that much longer.

Then again...

Something taps at the corner of my brain, and I slow my pace.

What if I took this as an opportunity to learn? To grow, like Gramma's always saying.

I straighten my spine, shake out my free hand, and look down at Koa. What if I tried to see him the way everybody else does—as a sweet, lovable little pup that needs someone to care about him?

The stiffening fear begins to seep from my shoulders as I relax, and I almost smile at the pup.

But before I can, a dark, furry figure darts across the road, and Koa snaps to attention.

A cat.

Run, kitty. Run. My shoulders shoot back up until they've nearly replaced my earrings. The cat disappears into the bushes on my left, and Koa follows. My hand clamps around the leash.

Now or never.

I tug backwards with everything in me, and Koa yelps. He casts one last glance at where the cat disappeared, then dips his head to inspect his injured leg.

"Sorry, bud." Keeping a grip on his leash, I take a step closer, kneel, and—wait. I freeze, my hand in the air halfway between me and Koa, then scramble to my feet before the mutt can attack. "Let's get you home."

"Grams?" I nudge the front door open with one bare foot and keep a healthy distance between myself and Koa as we step inside. Once the front door has swung shut behind us, I take a moment to revel in the gentle tranquility.

The tile floor is smooth beneath my feet, probably freshly scrubbed, and the air is tinged with ribbons of cinnamon and sugar. "Grams?" The word seeps into the cool darkness, but no one answers.

Her car was in the driveway, so she couldn't have gone anywhere. I finger my necklace and wait for an answer. Koa whines and paws at the floor, his toenails scraping against those nicely polished tiles. "No-no." I wag my finger at him and harden my tone, but my heart softens a teeny bit when he stares up at me with wide, wondering eyes. It can't be easy for him, getting shuffled around from place to place like someone's unwanted junk—especially with that sore leg. At least Macie and I had Gramma to come to after Mom died.

"Olive?" Gramma's voice comes from above, and I look up as she hustles down the stairs, holding an over-stuffed pillow and a ratty quilt. "I thought we could use this as a doggy bed for Koa. Did Jazz say anything to you about what's going on?"

I shake my head. "Nada. But I think Ruby was drunk." I sag against the wall and recount the bizarreness of the scene as Gramma's face roils and darkens.

"I'd better call Pastor Dave. Someone needs to check up on them."

"Why bring Pastor Dave into it? Just go over yourself."

Gramma glances over her shoulder at me on her way to the kitchen phone. "It's not my place."

"Can't you make it your place?"

Gramma sighs and hangs her head. "There's only so much I can do. Sometimes we have to hand things over to God and trust that He has someone else picked out that can take better care of them than we can."

"If you say so." I bend and unsnap Koa's leash. He stares at me with wide eyes and takes a few stiff steps away. "But look at Koa. I don't know what Ruby did to him, but I sure don't want Jazz to end up like him. She has enough problems with her legs already." Koa whines, as if in agreement, and hobbles over to inspect a pile of shoes by the hall closet.

Gramma raises a finger to her lips and grabs her clunky landline. She punches in the number from memory, then presses the phone against her tanned, wrinkled face. "Hello? David?" She listens, twisting her finger around the cord for a few minutes, then flaps her hand, as if shooing me away.

I shake my head, but Gramma continues the motion. *For Jazz*, she mouths, pointing to the hallway.

Bowing my head in resignation, I tromp outside to the front porch, leaving the door ajar in case Koa feels like exploring the great outdoors. I collapse onto the swing and peek at my watch. Not even eight in the morning, but it feels like I've lived an entire day already.

Macie comes outside after a few minutes, princess-kitty backpack slung around her sturdy shoulders, her hair pulled into two tight ponytails. "Why do we have the puppy? Doesn't Jazzie want him anymore?"

I sigh and grit my teeth. "Jazz loves Koa. But she needs help taking care of him."

"You mean he's ours?" Macie spins in a circle.

"No, thank goodness. Only for a week. Then he's on to someone else from the support group."

"Oh." Macie's face falls. "But at least we have him for now."

"Right." I close my eyes tight. When I open them, I find Koa out on the porch beside Macie. He nuzzles her sparkly sneakers, and Macie giggles, her voice so loud, so free, that I can't help smiling. Until Koa fixes his attention on me.

He saunters across the porch, leg still a bit stiff, and sniffs the air like I'm an extra-juicy steak. I yank my legs onto the swing next to me, but that doesn't deter him. He lifts his head and runs his tongue over my toes. I swallow a scream, tightening my grip around the swing's weathered wooden slats. *Stay away, beast.*

"What's wrong?" Macie steps forward to pat Koa again. "Don't you like him?"

"Isn't it time for you to head off to the bus stop?" I raise an eyebrow at Macie, and she moans.

"Yeah. But I wanna play with Koa as soon as I get home."

"That's fine."

Maybe by then, I can convince myself to not break out in mental hives every time Koa oversteps my ten-foot, dog-free radius.

After spending all morning and part of the afternoon slugging through my schoolwork and creeping around so as to not attract any unwanted attention from Koa, I sneak across the street to the beach, where I pick a shady spot and sit, leaning against the smooth bark of one of the palms.

Pulling out my phone, I text Dad.

Can we talk?

I cross my fingers as I wait for his response.

Not now.

So much for that. I snort, then tap on Brander's icon. Maybe he's around.

You free?

His reply is almost instant:

Sure. What' s up?

I bite my lip and stare at the glistening waters for a minute.

Too much to explain. Meet at the Shave Ice Shack?

A trio of dots appear, and I wait for his response.

Where are you now?

A dove coos overhead as I type, and I can't help smiling.

The beach by Gramma' s.

Only a moment later, a response from Brander pops up.

Wait there.

I do as I'm told. Within a few minutes, Brander's Porsche pulls up to the curb, and he jumps out. Sunglasses veil his expression, but his head wags from side to side as he scans the beach.

"Over here." I jump to my feet and wave.

Brander returns the gesture with a *shaka* as he jogs over, his shoes shining in the afternoon sunshine. "Are you okay?" He pushes his sunglasses onto his head, flattening his cowlick.

"I'm fine. I guess. Except for the dog. It's Jazz I'm worried about."

"Huh?" Brander wrinkles his forehead at me as we head toward his car. "What's up with Jazz? And what does Koa have to do with anything?" He stops in front of the passenger's side and opens the door for me.

"Long story." I collapse into the seat and wait for Brander to get in the driver's side before explaining. By the time I'm done, Brander has taken me for a spin down the main highway to a ramshackle farmers' market with a food truck covered in a medley of painted fruits and flowers.

"I don't know what to do." I crack open the car door and step onto the dirt patch.

Brander hops out and joins me, resting a hand ever-so-lightly on my shoulder. "Want a smoothie?"

"Um…" I peek again at the truck out of the corner of my eye. It's a bizarre cross between a hippy peace bus and one of those food trucks that could give a person E. coli, but Brander nudges me toward it. If Mr. Fancy-Pants is okay eating here, then I guess…

"I promise, it's way better than it looks."

I purse my lips and follow him to the order window.

A few minutes later, we're in Brander's car again, both of us holding coconut-banana smoothies. "Now what?" Brander glances at me as he pulls onto the crowded little highway.

"What do you mean? You're the one who took me on this—excursion." Did I almost say *date*? Why would I call this a date? Except for the fact that he paid for me, and I didn't even try to buy. And—

"About Jazz?" Brander cocks his head at me. Obviously I'm supposed to say something. Whatever that *something* is supposed to be, I haven't a clue.

"Sorry. What'd you say?"

"What are we going to do about Jazz?" Brander frowns and guns the gas so hard I'm thrown back in the seat.

"Thanks for the whiplash." I grin, then take a drink of my smoothie. "And Jazz? No clue. I've tried to get her to talk, but she won't. It's like she's afraid saying anything will make the entire island erupt. I don't get it."

"Really?" Brander *harrumphs* under his breath, and I scoff.

"What do you mean *really*? Why wouldn't Jazz want to talk to me about whatever it is that's going on? I'm one of her closest friends."

Brander shrugs. "Why wouldn't you talk to me?"

"Huh?" I stare at Brander like he's sprouted another cowlick.

"About the support group. Why didn't you tell me the truth?" His voice cuts like sharpened flint, and I wince.

"You're not still holding on to that, are you? I thought you'd forgiven me."

Brander sighs and runs a hand through his hair. "I did. But that doesn't mean what you did is right."

"I know." I clench my fist and huff out a sigh. "Whatever. That's not what this is about. You think Jazz is—what? Embarrassed?"

"Possibly."

"Come on, you've known Jazz way longer than I have. You've got to have more of an explanation than that. Spill it." Something I've never felt around Brander boils up in my chest—frustration? Irritation? I don't know. All I know is, if we keep going this way, I might blow my cork.

Brander guns the gas again—hard enough to make me think that maybe he feels the same way. "Jazz has a tough life. It hasn't always been easy for her to fit in with the other kids. Some of them see her as, you know."

"But I *don't* know. And I'd appreciate it if you told me." My tone is at once ice-cold steel and boiling hot magma.

"I can't. Not unless I want to break Jazz's trust. There are things meant to stay between friends."

"Whatever."

"What's that supposed to mean?" Brander pulls off the main highway and screeches to a halt at a red light before turning to look at me, something brewing beneath his gaze.

"It means that you're giving Jazz a get-out-of-jail-free card, but not me. You're still dredging *my* mistake up to justify Jazz's bad behavior. Pardon me, but something about that seems kind of off." I take another slurp of my smoothie, sucking so hard it shoots down the wrong side of my throat. I choke, banana froth going where no liquid should ever go, and sit there, coughing and sputtering like a fool.

"Sorry." The light turns green, and Brander zips across the intersection. He keeps his eyes fixed straight ahead, but nothing on his face says *sorry* to me. "You don't know Jazz like I do. Trust me, if my hunch is right, she has every right to a bit of privacy."

So now he's calling me nosy?

I scoff.

"And what you did hurt. I thought we were getting close. After everything we went through this summer, and, well, you know..." Brander pulls onto Gramma's street. "I thought we'd be honest with each other. And then for you to—yeah.

Whatever."

"It's obviously not *whatever* to you." I cough again and strain against the urge to thrust my nose into the air like a spoiled rotten diva. "And I'm sorry. I really am. I thought you knew that."

"I *do* know that." Brander sighs and kills the engine in front of Gramma's place. "But sometimes *sorry* isn't enough. You know what I mean?"

Yes. I hang my head, not quite ready to admit it aloud. Grams is right. Brander is right. This rebuilding-trust business is way tougher than I ever could have imagined. *God, help me stop messing this kind of stuff up.*

Brander groans and shakes his head. "This is complicated. I—" his phone beeps, and he grimaces. "I've gotta go. I have an interview with the news for Koa's party. Can I call you tonight?"

His brush-off wraps my heart in barbed wire, and my throat burns with a mix of frustration and half-stuck smoothie. "If you want." I push the door open and hop out. "Thanks for the smoothie."

I slam the door shut, and Brander's eyes balloon. "Don't take this the wrong way. All I want is for you to see how—"

"Can we talk about it later? Please?" I step toward Gramma's house. "I'm not worried about me right now, just Jazz. And since you aren't going to give me any ideas on how to help her..." I make a fist, Brander's words boiling in my chest, fueling me as I stalk up the front walk and into Gramma's house.

Koa comes scrabbling down the stairs to greet me, but I barely blink at him. Brander's stony-eyed gaze is burned into my own memory, and—I'll admit it—it stings.

It's no fun being shut out by Jazz, but supposedly she has a good reason. Brander, on the other hand...

I've apologized and asked for forgiveness, but the friendship that we had—the one I thought we were rebuilding—is crumbling once again.

Why can't I do like Gramma said? Share the deepest, most painful parts of myself and form relationships built on more than mere pleasantries?

Because I'm a coward. The truth roars in my mind like a jet engine, and I cringe.

I'm a coward, and I know it.

My chest burns as I brush past Koa on my way upstairs, flop onto my bed, and cradle the necklace Brander got me in my palm.

God help me. I don't want to be afraid.

Chapter Nineteen

What a surprise—Brander never calls.

I spend all evening sitting with my phone turned on, waiting around like an anxiety-addled idiot, but I don't get so much as a text from anyone.

Now that's two people who aren't talking to me.

"Gramma?" I knock on the doorframe of her bedroom downstairs.

"What is it?" Grams steps out from her master bath, wearing an oversized nightshirt advertising Kimo's famous Hula Pie.

"Everything is a complete disaster." I lean against the wall and cross my arms over my chest. I'm being melodramatic, but who cares at this point? "Jazz is ignoring me, and so is Brander. For good reason, but still."

"Brander?" Gramma's brow folds, and she sinks onto the edge of her bed.

I groan and shake my head. "I was trying to find a better way to help Jazz, but then Brander went off on me about how I broke his trust, and how sorry isn't enough." The breeze coming through Gramma's window ruffles my bangs, and I swipe them out of my eyes. "But he's totally fine with *Jazz* being all sneaky and secretive."

Gramma's expression morphs into a frown, and she pats the side of the bed next to her. "Come have a seat, sweetie."

I cross the room in a few short steps and flop onto the plumeria-patterned quilt atop Gramma's cushy mattress. "Brander and I were so close this summer. But now that he's at school, and working the Shave Ice Shack without me, and

I messed up by tiptoeing around the support group thing...everything is different. I hate it."

"Have you told him any of that?"

I shake my head. "All we did was grab a smoothie. By the time we did that, he was running off to do some fancy-pants interview." I scowl and pick at a loose thread on my pajama pants. "It's not like him."

For one long moment, all the answer I get is the gentle creaking and groaning of the house settling. From far beyond Gramma's open window, Polynesian drums beat out a rhythm in perfect counterpoint with my heart. I close my eyes and twine my necklace around my fingers as the rhythm echoes in my chest. Breathing in deep, I let my shoulders unwind, and I lean my head against Gramma's shoulder.

"I hate fighting with Brander. I hate watching Jazz struggle. I hate creeping around the house because of Koa, and I—" I stop before I can get started on how much I miss Mom. Best to keep that out of the picture, if I want to have any hope of surviving this conversation without crying.

"Life's never easy, is it?" Gramma brushes my hair away from my face and finger-combs a tangled patch. The smell of plumeria wafts through the window, and my shoulders droop. "If I could tell you everything that was going on with Jazz, I would. But breaking her trust wouldn't be right, especially now."

"Then how can I—"

"You wait." Gramma pats my shoulder. "And pray. But mostly just wait—be there for her. And, when she's ready to talk, make sure you're ready to listen."

Oh, I'm ready all right. I roll my head off of Gramma's shoulder and straighten. "And Brander? All I want is for us to go back to the way we were this summer. But I blew it. He says he's forgiven me, but I don't know how to make him forget."

Gramma chuckles. "Time. I know that's not what you want to hear, but it's the truth. Show him you're trustworthy—that you care about your friendship and want to see it succeed. And don't assume it's up to him to take the first step. You want to talk? Call him."

"You mean right now?"

"I don't see anything stopping you."

"I guess...you're right." I stand and take a step toward the hall. "Thanks for talking. I needed that."

"Any time." Gramma blows me a kiss before I leave.

After a quick trip upstairs to grab my phone from its charger and a tiptoe through the living room so as to not wake a slumbering Koa, I step onto the porch and press the phone to my ear.

"Hey." Brander's voice hitches when he picks up. "Sorry I didn't call. My parents had dinner guests, and they wanted me to sing for them, and—"

"It's okay." I work to keep my voice light, to keep from asking why he couldn't at least have texted. It's about time I start showing people the same kind of grace I wish they'd give me. Even if it's over something as silly as a text message. "If it's not too late, maybe we can talk now?"

"Sure."

I take a deep breath, and then the words come tumbling out. "I don't get it. I want us to be good friends. Forever friends. I want us to trust each other."

"That's why you lied?"

"No. That's why I asked for forgiveness. That's why I didn't stick my head in the sand and hide out of extreme mortification. Because I could have done that, you know." Would've *rather* done that, actually.

"I know." Brander sighs. "And I shouldn't have come down so hard on you. I've got a lot on my mind lately."

"Everything okay?"

"I guess. But busy. I had to do three different interviews

for the Koa-fundraiser thing today, and I've got a huge paper due at the end of the week. My parents are nagging me to get it done, but I have to practice my worship set, and—"

"Okay, whoa. I get it." A breath of fresh air enters my chest, filling me with hope. "I didn't realize you had that much on your plate. Anything I can do to help?"

"Nah." Something rustles on Brander's side. I can almost picture that cowlick of his wagging back and forth. "Knowing you're here for me means a lot. I miss working with you." He draws in a deep breath.

The wind whispers over the porch, and the swing squeaks as it sways in the breeze. I drink in the cool sea air and wait for Brander to finish. "And I'm sorry." Those three words, spoken softly without a hint of resentment, nearly send me toppling off the porch into the bushes.

"Sorry?"

"I shouldn't have made such a huge deal about things today. You apologized. I forgave you."

"That's why I thought we were good."

"We are. We really are."

Then why didn't he tell me that earlier today? *Why can't I understand?* "Thanks. I'm glad to hear it. So—still friends?"

"We never stopped. I shouldn't have acted the way I did today. Honest." Brander's words fill me with warmth despite the evening chill, and we talk for a while longer before my yawns begin to sneak in around every other word.

"Guess I'd better call it a night." I smother another yawn and step inside.

"Yeah." Brander sighs. "I'd better get cracking on this paper unless I want to deal with Okasan's wrath in the morning."

"Good luck." Poor guy—he'll need it. I haven't been around his mom much, but from what I know of her, she's the queen of Japanese tiger parents. Unlike my own mom. My breath falters. Brander and I say goodbye, but my heart is suddenly a million miles away.

I slog upstairs to my room, quiet so as not to wake Macie. But in my mind I'm back in Boston, Mom sitting next to me—keeping me company while I do my homework. She used to take whatever craft project she was working on into my room, and we'd share my desk. Math was never my thing like it was Mom's. Whenever I had a question, she'd walk me through it, and—I stop at the top of the stairs, my heart swelling until it creeps into my throat.

I don't need these memories tonight. This entire day has left me too fragile, too frayed to think about Mom.

Instead, I crawl into bed, pull the covers over my head, and will myself to fall asleep.

Sleep might come, but it's not for long.

I'm pulled from a bizarre dream involving a fire truck and an angry dogcatcher when someone nearly yanks a strand of hair out of my head. "Hey!" I yelp, then slap a hand over my mouth.

"*Macie.*" I flick on a light, squint at the clock, and groan. This is no time of night to be dealing with pesky little sisters.

Before I can ask what on earth she's doing, another wail, the same one the fire truck was making in my dream, splits the air. "What *is* that?" The howling continues, and I lift my hands to cover my ears.

"It's Koa." Macie yanks on my hair again. "He's lonely by himself."

"Oh, good grief." Sleep muddling my good reason, I swing my legs over the bed and pad downstairs to the living room, Macie close behind. Sure enough, there's Koa, pacing in circles around the couch, lifting his snout and howling every couple of seconds.

"I told you he was lonely." Macie bounds into the room

and throws her arms around Koa's neck. Which is when it happens.

Koa piddles.

"Ew! Koa!" Macie darts away, then throws back her head and laughs. "He had to go *potty*."

"Hilarious." I spit the word out under my breath as I move to the kitchen to grab a roll of paper towel. Moonlight floods the living room, reflecting off the puddle of piddle, and I groan. "Go take him outside and let him do the rest of his business."

"Okey dokey." Macie grabs onto Koa's collar and half-skips, half-drags Koa out of the room as I get to work cleaning up. By the time Gramma's floor is appropriately sanitized, Macie and Koa have returned.

Not surprisingly, Macie is wound up tighter than her knotted curls. "I still think he's lonely. Doesn't he look lonely? Can we take him upstairs to sleep with us? Please?" She squeals and bounces on her tippy-toes, craning her neck to look at the clock. "What time is it? Is it past midnight? I've never been awake past midnight."

"Shh." I lay my hand on her head and press a finger to my mouth. "We've got to be quiet or we'll wake Gramma." It's a miracle that she's stayed asleep so far.

"Okay." Macie's voice drops to a nice, healthy outdoor voice, and she takes my hand. "Pleeeeaze? He can sleep in my bed. I promise it won't be scary."

The whole scene is so pathetic I almost cry. Here I am, sixteen years old, and I need my baby sister to keep me from having a panic attack. "Fine." I dip my head in defeat. "Bring him up."

Macie claps her hands together and spins in a circle before thundering up the stairs, Koa close behind. I follow at a much more appropriate pace, considering it's only one o'clock in the morning, and creep into the bedroom.

True to Macie's word, Koa is already curled up on her

bed, slipping off into puppy dreamland. I hold my breath and sneak across the room, releasing a sigh of relief when he doesn't stir.

I collapse into bed with every intention of keeping a close watch on that dog until daybreak, but the night's excitement must catch up with me. In what feels like minutes, my eyelids are sagging. Then the darkness rushes forward, wrapping its arms around me and pulling me into a deep slumber.

Chapter Twenty

"SWEETIE, IT'S TIME TO GET UP." Someone raps on a door far, far away from my dreamland, but the noise cuts through my sleep. I roll over in bed, my brain in a fog from last night's adventures, and crack one eye open.

"Sorry, Grams." I yawn and sit up. Macie's bed is already empty, and water is running in the bathroom down the hall. "I had a crazy night."

"So I gather." Gramma's smile hints that she knows a bit more than she's letting on, and she nods at the lump of blankets at the foot of my bed.

And then...

The blankets *move*.

Koa's tawny head pops up, and I choke on my own breath, yanking my trembling legs to my chest. Sitting there in a half-fetal position, I stare at Koa like he's a poisonous sea snake or hungry tiger shark. "How'd he—I mean, Macie—" My lips move, but no air, no words, come out.

"Don't panic." Gramma ruffles Koa's ears before turning toward the door. "He's harmless. You're running late, you know."

I peek at the clock and hiss. Yes, I'm late. Normally, Jazz would be here any minute, but now that everything's been turned upside-down...

The doorbell chimes, and Macie bursts out of the bathroom with nothing more than her sparkle-mermaid towel wrapped around herself. "I'll get it." She races down the stairs, leaving a trail of wet footprints behind.

Gramma looks at me.

I look at Gramma.

We both burst out laughing.

Koa's ears perk up, and his head whips around so he's facing me. I snap my mouth shut mid-giggle, but it's too late.

Koa gets to his feet and pads toward me. Heart hitching, I stay stone still as Koa bumps my arm with his head, then reaches out with his tongue to lick my elbow. "Gross. Grams?" I peer up at her with my best attempt at puppy-dog eyes, but she offers me nothing more than a bob of her shoulders before she turns to leave.

A snicker escapes through my nose, and Koa cocks his head at me.

Stiff as a wooden puppet, I lift a hand and rest it atop Koa's head. His fur is warm and downy, and the extra-long whiskers above his eyes tickle my fingers. An unbidden smile finds its way onto my face, and I don't bother to try and chase it away.

Using my index finger, I draw small circles all over Koa's fluffy head. Within a few minutes, he's got his snout nestled in the blankets, and his snoring is louder than an overloaded semi.

"Yoo-hoo!" The voice comes from downstairs, and I nearly jump out of my skin for the second time that morning.

I scramble out of bed, jolting my nightstand with my hip and sending my shave-ice-necklace swinging from the lamp. My hip burns from the impact, but I grit my teeth and jog into the hallway, Koa following close behind. "Jazz?"

"Ready to work?" Her voice is edged in something that wasn't there when I met her—a lack of innocence, perhaps, but her words are still sunny.

"You're here." I skitter down the stairs, scanning Jazz's face for any clues that might help me better understand yesterday's events. "How are you?'

"Okay." Jazz squares her jaw, and in that moment I see it—the secret. It's weighing down her smile, filling the bags beneath her eyes. But at least she's here. "How's Koa?"

"Good. Even after our sleepover." I angle my gaze at the mutt, but I also can't resist smiling. Just a bit.

"You and Koa had a sleepover? No way." Jazz tosses her head, sending her braid flopping over one shoulder.

"Koa had an accident in the living room in the middle of the night, and Macie convinced Olive to let him sleep upstairs." Grams winks at me, and I return the gesture. I never told her any of that—guess I didn't manage to keep from waking her after all. And she made us deal with the mess ourselves? I snort.

Of course, it all worked out in the end—which, I'm sure, is what she knew would happen all along. Typical Gramma.

"Wow." Jazz's eyes grow wide, and she fixes them on me as she takes a step toward the living room. "I'm glad you're getting along with him."

I shrug. "Yeah, I guess. Sorry I'm running behind this morning. I'll be right back." I take the stairs two at a time and fly through my morning routine. I'm snapping an elastic around my ponytail when there's a soft tap on the bathroom door.

"Yeah?" I poke my head into the hall to look at Grams. "How is Jazz? Did she tell you anything about what's going on?"

Gramma purses her lips. "Things aren't good at her place right now, but she's not in any danger. Pastor Dave dropped by, and he's going to visit every couple of days for a while."

"But what is going on? Is it all Ruby's problem?" I make a fist and press it against my leg. "It can't be. I mean, I met her. She didn't seem *that* psycho."

Gramma bites her lip. "Now isn't the time to discuss this. I think it's more important that you go be a good friend to Jazz. Give her a hug. Pray for her. Help her catch up on her schoolwork. Macie missed the bus, so I'm going to run her over to the school. I'll be back in a jiffy."

I slip out of the bathroom, fear nipping at my heels. What else does Jazz need? How can I help her if I don't even know what's wrong?

A little help here, God?

An irritable floorboard creaks as I step into the living room, and Jazz's head shoots up. Her eyes are wide, something in her face reminiscent of the way she looked the day she told me she had cancer. "Before we start, can we—would you..."

I cross over to the couch and sit beside Jazz. "What do you need?"

Jazz swallows hard. I can almost see her secrets, her fears, building up behind a giant lump in her throat. "Would you mind praying with me?"

"Oh." A tiny part of my heart sags. Guess I'm not getting the scoop today after all. But I lean into Jazz and bow my head. "Dear God, I don't know what's going on with Jazz, but You do. Please help her and her aunt deal with whatever's going on." *And God, can You keep my curiosity from killing me? I'd appreciate it.* "Amen."

Jazz prays too, asking for peace and wisdom. When she's done, she looks up at me with wide eyes. "Thanks again for everything yesterday. I probably didn't say so when you came over, but it meant a lot to me."

"You're welcome." I swallow against the weight of a million unasked questions and nudge Jazz's shoulder again before pulling away. "Now—ready to work?"

"Sure." Jazz pulls out her biology book, and I hesitate for a moment, hand hovering over *Pride and Prejudice*. That literary analysis essay is due at the end of the week. I'm not worried about the deadline. After all, it's nearly done. But something about it seems off—dry, maybe. Like *Pride and Prejudice* is anything but my favorite book.

Maybe I should add an analysis of a few more quotes—Mom's quotes.

No way.

My emotions are already running wild, and I need to keep a clear head if I'm going to help Jazz. No essay for now.

My gaze hovers over the stack of books on the coffee table, and I reach for my algebra book, heart crunching at the memory of my study sessions with Mom. Math can wait too.

I straighten my shoulders before grabbing my history textbook. Why not start the morning off with something guaranteed to put me to sleep by page two?

"You're starting with *history*?" Jazz fake-gags and crosses her eyes at me. "Yuck."

"Better than literature."

"I thought you liked that *Pride and Prejudice* junk." Jazz raises an eyebrow.

"I love it. But that doesn't mean I want to analyze and 'relate several scenes and quotations to my own life.'"

"Ohhh." Jazz nods, but she shoots me another glance before paging through her bio textbook. "If you get bored, you can always help me. This stuff is seriously wacko." She crosses her eyes again, sticking out her tongue this time. I laugh before scooting over to help her.

Morning light illuminates the pages of Jazz's textbook, and the birds outside are tuning up for a day's worth of chirping and warbling. Even with the gray cloud that is literature hanging over my head, something soft and warm fills my heart.

I'll never hang out and do schoolwork with Mom again, but God gave me someone else to do it with—Jazz. And now it's my turn to be the tutor.

And maybe—maybe that's why change isn't always such a bad thing.

"Let's take Koa for a walk."

I nearly fall off the couch at Jazz's suggestion the next afternoon. Like clockwork, she showed up this morning, ready to do school, but now that we're done... "Why would we do that?" I'm no longer turning into a ball of terrified jelly every time Koa steps into the room, but it's not like I want to be his new best friend either.

"We'd do it because he needs love and attention." Jazz whistles for Koa, and he scampers around the corner, collar swinging around his fuzzy neck. "I miss hanging out with him."

"Yeah?" I look first to Jazz and Koa, then to my laptop. Sitting on that hard drive is a D-for-effort literary analysis essay. And it's due in two days. I have a lot of faults— probably more than I know—but procrastination has never been one of them.

"I'm sorry, Jazz, but I've gotta work on that essay. Grams expects me to keep my grades up, and I'm not giving her any reason to put me in public school." I suck in a breath, then frown. "But you can take him for a spin, if you don't think he'll be too much to manage on your own."

"Okay." Jazz slides off the couch.

"Have fun." I crack open my laptop and click over to my word processor. "Say hi to the beach for me."

"Will do." Jazz shimmies her wrist in a *shaka* before heading out, Koa prancing at her heels.

The second the front door slams shut, a little bit of light seems to leave the room. I stare at my favorite picture of Mom—the one hung oh-so-conspicuously next to the stairs— and sigh.

"I miss you, Mom." My voice cracks, and my vision floods. Everything shimmers behind a veil of tears, and a sob swells in my chest.

No matter how crazy life is on this island, it's never enough to chase away the memories—both good and bad—of

Mom. And on days like today, that's *not* a good thing.

My breath comes in shuddering half-sniffles as I skim what I've written so far. My points are weak, the quotations and scenes I've picked are ones I hardly care about, let alone can relate to. The writing is tight, the prose is good, but it needs something. It needs...

Mom.

The thought wraps around my chest, almost choking me, and I'm swept back to that first day at support group, when I spilled my guts in my notebook. It felt so good, so *freeing.* Maybe writing about Mom here, now, could help.

Guess there's only one way to find out.

I tap to create a new document, take a gulp of air that's as much a prayer as it is a necessity, and bring my hands to the keyboard.

It is a truth universally acknowledged that a single young lady in possession of a large amount of grief must also be in want of her mom...

"Knock-knock."

I glance up at Jazz, who stands in front of the couch with her hand mere inches from my face.

"Anyone home?" She snorts, then points to my laptop. "How's it coming?"

"It's..." I shake the mouse, waking the computer, and scrolling through my essay. "Done."

"Done?" Jazz's eyes balloon on her face. "You write fast."

"Not as fast as you'd think." Writing this essay took a lifetime. And now that I've put it all on paper...wow. Part of me feels empty. Gutted, even. But my heart, of all things, is strangely full.

"Wanna stay for dinner?" I look up at Jazz and cross my fingers she'll say yes. "I could use the company."

"Sure. Can I read the essay?"

"Later." I bite my lip against a fib—that it still needs proofreading.

They say the truth's always better, huh? We'll see about that. Right...now. "It's kinda personal. About Mom. You know what I mean?"

"Oh. Okay." Jazz flops onto the couch next to me. Her sun-bleached hair is slip-sliding out of its braid, but there's a certain closed-mouth smile on her face that I haven't seen in a while. "Gotcha. Maybe later."

"Maybe." I start to close the lid of my laptop, then stop. If I was back in Boston, if my heart had been through as much turmoil as it's endured today, there'd be only one thing I would want to do. "Wanna know a secret?"

Jazz raises both eyebrows and scoots closer. "Sure." Her whisper is so overly dramatic, I have to smother a laugh.

"Not *that* big of a secret." I click over to my Internet browser and run a quick web search. "Back home, when I had a rough day, I used to binge-watch bad cat videos."

"Honest?"

I shrug, and a handful of seconds tick by on Gramma's wall clock, echoing in the quiet of the room, before a spark lights in Jazz's eyes. "Have you seen the one with the cat and the cucumber?"

I shake my head and position my fingers above the keyboard, ready to search, when Jazz yelps.

"Hawaii's heartthrob!" She jabs a finger at the screen.

"What?" I squint at her. Somehow, I never pictured Jazz as one to have a celebrity crush.

"See?" She taps a video thumbnail, leaving a sweaty fingerprint on my screen. "It looks like Brander." Jazz snickers.

"What?" My thumb jerks, and the video clip starts playing.

"Deep in the heart of Maui's most scenic seaside town,

locals have been hiding a star," a woman's voice intones as the camera pans across stretch of beach, coming to rest on—

"That's the Shave Ice Shack!" Jazz's leg jerks, and her prosthesis whacks against the coffee table.

"Shh." I bring a finger to my lips and turn up the volume.

In the background, someone twangs on a guitar as the lady keeps talking. "Young pop singer Brander Delacroix has skyrocketed to Internet fame after appearing on *Aloha Oahu* yesterday morning to raise awareness for a charity event he's hosting."

"Hosting?" I squeak as the camera cuts to a shot of Brander, looking snazzy in a gray button-down and loosely knotted blue tie, playing his guitar in a stuffy TV studio. "Good grief."

"And Delacroix has raised plenty of awareness for that event, but even more awareness about his music." The twanging of the guitar grows louder, and Brander's voice fades in.

"He sounds great." Jazz taps her good foot along with the beat of Brander's stylized version of *Amazing Grace.*

I open my mouth, but no words come out. The lady's voiceover cuts in again, touching on Brander's millionaire-mogul parents and once again referring to him as one of Hawaii's hidden gems.

"Five hundred *thousand* views?" Jazz's prosthesis bangs against the table again. "It was only uploaded this morning."

My head spins as I scroll through the comments, many of them including plenty of goo-goo-heart-eye emojis. "Of course, they conveniently managed to forget that their new TV heartthrob is a *worship leader.*"

Jazz giggles. "You aren't jealous, are you?"

"What? No. But look at this." I wave a hand over the comments. "They're acting like he's a major celebrity. What happened?"

The news clip ends, and another one starts playing. I

take a peek at the logo in the corner and yelp. "Jazz, this is *national* news."

"Think about it." Jazz leans against the couch cushions. "When he goes off to make his fortune in Hollywood, we can say we knew him when."

"I'd rather he stay right here, thank you very much." I slam my laptop shut and slide it onto the table. "Do you think he knows?"

"If not, there's no better time for him *to* know than now." Jazz pulls out her phone, dials, and puts it on speaker.

The rings echo in a suddenly eerie silence, and Gramma pokes her head into the room. "What's going on?"

"Hello?" Brander's voice booms through the phone's speaker, and Gramma's eyes widen.

"Brander!" Jazz and I speak at the same time.

"What on earth is going on?" I stare at the phone and wait for Brander's words.

"Huh?" He laughs. "I'm getting ready for youth group. Are you coming?"

"But what about Hollywood?" Jazz squeaks, then slaps a hand over her mouth. "I mean...do you not even know?"

"Know what?"

"How can you *not* know when you've gone viral?" I smother a laugh. For someone so rich, Brander seems to live under a very large, dense rock most of the time.

"What? You mean the spot on *Aloha Oahu?* My dad knew a guy."

"No." Jazz shakes her head so hard her braid swings around to swat me on the nose. "I mean the spots on every trending pop culture channel on YouTube."

"And..." I pull out my phone, run a quick search, and nearly yelp. "You're trending on Twitter. I didn't think people even used Twitter anymore." But obviously people do—at least the fifty thousand people who retweeted *Aloha Oahu's* original post.

Something sour stirs in my stomach as Gramma leans over my shoulder to speak into the phone. "I'll be proud to say I knew you when, Brander."

"Why are you acting like he's going anywhere?" I cross my arms. "Just because someone's cat goes viral on YouTube doesn't mean they ship it off to Hollywood to star in one of those talking animal videos."

Something that sounds suspiciously like a snort comes from the phone, and I half-glare at it.

"I don't believe you guys." Something click-clacks on Brander's side of the phone. "I'm getting on Twitter now, but I highly doubt anything of mine has gone"—his voice rasps on the other end of the phone—"*viral.*"

"Found it?" Jazz jiggles her good leg

"Yeah. Wow." A beep echoes on the phone. "Sorry guys, but Okasan's on the other line. I've gotta take this."

"Go ahead." Jazz waves a hand in the air. "You're famous, now, *daaarling,* you can do whatever you want." This last line is delivered in such an ostensibly dramatic tone that I have to laugh.

Jazz ends the call, but the quiet stillness echoes in the room for only a moment before Grams clicks her tongue and sighs. "What do you know about that? Brander's gone viral."

"He isn't only viral, Grams. He's *famous.*" My chest constricts as I skim the comments. Girls want Brander to write songs for them, take them to prom, and...worse.

This is disgusting.

I glance from Jazz to Gramma as they share excited chatter about Lahaina's newest rising star. Macie wanders in, and the excitement intensifies. Will Brander get a record deal? Will he move to Hollywood? How many lives will he touch with his music? But all I can do is sit, stomach churning.

All of a sudden, Brander is way more than a worship leader.

He's a star.

An icon.

A social media sensation.

If Grams and Jazz are right, he could get way more than his five minutes of fame from this. What if he decides to chase it—run off to Hollywood and try out for one of those singing shows with the celebrity judges? I'd have to say another goodbye.

When the loss of Mom is still a raw, ravaged place in my heart. When Brander and I are still remembering how to be friends. When I'm still stumbling down the long, winding path to normal.

God, please don't take him away from me, too.

Chapter Twenty-One

THE NEXT AFTERNOON, I'M CURLED UP on the porch swing with *Pride and Prejudice* and a box of tissues. Jazz left immediately after she finished her work for the day, but I've got more catch-up to do. Sure, I've read this book half a dozen times—probably more. I don't technically need to finish it this time around. But I'm going to. For Mom, who will never get to read it again, and for myself, who at some point, has to move on.

Mom's voice echoes in my ears with every line of dialogue. I can almost see the sparkle in her eyes when she read the part where Lydia Bennett elopes. My heart brims with unshed tears, swelling until it's nearly full, and I grab a tissue.

"Aloha."

A tear leaks from my eye, and I jerk my head up. I squint at the person, their form a silhouette against the golden afternoon sun. Even though I can't make out a face, a cowlick springing up from their head is a good clue.

"Hey, Brander." I swipe at my eye with the tissue, then scooch over on the swing to make room for him. Brander sticks his hands in his pockets and shuffles his Oxfords against the splintery porch, and I pat the swing for him to sit. "What's up?"

"Can we bring Koa out with us?"

"Why?" I finger my necklace.

"It's no fair for him to have to stay cooped up inside all day."

"Macie and Jazz take him for a walk most afternoons.

And Macie'll be home from school soon." I stare at Brander—or, more specifically, at the bags beneath his eyes. Is that what being a celebrity does to people, or is something else going on? I sigh and jerk a thumb toward the front door. "Go ahead. Bring him out. As long as you're willing to resuscitate me if I have a heart attack."

"Uh, okay." Brander's cheeks flame like an out-of-control tiki torch, and he takes a step toward me, then falters.

"What?" I squint at him before the realization drops on my head like a coconut. Did I seriously say he'd have to give me mouth-to-mouth...oh, brother. I groan and bury my head in my hands. "I didn't mean it *that* way."

"I know." Brander shakes his shoulders and brushes off his shirt before walking over to the front door. When he does, Koa explodes from inside like a supercharged atom bomb. I wince as he buries his head in Brander's dark wash jeans, covering them in wispy puppy hairs.

"Koa, stop bugging him." I reach out and grab the pup by his collar to drag him away while Brander takes a seat next to me on the swing.

I brush off my hands and turn my face to his after Koa has gotten settled. "How does it feel to be famous? Did you have to sign every girl's *slippa* at school today?" The Hawaiian word pops out of my mouth without me thinking about it, and it rolls off my tongue so easily I almost laugh at myself. "Or do Hawaiian people not do viral videos?"

Brander plants his hands on his knees and sighs, eyes wide. "They watch them, all right. So do record labels, obviously."

"Huh?"

"One of the biggies from Nashville got hold of my dad. That's why my mom beeped in yesterday. They're looking to branch out and start a Christian music label. I guess the head honcho got them all excited, talking about albums and tours and that stuff." Brander waves a hand in the air, as though dismissing the idea, but his fingers tremble. There's a spark in his voice that lights his entire face. A lump of mushrooms grows in my stomach as he continues, rattling off a list of people signed with this mighty music group.

"Nothing's for sure yet, but it's definitely something to consider—to pray about." Brander's breath whooshes out from between pursed lips. "Ever since I was little, I've wanted to touch lives with my music. Maybe this is it."

"Cool." The word croaks as it leaves my mouth, and I swallow against the dryness of my throat. "I mean, good for you. I mean—yeah, congrats. That's amazing."

"Thanks." Brander takes his fingers and laces them through my own. "But I don't know. For one, it's pretty far-fetched. For two, I don't really know if I'd be up for living in Nashville."

"Like, for good?" That lump in my stomach nearly doubles in size.

Brander nods in slow motion. "The label likes to be hands-on with all of their artists. They'd set me up in a good place, help me get plugged into the scene there."

"You mean you'd, live there? Full time?"

"Maybe. My dad didn't ask. I bet I can make it home for holidays, at least."

"Oh. You'll probably get a private jet."

Brander laughs, obviously not sensing my sarcasm. "Yeah, right. I'm not that big. Probably won't be for a long time"

"I know a ton of people that think differently." My hand drifts to the phone in my pocket. Last time I checked, I had over a dozen texts from people in Boston, asking if I knew the elusive Hawaiian Heartthrob. The first time I've heard from them since I left. "And I don't blame them. You've got a great voice."

"Yeah, but—" Brander dips his head. "That's not the point. I don't even know if I'm going yet."

"You don't?" My head pops up.

Brander shakes his head, runs his fingers through his hair. "I want to touch lives with my music, but that doesn't mean I have to get famous while doing it. Right now, I'm leaving it up to God to see what He wants from me. Part of me hopes it's Nashville"—he squeezes my hand— "and a lot of me wants to stay right here."

Then do it! My brain practically screams. *Call the label and tell them thanks, but no. That you have family and friends here who would miss you. Forget about being famous and just be* Brander.

"How long do you have to decide?"

He frowns. "This kind of thing is time-sensitive. If I want to make a go of it, I've gotta move fast. Before the Internet forgets about me."

"For what it's worth, I'll never forget about you. In fact, I'll miss you if you leave. I'll miss you a lot."

"I know." Brander moves his thumb in small circles over the back of my hand. He stares past the porch, the beach, the boats in the harbor, to—where? His future? What does he see laid out for himself?

A cloud of fog creeps over the top of one of the neighboring islands. It rolls over the hills, rushing to meet the sea. A stiff wind brushes my shoulders and tousles Brander's cowlick as we sit in silence.

"Listen." Brander pulls away from me and clasps his hands, leaning his elbows on his knees, head bowed. "If I leave, I think you should know something about Jazz."

"Okay..." I lean forward along with Brander, waiting for his words to spill out into the afternoon. Jazz's secret—the one that's been killing me since I got here—will be hidden no more. My heart thrums in my chest as Brander hesitates, mouth open. I can practically see the words balancing on his tongue. "Jazz's—"

Bzzzt.

The spell of the afternoon is broken. Koa jumps to his feet and lets out an earsplitting howl. Brander winces and pulls his phone from his pocket, then presses it to his ear. He holds a finger in the air, and I sit as though slapped in the face. Whoever is on the phone—couldn't he have called them back another time? Isn't real life right here more important? Or are things different now?

I press my lips together and turn my head to the side, but it's impossible not to eavesdrop. The guy on the other end of the phone seems to have only two volumes—loud and louder.

"Brander Delacroix? This is Mike Parker, with the label. You done your soul-searching yet?"

"Uh—"

"Son, you'd better learn something. In this business, hesitating is the same as saying no. If you want to make it, we have to act fast. There's already a high school choir prima donna making the rounds on YouTube today. My offer still stands, but if you're going to say yes, I need you out here pronto. Got it?"

Brander blinks.

"I'll check in tomorrow morning. Let's try to have an answer by then, okay son?"

"Okay." The word seems to break Brander's voice, snapping it in two over those small syllables. He pulls the phone away from his face and shoves it in his pocket before looking at me. "Sorry."

"Don't be. You're famous now." I wave a hand in the air, parroting Jazz's words from yesterday. "You can get away with that kind of thing." I test out a smile, but I probably look more like one of those angry tiki totems. "Are you going to be at youth group?"

Brander sighs and shakes his head. "I think God and I'd better spend some one-on-one time tonight. What about you?"

"Nah." I lift a shoulder and stand with Brander as he moves to leave. Koa whines and takes a step toward him, but I push the mutt away. "Wait." I reach for Brander's arm before he can make a move for the stairs. "Do you mind— could I pray with you? Before you leave?"

A smile washes over Brander's face, but it wobbles as I place a hand on his arm. No matter—I bow my head and wait for him to do the same. "Dear God, please give Brander wisdom. He doesn't know what You want from him, but he needs to know—and quick." *And I think You and I both know what I'd like the answer to be.* "Amen."

"Thanks." Brander lifts his head and looks at me with a watery gaze. His phone beeps again, and his hand moves to his pants pocket. "I'd better go. This is all so weird."

"Tell me about it." I cross my arms and scuff at a warped floorboard as Brander descends the stairs, phone in hand. "See ya."

"See ya." Brander pauses for a millisecond, lifting his hand in a wave before turning down the street. He must have come on foot—neither the Porsche nor his moped is within sight—and I watch as he shuffles along at about half the pace of a turtle.

This decision must be killing him.

So much for *Pride and Prejudice.* Sure, I know I need to suck it up and finish that book—for Mom's sake, if not my own—but right now...

I've got some more praying to do.

After I've spent a sufficiently long time doing my fair share of moping and praying, I trace Brander's path to the sidewalk. When I hit the walkway, though, I head in the opposite direction than he went.

Before I reach the intersection, Macie's school bus pulls

to the curb in a puff of exhaust, and I stop. Macie hops to the ground, and I reach out to ruffle her curls. "Hey, squirt."

"Where are you going?" She ducks away from my hand and tugs at her hair.

"Jazz's house."

"Can I come? I wanna tell her about what happened at school today with Kanani." Macie jumps from foot-to-foot, the sparkly flowers on her flip-flops glittering in the sunlight.

Kanani again? I peer at Macie. "What's going on with you two this time?"

"She's my new best friend." Macie bounces on her heels and lifts her wrist, revealing a garish, purple-and-orange bracelet. "We traded crafts today. I'm gonna ask Grammy if she can come for dinner sometime."

"Oh." I shake my head. Why can't all friendships be as easy as they are for grade-schoolers? "Good for you two."

"So can I come to Jazzie's?" Macie clasps her hands over her heart and blinks up at me.

"Not this time. But I bet Koa would love to take a—"

A puppy yips in the not-too-far-off distance, and Macie and I both spin around.

"Koa!" Macie squeals and falls to her knees, stretching her arms out wide. A quick glance over my shoulder reveals Koa, leash trailing behind, running pell-mell toward Macie. Grams chugs down the sidewalk after him, but she's no match for that wild puppy. Koa attacks Macie with slobbery kisses, and Macie returns the gesture, with plenty of giggles thrown in.

Gramma wags a finger at me as she approaches. "You shouldn't take off like that without putting Koa inside. Thank goodness I went out to check on him when I did. He was already halfway to the beach."

"Sorry." I nudge Koa with my foot in apology, but he shoots me a puppy version of the famous Hawaiian stink eye. "You wanna take him home, Mace? I've got to get to Jazz's."

"Actually..." Grams presses Koa's leash into my hand. "I think you should take him. He could use the exercise, and Jazz will be glad to see him."

Great. Macie's face crumples, and she scuffs her feet along the sidewalk as Gramma takes her by the hand and leads her home, leaving me alone with Koa.

"Okay, buddy." I wrap the leash around my hand and take a step toward Jazz's, then another. Koa follows suit. With the sun warm on my shoulders, a breeze in the air, and a spring in Koa's step, it could almost be nice.

Except for the fact that Brander's decision hangs heavily on me, and the longer it stays there, the tighter my nerves coil. By the time I turn onto Jazz's street, I'm huffing and puffing like a steam engine—and it's not from the exercise.

God, what are you doing?

Chapter Twenty-Two

"HEY, KNOCK IT OFF." JAZZ'S VOICE spills out onto the street from Ruby's open door, and a crash resounds from within. "Watch it!"

A second voice responds, spouting off more curse words than I've ever heard in my life, let alone in one sentence. I drop Koa's leash and shove my fingers in my ears, but it doesn't help. The ugly words—as well as the speaker's red-hot tone of voice—stick in my brain like a bad commercial jingle.

"Jazz?" I remove a finger from one ear and grab Koa's leash before he can get any ideas about running inside and playing Superdog.

"I told you. Don't you ever—" the voice hiccups.

My heart pounds in my chest, my gut, my ears. Jazz said Ruby drinks too much sometimes, but does she get this drunk? On a regular basis? Fingers shaking, I tie Koa's leash to an overgrown hibiscus bush before leaping up the steps and stepping inside.

The curtains are drawn and without the aid of the fluorescent afternoon sunlight, I'm half blind. I hover in the entryway, rank with the stench of beer and cigarettes, and stare into the blackness.

The darkness fades as my eyes adjust, and I poke my head around the corner, blinking at the scene before me. Jazz and Ruby are both huddled on one overstuffed couch, Ruby's arm wrapped tightly around Jazz's shoulders. Before them, a tall, beer-bellied woman sways on her feet. Her blonde hair is matted, her red-painted mouth spews yet another string of profanities. She gestures wildly with both hands, one clutching a beer bottle, the other a smoldering cigarette.

A cry escapes me, and the lady reels around. Her gray eyes spin as though searching for something to focus on yet finding nothing. And then the expression clears, and she squints in my direction.

"You." The woman stumbles toward me. "She told you about me?"

She who? I shake my head.

"She didn't?" The woman raises the bottle to her mouth to drink, but it's empty. She mutters something—I have a feeling it's a good thing I can't make it out—and turns, smashing the bottle against the wall.

Glass shatters, clinking against the linoleum as it falls, and the woman fixes her reeling gaze on me. I avert my eyes and shove one trembling hand into my pocket for my phone. My heart pounds against my ribcage, every nerve on alert, as I enter in the passcode and tap to dial 911.

But before I can make the call, Ruby leaps from the couch, tumbles across the living room, and half-tackles the other woman. She drags her through the room and pushes her onto the couch. "Go, Jazz. I'll take care of her."

I take a step forward as Jazz stumbles off the couch and clunks across the living room on her prosthesis. She looks to me with wide, wounded eyes, and I offer her as much of a smile as I can muster, considering the circumstances.

I motion Jazz forward, but she falters when she reaches me. She stands on her good leg for a moment, prosthesis dangling in the air, and looks at Ruby and the other lady before hooking my arm in hers and pulling me out of the house.

Once we're outside, she releases my arm and half-falls down the steps before throwing herself across the overgrown front walk. She nearly trips over the sidewalk, but she keeps going. If I couldn't see it myself, I would never know she had a prosthetic leg.

I untie Koa's leash, and he leaps against me, his tiny claws scraping my bare legs. I bite my lip and tug on the leash. "Jazz! Stop! You'll hurt yourself." I jog after her, my feet pounding the sidewalk, a brisk wind filling my lungs. "Wait for me."

Jazz falters at the end of the street and bends over, planting her hands on her knees and wheezing as Koa and I catch up to her.

"What was *happening* in there?" The words burst out of my mouth, their raw bluntness whistling through the air. I'm knocking on the door of Jazz's secret. And she's cowering in the corner.

Jazz curls into herself and picks at a hangnail for what feels like a century before lifting her head and focusing her silvery eyes on me. "I guess...I guess you met my mom."

"Gramma?" I press the phone against my face with one hand and hold tight to Jazz with the other as we walk to the beach. "Jazz is coming for dinner, and you'd better make a key lime pie."

Thank goodness, Gramma promises to set an extra place and get a piecrust in the oven. No questions asked. When I pocket my phone and glance over at Jazz, her eyes are wide and flooded with tears.

"You didn't have to do that."

"Of course I did." I squeeze Jazz's hand, and she leans against my arm. Key lime pie is Jazz's favorite, and it also seems to be a good dessert for wound-licking. I bet there'll be a lot of that going on tonight. "Do you want to talk?"

"What is there to say?" Jazz's shoulders sag, and we wind our way through a quiet side street before stepping onto the beach. She releases her arm from mine and, keeping a firm hold on Koa's leash with her other hand, shuffles through the sand to a picnic table.

The wind tosses a stray lock of hair in my face, and I brush it out of my eyes as I sit on the bench across from Jazz. All around us, families frolic in the foamy surf. Frisbees fly across the shore, and a group of grade-schoolers seem to be intent on constructing an entire sand city before sunset. Even a few stray chickens get in on the action, clucking and scuffling through the sand.

It's the perfect afternoon, but Jazz's frown makes it seem more like we're at a funeral than the beach. I give her arm a squeeze, then turn my attention to the bay. Mist spreads over the neighbor islands like a thick blanket, but the sky above Lahaina is crystal clear. If only there was something I could do to break through the mist enshrouding Jazz. If only there was a way to—

"Maybe I do want to talk." Jazz's words knife through the sense of almost-calm, and I whip around to face her. She twists Koa's leash in her hands as he plops onto his haunches at her feet. I nod for Jazz to continue, and she runs her tongue over her lips. "My mom is a monster."

"Whoa, I don't—"

"Hear me out." She holds up a hand. "You know my dad left when I was a baby, and Mom made a life for us on the boat. For a while, it was good. She went to counseling at the church, had nice, normal friends, and—yeah."

"But what *happened*?"

A veil falls across Jazz's gaze, and I nearly slap myself. Now isn't the time to ask questions—it's time to let Jazz do the talking. All of it.

The ocean waves pound in my ears for several long moments before Jazz starts again, telling me all about her mom's sudden career change years ago—when she took a job at a bar. She developed a tendency to stay late after work, to get tipsy. Before long, she was in over her head.

"At first, I think she honestly wanted to change. She went to those AA meetings, and kept doing counseling with the pastor. But then, even though she lost her job, she kept going to the bar—every night." Jazz's eyes widen and her focus slips, as though she's looking straight through me and into days gone by. "Mom's always had a temper. But the drinking..." She shudders.

Before Jazz can continue, I leap to my feet and slide next to her on the bench, giving her a nudge with my shoulder. She offers a weak smile in return. "When my leg started going bad, it was up to Ruby to take me to the doctor. She's always been there to look out for me. Not that she's probably the best person for the job, but she's my aunt. The only family I have. When we found out it was cancer, Mom flipped. She wasn't safe. Not that she had been for a while, but...whatever. That's why I moved in with Ruby."

"What about social services?" The words burst out, despite my zipped lips. "Didn't they ever get wind of all that?"

Jazz wags her head from side to side and bends to stroke Koa's silky ears. "Mom always managed to keep it together enough to pull off the façade. She never actually went so far as to hurt me, so there wasn't enough evidence for them to put me in the system."

Ouch. "And Ruby? Is she..."

"Teetotaler." Jazz's cheeks burn red. "I'm sorry I lied. I should have explained everything that day, but it's mortifying. At first, I thought things would be okay. When Mom showed up at Ruby's, she said she'd quit, that she was looking for a job."

"Then what—"

"That lasted for all of about the first week." Jazz scoffs. "She went out one night after a day of bad interviews, and the rest..." She waves a hand in the air.

"Can't Ruby kick her out?"

"Not when Mom's drunk. She'd knock Ruby into next week." She bends to pat Koa again. "That's why Koa was limping. Mom was stoned the night before you came to get him, and Koa got one step too close."

I cringe on Koa's behalf. "You can't go back there with her."

"Where else can I go? Not the boat."

"Have you talked to anyone at the church?"

Jazz shakes her head. "You don't get it. Mom and Dad weren't even married when she found out she was pregnant with me. Even when they tried to do the right thing, it didn't last." Tears fill her eyes, and she lowers her head. "People look at you funny when you have *that* kind of a history."

"Even Pastor Dave? Jonah?"

"It's not worth telling them. I can take care of myself."

I wrap an arm around Jazz's shoulders and hug her. Hard. "For the record, I would never look at you differently because of a dumb mistake your parents made. And I know Grams and Brander wouldn't, either. Do they know?"

"The important parts." Jazz takes one long, shuddery breath. "At least all this drama keeps my mind off my leg. And swim team."

"Do you have to find a positive for everything?" I groan and lean my head on the table. "But seriously. You should talk about this kind of thing. It can't be good to keep it all bottled up inside. Maybe—"

"Maybe you should do the same." A glimmer lights the corner of Jazz's eye.

"Oh, no. This is about *you*."

Jazz sighs. "But what if I told everyone, and they started looking at me funny? I—I don't know."

"It's okay to not know." I tug Jazz's long, ropelike braid and twine it between my fingers. "You don't have to have all the answers. But I don't like the idea of you being in that house with your mom. Maybe Gramma should talk to Ruby."

"But..." Jazz peers at me, eyebrows scrunched together. "Sometimes we have to take things slow and see what God does. I'm praying for my mom, Tutu Bonnie and Brander are praying for her, and Pastor Dave knows enough to keep me high on his list."

"Don't forget about me."

"Okay, so you're praying too." Jazz digs her foot into the sand. "But I've got to consider that maybe this is where God wants me. Maybe I'm the light that'll guide Mom home."

"Maybe." But why? Why would God put Jazz—good, sweet, sunny Jazz—in such a dark place? I can see why God would put other people in that kind of a situation. People like me, who could use a bit of a comeuppance. But Jazz?

"Maybe you could stay over at Gramma's tonight? For my sake?"

"For tonight. And..." She picks at a hangnail. "I'm sorry. I should have told you everything when you first showed up."

"It's okay." I stare Jazz straight in the eye. "I get it. I'm not saying that it's the right thing to do. For either of us. But *I get it.*"

A tear glimmers in Jazz's eye, and she reaches out, pulling me into an embrace. "And I'm so glad you do."

Chapter Twenty-Three

"I—I HAVE SOMETHING TO SAY." Jazz's voice wavers and shimmers in the midmorning sunlight at the support group on Saturday. Koa is nearly glued to her side, and I might as well be. The scrubby park grass tickles my bare feet as I grab her hand in a silent show of support. After our talk on Wednesday, I've been doing my best to stay out of Jazz's business. After all, who am I to try and get her to spill her guts to a group of near-strangers when I'm afraid to talk to my closest friends?

"Go ahead, Jazz." Jonah gives her a thumbs-up. "We're here for you."

Inwardly, I groan at Jonah's extra-cheery tone of voice and overly welcoming smile, but I snap to attention when Jazz clears her throat. "It's nothing big. But I do want to apologize. When we first started out and introduced ourselves, I—I wasn't completely honest. I'm not here because of my leg. I mean, that's part of it, but also...see, there's this thing with my mom..." Her cheeks flush all the colors of a sunset, and she curls her shoulders inward.

"Come on, spit it out. Some of us want to get this thing over with." Malia rolls her neck and picks at her chipped black nail polish. Jonah shoots her a gaze tainted with stink eye, but Malia tosses her hair and turns her head.

"Sorry." Jazz tugs on the end of her braid. "The thing is— my mom, she's...she drinks. A lot."

"You mean like an alcoholic?" A surfer guy with a thick neck and even thicker black hair—Oke, I think his name is— pops his knuckles. "Dude, that reeks. My dad's been a boozer since I was in grade school." His usual hard mask of indifference cracks, and Jazz's shoulders drop a couple of inches.

"I'm sorry, Oke. It's tough, isn't it?" Jazz bites the inside of her cheek and stares at the ground. "It's like...was I not enough for her? Does she really need the beer too?" Her voice breaks, and my heart snaps right along with it. How can I call myself Jazz's friend and not know these things about her?

How can I call myself Jazz's friend and hide all of my own hurts from her?

Brander looks up from where he's been pecking on his phone half the morning and shoots a smile in Jazz's direction. He's been eerily silent about the whole Nashville thing, but if the amount of time he's spent on his phone today is anything to go by, an answer must be coming soon. My stomach clenches at the thought, so I push it away and focus on the conversation.

Other kids chime in and share their own hardships, most of them connected to a parent or sibling struggling with an addiction. Something stirs deep in my stomach. Some of these kids have been silent as sea turtles since they introduced themselves that first group meeting. It's time for them to get their stories out—and maybe it's mine.

A lull hits the conversation, and I open my mouth, but I'm not fast enough. Malia cuts in with a snort and a roll of her eyes. She shakes her mane of hair and casts her darkened gaze over the group. "This little pity party has been nice and all, but I've gotta go." She stands, slinging a worn leather backpack over one shoulder, and inches away from the group. "Have fun sharing all of your sob stories."

"Wait—Malia." Jazz plants her hands on the bench and makes a move to push to her feet, but I stand first.

"I'll get her." I jog away from the group, following Malia down the gently curving seaside path. "Hey, wait up!"

Malia trips over her own feet, and the strap on one of her flip-flops breaks. She narrows her eyes and mutters something as I draw closer.

"Is everything okay?"

"No." She spits the word out like it's a piece of rotten pineapple and kicks off the useless shoe. "Nothing's okay. Not that you have any experience with *that*." Sparks shoot from her gaze, and she snorts in my direction before taking off again.

I stand like an ice pop and stare after her. I could try to catch up again, but sometimes...sometimes, it's best to be alone.

Turning toward the group, I keep my head low as I approach them. "Sorry." I take a seat next to Jazz again, and Koa stretches his neck to snuffle my knee, his whiskers tickling my bare leg. A giggle bubbles up, but I swallow it. Now's not the time. "I tried to catch her, but I don't think she's in the mood to talk."

"That's okay." Jonah scratches his head, rumpling his messy man-bun, and flips through a folder. "I'm sure she'll come to us when she's ready. And until then, we can keep praying for her. Let's do that now."

We all bow our heads, and Jonah delivers a prayer— short and sweet—asking God to comfort Malia. When I open my eyes again, Jonah's face is drawn. "Now, we have another problem to take care of—Koa."

"Koa?" Brander pockets his phone and cocks his head at Jonah before reaching over to pat the furry mutt's muzzle. "Is he okay?"

Jonah frowns and erases something in his folder. "He was supposed to go to Malia's place for the week."

Oh no. My stomach churns at his words, and I glance around at the others. Surely there's someone here who can take him this week. There must be. "Can you do it, Brander?" I cast him a hopeful glance. "He'd have a blast hanging out with Rosco."

At that moment, Brander's cellphone buzzes, cutting him off before he can even begin. He pulls out his phone again and glances at the screen, his expression tightening. "Sorry, guys. I've gotta take this."

He jogs toward the beach, away from the group, but the caller's voice floats toward us on the air anyway. "Son? This is it. Do you have an answer or not?"

I cringe, the speaker's words drilling a hole straight through my heart as Brander's response is lost in the wind. Jazz's brows shoot up as I lean in close to whisper. "The record guy."

Though my words are soft, barely more than a breath, a good half dozen of the others perk up. "Is he really going to Nashville?" One of the girls gazes after Brander, then turns to me. I shrug and lift my hands, palms up.

"Come on, let's focus on Koa." Jonah claps his hands and lifts the old clipboard with the signup sheet. "Who's it gonna be? Koa needs a landing pad this week. I'd take him home myself, but my roommate's allergic."

An eerie silence falls over the group. "I—I guess I could take him. If no one else can, I mean. But I'd rather not." The second the words have left my mouth, I make a fist and press it against my leg. What was I thinking?

My gaze drifts to Koa, in all of his fluffy-puppy-eared charm. Maybe—somewhere deep inside—I was thinking that pup can be mighty cute. When he's not terrorizing the human race, that is.

How 'bout it, gang?" Jonah scans the group gathered on the lawn. "Any other takers?"

"Sorry." A dark-skinned girl with a row of scars on one arm frowns. "I'd love to take him, but we have neighbor island friends coming to stay. Things are crazy enough without a puppy in the mix."

"That's okay." Jonah fixes his attention on me. "Looks

like he's all yours."

"What happened?" Brander returns from the beach at the end of the session, and his eyes balloon as he looks from me to Koa, then back again. "You're taking him again?"

"Everyone else was busy, and you..." I wave a hand in the air.

"Right." Brander shoves his hands in his pockets and shuffles his feet. "Could we maybe go for a walk? I can drop you off at Tutu's afterwards."

"Sure." I walk over to say goodbye to Jazz, who appears to be in the middle of a heart-to-heart with Jonah and that other guy, Oke. "You have a ride?"

Jazz shoots me a thumbs-up, so I follow Brander to the beach, the nerves in my stomach tightening with every step. I wrap my hand around Koa's leash and take in a shuddery breath of plumeria-scented air.

Brander hangs his head and looks at me, eyebrows folding into each other. "Olive, I—"

"You're leaving." I kick at the sand as we step onto the beach. "Aren't you?"

Brander groans. "It's not like I'm never coming back. I'm only going over with my dad for a while—to check it out, maybe try dropping a single with Mike's label. Spend a couple of months seeing what I think before I make any big commitment. They'll fly me back here for holidays. If I decide not to go on tour, I mean."

"Tour?" I stop walking and stare at him. Light filters through the leaves of a palm tree, highlighting the soft angles of his face. His chocolate-covered-almond eyes shimmer with the possibility of a new chapter. His cowlick stands at attention. "You're really doing this, aren't you?"

Brander nods, and a tiny part of my heart shrivels up

like a prune. "Dad's getting us tickets right now. I've gotta at least explore the option. See if it's where God wants me." He shoves his hands deeper in his pockets and bows his head. "I was going to talk about it at group today, ask for prayer. Then everyone got going about substance abuse. They needed that talk more than I needed prayer. The next thing I knew, Mike called."

"And you said yes." My voice cracks over the words, but how can I blame him? "It's got to be pretty nice, knowing you're headed for fame and fortune." No matter how hard I try, I can't keep that note of bitterness from creeping into my tone. How can he say goodbye like this, when he doesn't need to—when he could call Mike, tell him no, and send everything hurtling back toward *normal*.

Except, I guess in life there is no *normal*.

Something pricks my throat. I lift my eyes to meet Brander's gaze. He rests his hand on my shoulder, his touch as light as that of a butterfly. He pulls me toward him, looks me straight in the eye. Koa tugs at the leash, but I ignore him. My heart thrums in my chest as I stand there, waiting for one of us to say something.

"I'm going to miss you so much." The words burst from between my tightly closed lips, and I take a step closer.

"I know." Brander pulls me in, and I get a whiff of his omnipresent guy-smell—eau de hair gel?—before his lips come to rest on my forehead.

The movement is so swift, so sudden, that I don't even have time to close my eyes before he's pulling away, a sheepish smile on the lips that were kissing me moments before.

A million questions teeter on the tip of my tongue—this is the third time he's kissed me like that, with never a word about what it means to him, to *us*. If there still is—ever was—an *us*, that is.

And now I guess I'll never know.

Because he's going...going...

Gone.

I stand on Gramma's porch a quarter of an hour later as Brander's Porsche whooshes away from the curb. Will he even glance at me in the rearview mirror? Or is he too busy looking through the windshield of his dreams, his hopes—his new *life*?

Something in my heart snaps. I drop to my knees, splinters from the old porch digging into my bare legs. Tears well up and choke me. A raw sob bursts from deep within, cutting my throat like a million shards of glass. Another one follows and then the tears come spilling, cascading down my cheeks in a silent waterfall.

The entire world shimmers as I swipe at my overflowing eyes. Thank goodness, Gramma's rattly old station wagon isn't in the driveway. I can make a total blubbering fool out of myself and no one's around to notice. To care.

I sniff and bury my head in my knees, a ball of fire churning in my gut. How can Brander do this? Leave me, leave his home, leave everything for the fame game? It's not—it's not *right*. It can't be.

Something cold and wet bumps against my neck and I whirl around, garnering a whole new pincushion of splinters. There's Koa, sitting on the porch next to me, damp, slimy nose twitching. He cocks his head at me, as if to ask what's wrong.

Everything. Everything's wrong.

The words stir something in my chest, breaking another wall—one I thought I'd plastered over. Koa nuzzles me and more tears come, then turn to hiccups as my fountain runs dry.

This isn't only about Brander.

It's about what I've gained, what I've lost, and the changing winds that never seem to stop. The dreams that came true, and the ones that got washed away like a sand castle at high tide. It's about life and all of its terrible messiness.

And, despite the great lengths I've gone to these past few months to stuff my feelings, to play it cool and act like everything's okay—despite the smiles I've pasted on, the little white lies I've let slip past my lips.

I'm *not* okay.

So I sit, a fresh wave of tears washing my face, leaving salty trails down my sunburned cheeks. I sit, arms around Koa's neck, face buried in his stinky doggie fur. I sit on that porch—the one where, in less than five months, I've been abandoned, I've been saved, I've been kissed—and I cry.

I cry for Mom, for Jazz, for Brander.

For Macie, who will someday forget the sound of her mommy's voice. For Gramma, who outlived her only daughter. For Dad, who's swimming upstream against a midlife crisis.

I cry for Jazz's mom and Ruby and Malia.

I cry for all of them. And I cry for me.

Chapter Twenty-Four

TURNS OUT, GRIEF ISN'T SOMETHING TO be dealt with in a day, or a couple of days, or even a month. It also isn't a thing to be locked away, pushed aside. Grief is to be dealt with, in all of its beautiful agony. It's something to be embraced, understood. Challenged by the knowledge that, someday, we *will* overcome.

I wish I could say I came up with all that on my own, but I didn't. That pearly bit of wisdom came straight from Gramma, who found me and Koa curled up together on the front porch swing when she and Macie came home from the beach later that afternoon.

"How are you doing?" She pats my shoulder and stands from the porch swing after we've talked the better part of the afternoon away.

"Awful." I scuff my shoe along the floorboards and give Koa's ears a ruffle before rising and following Gramma inside. "But better than I was when you found me."

"Considering the circumstances..." Gramma opens the door to go inside. "I'd say that *better* is a pretty good place to be."

"If you say so." I kick off my shoes and trudge in after her. Macie scampers out from the living room, where she's no doubt been spying on us all along, and throws herself at Gramma. Her brown eyes are swirled with a thousand different emotions, and her face is crumpled in a frown.

"Is Brander really going away?" She buries her face in Gramma's shirt.

I lift my shoulders, the truth churning in my stomach.

"Yeah, squirt. But he'll try and make it home for Thanksgiving. That's only"—I count on my fingers— "four weeks. Not so bad, huh?" My voice breaks as I say it, and Macie squints at me like she's not sure whether I'm telling the truth or not. Thankfully the mention of one of her favorite holidays seems to be enough to distract her. She detaches herself from Grams and takes a step toward the kitchen.

"What do you make for Thanksgiving dinner, Gramma? Do you eat turkey, or do you roast Spam? Thanksgiving is my favorite." She rests a finger alongside her chin. "And this is the first time I'll ever spend it in Hawaii."

A tremor runs through my veins as I follow Macie farther into the house. This Thanksgiving is more than my first Thanksgiving on Maui—it's my first one *without.*

Without Mom, without Dad, without the life I used to call my own.

How will I survive? Put on a happy face and act like things are all hunky-dory when Mom's special corn relish and cranberry salad aren't on the table with the turkey and gravy? How can I even begin to start thinking about Christmas, about taking over Mom's role as Santa Claus?

Grams had better be right—that this grieving thing will get a whole lot easier. Thankfully, Gramma's advice has never failed me. I have to believe that it won't start now.

"Jazz?" I call her late the next night, when the rest of the world is fast asleep, but she answers anyway. "Are you good to talk?"

"Sure." Something rustles on the other end, and I picture Jazz rolling over in bed. "Brander told me the whole Nashville story. Sounds like he's pretty pumped about it. I'm guessing that's what you want to talk about?"

"Actually, no." My resolve quivers as a cool night breeze caresses my shoulders. Koa woofs in his sleep and snuggles up against me. I bury one hand in his tawny fur. Might as well get it all out now. "Remember a certain apology you gave me? A couple of days ago?"

"What about it?" Jazz's words tiptoe across the line.

"I need to give you the same one. I'm a mess, Jazz."

"Aren't we all?" Jazz snorts. "Mom came home tonight, raving drunk again."

"She did?" My stomach plunges to my toes. What should I have thought—that things would magically get easier for Jazz after a handful of extra prayers?

"She did. Except, this time, Ruby finally got enough guts to kick her out."

"You mean she's gone?" A weight lifts from my shoulders, and I lean against the top step. "What happened?"

"A miracle, I guess. Jonah and Oke and I had a good talk yesterday. Jonah talked a lot about how we can love someone and still hate what they're doing. I told that to Ruby when I got home. Maybe something clicked."

"Whatever. It doesn't matter. I can breathe a whole lot easier knowing that you're safe." I send up a silent prayer of thanks before turning my attention to the conversation at hand. "But whatever. Remember a while ago, when you got down on me for not being honest with you?"

Jazz *hmm*s on the other end. "That was a rough day for me. I'm sure I said stuff I shouldn't have. Would you please—"

"That's not what I'm getting at. You were right to say what you did. I was begging you to spill your guts about what was going on over at Ruby's place when I had no intention of spilling any secrets of my own."

"Yeah?"

"So, now I'm ready. I mean, if you want to talk."

"Sure, but—I don't want you to think you have to do this or anything. Even though I was ready to talk at youth group today, that doesn't mean—"

"No. Listen. I've been ready for a long time. But it took a lot to make me realize it." And then, almost without my own bidding, the words start coming, pouring out of me, coming from someplace deep in my heart—my soul.

I tell Jazz the same story Brander pried out of me months ago. About how I watched my mom die, my dad turn into a shell of the person he once was. I tell her about *Pride and Prejudice*, why it's been so hard to write that measly little essay. I tell her about Brander's kiss, his promise to return for Thanksgiving.

"But even if he does make it back this year, there'll be someone else missing. Forever." My voice cracks as I finish to stark silence on the other end.

I take the phone away from my face and shake it a few times—we're still connected. Leave it to me to put Jazz to sleep with my own bellyaching. But then, from the other end of the phone, comes a sigh.

"Wow. You didn't *have* to tell me all of that, you know. But I'm glad you did. I wish there was something I could say to make it better, though."

"There's not. And I guess it's no use sitting around moping about it, but I don't get it. Can't there at least be some light? Somewhere?" The lights in the bay twinkle in the darkness, as though mocking my simple wish. "Gramma says it'll get easier, that I can put my trust in God and all that good stuff, so maybe..." I yawn. "Whatever. I should let you go."

"No." I can picture Jazz shaking her head, her braid cutting through the air with whiplike precision. "Let me pray with you first."

"Okay." My heart swells for this girl, this friend who doesn't give up on me, on God—on *anyone*—and I bow my head as she prays.

"We're both in a rough spot right now, God. Can You

show us where you want us? Help us see Your plan? Because, if Olive is anything like me, she doesn't want to hurt anymore. And right now, life is a whole lot of messy. Amen."

"Thanks, Jazz." I take a gulp of heavy nighttime air like it's the first breath I've had in years. "I'm so glad your mom's gone."

"Yeah—um..." Jazz's voice catches, and I almost slap myself. After all, alcoholic or not, that crazy lady *is* still Jazz's mom.

"Can I pray for her?" I barely wait for an answer before diving in. "Dear God, please be with Jazz's mom wherever she is. And be with the rest of us too."

The words rattle my chest, but they go even deeper than that. They fill me up and flow into my heart, into the hole that was created when Mom took her final breath. They crash over me, wash away a small amount of the pain that's been hanging over me since I said Goodbye.

And then—right as Jazz and I wish each other goodnight—the sky splits open. Rain comes pouring down in what has to be the biggest squall this island's ever seen. I set my phone on the top step, then dash into the front yard, letting the rain drench me, wash me.

I lift my head to the sky as raindrops mixed with tears run down my cheek. The wind blows in my hair, and Koa yaps at my ankles. I kneel and throw my arms around his neck. He reeks like wet dog—probably because that's what he is—but I don't care.

I stay there, water from the grass soaking through my pajama pants, rain trickling down my back, Koa wrapped in my arms, and I *breathe*.

I breathe with an overflowing heart, one so full of life that it doesn't know what to do with itself. So I let it spill over, let the bad memories gush out of me, drain away. That doesn't mean they won't come sneaking back, that I won't ever fight my grief again. But right now, in the middle of the night on an island I've learned to call my home, I am *new*.

The next morning, Gramma shoots me an extra-long glance when I stumble downstairs for breakfast with all the vim and vigor of a debilitated sloth. "Rough night?" Her tone is chipper, but her tight gaze reveals otherwise. Could she know more than she lets on?

Probably.

I slide onto a stool at the bar. Macie is already half done with her Spam and egg scramble, and she turns to look at me. "Koa stinks."

"So?" I grab a muffin from a tray on the counter and pinch off a piece to taste—coconut, yum. "Don't all dogs stink?"

Macie shrugs.

"Yes, they do. Which is why I don't like dogs." I bow my head for a quick prayer before taking an extra-big bite of muffin.

"You still don't like dogs?" Gramma crosses her arms over her generous middle and cocks an eyebrow. "Funny. Koa told me you two have been getting along pretty well."

I lower my head, mouth too full of muffin to answer even if I wanted to.

"How else could he have gotten himself soaked through last night unless someone took him out into the rain?" Gramma's eyes twinkle. "I'm glad to see you two are getting along better."

"Yeah. Well." I take another bite of muffin. "If he's going to be someone's therapy dog, he should at least be socialized."

"Right." Gramma slides her floral-print reading glasses onto her nose and eyes me over the tops of them. Before she can take her interrogation any further, the doorbell rings.

Macie jumps from her chair and scampers into the hallway, returning with Jazz only moments later. Despite our late-night phone call, Jazz is fresh-faced and chipper, her smile sunnier than ever. A shimmer of something deeper, heavier, still hides behind her eyes, but her stride seems ten times lighter as she clunks across the room, her prosthesis clattering cheerily on the tile floor.

"Aloha." She reaches past me for a muffin and crams half of it into her mouth. "Ready to get to school?" Without waiting for an answer, she plops her bag on the breakfast bar and unzips it to reveal, among her normal school books, her Bible.

Somehow, Gramma manages to corral Macie upstairs, and I help Jazz onto the stool next to me. "How are you?" Her eyes search my own, and I relax against the back of my stool. Finally, there's nothing to hide, no I'm-doing-fine façade to paste on, no pretense to keep her from digging deeper. There's just *me*, in all of my broken pieces. And next to me is *Jazz*. And, believe it or not, she's broken, too.

We stay that way, staring at each other for a few moments until giggles overtake our grave expressions. Jazz lifts her Bible. "Thought it might be a good way to start the morning."

"Sounds good to me."

Jazz opens the big book to the Psalms, leafing through a few pages before beginning to read. Her voice rolls over the words like waves over the shore. She reads verses and verses, all of them flowing over my ears but none of them lodging in my heart.

Until...

"My sacrifice, O God, is a broken spirit; a broken and contrite heart you, God, will not despise.'"

The words Jazz reads split the fog surrounding me and echo deep in my chest. Jazz's voice trails off, and she turns her head and looks to me. "Jonah showed me that verse after

you left for Boston, before I got my prosthesis. I felt broken—
I *was* broken." Her voice thickens. "But, even with all of my
problems and mess-ups, God can use me. He could use me
then, and He can use me now."

"You got half the support group to talk. Maybe..." I shake
my head. Malia's steely gaze flickers in my memory. Could it
work? "Maybe, if I share my story, I could help someone
else."

A smile stretches across Jazz's face, almost as though
I've found the point she was trying to make all along. She
nods. Slowly at first, then faster, until her head looks like it's
about to come flying off. "I think that's a great idea. And I
think you should do it this Saturday."

Chapter Twenty-Five

NEXT SATURDAY, RUBY DROPS us off at Ka'anapali Beach for the support group meeting. The young woman's eyes are noticeably brighter, her hair dyed a fresh shade of ketchup-red. The smile on her face is a near-copy of someone's trademark Cheshire-cat grin, and she hums along with the alt-rock station as she pulls into the parking lot. "I'll pick you girls up at noon?"

"Yep." I help Jazz out of the van before waving goodbye. "She seems different." I angle my eyes toward the van, then tighten my grip on Koa's leash as we walk toward the group's picnic table of choice.

"She is." Jazz swings her arms and throws her head back, breathing in deep. "We haven't heard from Mom all week."

My chest burns for Jazz, for another girl without a mom, but Jazz only shrugs. "I'm praying for her. Harder than I've ever prayed before. I think this could be the time when she turns around and gets herself right. For *good*. And when she does, we can finally start over."

I nod as we approach the table. How can a girl be so optimistic? Especially someone like Jazz, who's seen the very worst life has to offer?

But even more than that, how can I get that kind of optimistic spirit for myself? It might be something worth looking into—or, even better, praying about.

No time for that now, though. I help steady Jazz as she slides onto the last empty spot on a bench before settling onto the ground next to her. Koa curls up at my side, and my heart pinches a little. He won't be coming home with me this week. If memory serves me right, he's supposed to go with—

"Okay, gang. Let's get started." Jonah plops onto the grass across from me and claps his hands. The others stop chatting, and a hush falls over the group. "Anything to talk about before we get going? Praise reports? Deep, life-altering confessions?" He waggles his eyebrows.

My hand raises in the air, almost of its own accord. "I have one of those, actually." The words are dry in my mouth. All eyes fix on me. All of them except for Malia's, that is. She sits a handful of feet away from me, legs crisscrossed, picking at a clump of grass. Her gaze is cold, stony.

But at least she's here.

The others continue to stare at me. Waiting. I squirm under the sudden scrutiny, but I pat Koa's head for support.

"My mom died a few months ago. I feel like crying every day." My voice wavers. "Talking about it hurts. When I do, it's like I'm living her death all over again. But sometimes we have to talk. We have to get things out in the open before we can grieve."

The second I stop for a breath, Malia climbs to her feet and steps away. "Is this going to turn into a pity party again? Because if so, I'm outta here." She lifts her backpack and takes another step.

"Wait." I stand and gesture toward Malia. "This'll only take a minute."

I sit again, giving the sweetened condensed version of everything I've learned—about myself, grief, and God—then pause long enough to get my breath. "I'm not saying that grieving is easy or fun, but it has to happen before any one of us can truly begin to heal."

A handful of the kids nod along, as does Jonah. "Well said. Anyone want to add to that?"

A flurry ensues, with hands raised left and right. Before Jonah can get a word out, Malia spins on her heel and marches away without another word. I don't hesitate before jogging after her. And this time, I'm not going to give up so easily.

"Malia!" I tear down the path, weaving between groups of wandering tourists as my target disappears behind a surfboard rental hut.

My lungs burn as I continue to run. Why? Why chase after the girl who's given me and Jazz nothing but grief? Even if I do manage to catch an athlete like her, why would she bother talking to me?

The questions, though they tickle my brain, don't slow me. I pick up my speed and spy Malia's ebony mane bobbing a few paces ahead. She seems to disappear into a group of tourists with oversized maps and fanny packs, but only a moment later the crowd parts.

Heart pounding, I slow and scan the area—there. Leaning against a palm, arms wrapped around her six-pack abs, gaze hard and flinty, is Malia. I push my way through the Saturday crowd and stop in front of the palm.

I plant my hands on my knees and wheeze. I've never run that much in my life—not even in gym. Malia, of course, seems unaffected by the jog. She stares straight through me, eyes so blank she might as well hang a vacancy sign from her brows.

But at least she's staying put—for now.

"What do you want?" She spits out the words like they're poison, and I flinch. I was so focused on getting to Malia that I hadn't actually taken the time to consider what to say.

Help, God? I lower my head and scuff at a pebble before meeting Malia's gaze. "I don't want you to think that support group is one big pity party. It's not. It's okay to share our struggles. In fact, it's better than stuffing them inside." *Take it from experience.*

A child giggles farther down the shoreline and a bird caws overhead as Malia twirls a strand of hair around her finger. A single ray of light falls across her face. "Maybe it works better for you, but not me. And I'm sick of sitting around and listening to that group of bozos whine and whimper about their horrific, horrendous lives. I never would have come if my parents hadn't forced me to. Why can't everybody else leave me alone?"

I smirk at Malia's words. A few weeks ago, I sounded exactly like her—probably still do, sometimes. Maybe we aren't quite as different as I'd thought. "I can leave you alone, but I'm warning you. You might feel a whole lot better if you talk."

"Wanna bet?" She crosses her arms and squares her feet.

"Sure." I stick out my hand, as if to shake, but she waves it away and pushes off from the tree. "Come on."

I follow behind her, and we cross the path to an open-air restaurant patio on the edge of a swanky-looking shopping complex. Without so much as a second glance at the lunch-hour scene, Malia plops onto a chair at a two-top table and motions for me to do the same.

The music is pumping, and the patio is packed, but Malia flags down a waitress—more like her slightly older-looking doppelganger—and orders us both what sounds like a kind of tropical drink.

"You didn't have to do that." I keep an eye on the waitress as she disappears to place our order.

"Like you think I'm not gonna split the bill." Malia's eyes do a perfect pirouette. "Gimme a break. It's bad enough that you want to counsel me or whatever. I'm not paying for your drink."

"Figures." I dig a few bills out of my pocket and lay them on the table.

"Thanks." Malia adds her own cash, keeping her eyes on

me the whole time.

"Listen." I lay both hands on the table and lean across so my whisper can be heard over the happy-family chatter. "If you don't want to talk, it's fine. I wanted to give you the opportunity, but we don't *have* to."

"Yes." Malia's gaze grows dark. "We do."

"We...do?" I stare at her. *That* took a lot less persuasion than I'd thought would be necessary. *This is all You, God.*

"I'm going to go crazy if I don't talk to someone at some point. I guess I can trust you to not go squealing this all over the island. But if you do..." Her icy stare numbs me into submission.

The waitress returns and deposits our drinks, laying a kiss on Malia's head before bustling away. "Love ya too, Mom." Malia tosses the words over her shoulder like she couldn't care less, but the softness in her gaze reveals that she's closer to her mom than she might let on.

Malia's mom disappears around the corner, and I raise the drink to my mouth. Pineapple and coconut mingle in perfect harmony on my tongue, and I take another sip before setting my glass down and waiting for Malia to speak.

She twirls her straw between two ragged-nailed fingers and stares into her drink as though it contains the answers to all of life's problems. "We're homeless." Her lips barely move around the words, and they're flat and dull—wooden. As though her saying them without any emotion will somehow make the fact less real.

"You're—"

"Don't be a parrot." The words snap like a dry twig. "I'm homeless. No sense repeating it for the world to hear. My dad got laid off, and the economy stinks. My Tutu told my parents they'd bit off more they could chew, and she was right. We've been living out of our car since the start of the school year."

This time when I open my mouth, no words come.

"Not exactly the kind of thing I want to broadcast to the world. Especially when"—her lip quivers—"I'm swim team captain. I always get straight A's. I'm, like, way too perfect to be *homeless*. Or at least, I was." A kinky strand of hair falls into her face, and she swipes it behind her ear with one hand.

"But your mom—"

"Has a part-time gig? Sure." Malia snorts. "Think that's enough to keep a family of four fed, clothed, housed, and insured?"

My heart pinches in my stomach—for Malia, her parents, and that little rug rat sister of hers. "There's got to be a shelter around here. And maybe the people at the church could—"

"Hold it." Malia slurps on her straw and shakes her head. "I didn't ask for your help."

Oh.

"I said I wanted to talk. Are you going to let me?"

"Right. Go for it." I scoot my chair closer to hear Malia over the din of the restaurant patio.

"Please." Malia clutches her glass in both hands. "What I tell you cannot leave this table. Don't tell your grandma, or Jazz, or even that mangy mutt you're always hanging around." Despite the hard timbre of Malia's voice, her eyes soften when she mentions Koa.

"I promise. My lips are locked." I take another sip of my drink and motion for Malia to go on.

"I'm not a nice person, okay?" Her stony mask cracks a bit around the corners of her eyes. "But the rest of my family is. They don't deserve this. Not my mom or my dad, and especially not Kanani. And—sometimes—I wonder if this is all my fault."

I nearly laugh at the absurdity of *that* idea, but the gravity of Malia's expression keeps me from showing so much as a smile.

"My mom could come around this way any time, so I've gotta make this short." Malia chances a glance over her shoulder.

"Go for it."

"Dad always worked long hours. I hated it. He never made it to my swim meets—not even the important ones. So I got on him about it." Her face clouds. "It was ugly. I told him that, if he really loved me, he'd do whatever it took to see me swim. Then one day, he showed up. At the state qualifier."

The state qualifier...

I stare at my drink, Malia's words rolling through my brain. I've heard them somewhere before. *Jazz.* That's where her leg gave out, when she first discovered the tumor.

"We tanked. Not because of Jazz. We just...tanked." Malia's eyes pinch together. "And later, Dad got chewed out by his boss something fierce. He didn't even tell anyone what he was doing. Left the office in the middle of the day. Because of me."

"No way. Not even the world's worst boss would fire someone for a first-time offense."

"Maybe not. But if he did it again?" She dips her head and traces the condensation on the smoothie glass. "Kanani had a hula recital the next week. He left work for that too. And then he started coming home early. A lot of little things, but then the company's budget took a hit. I guess he was falling down on the job enough that they thought he'd be the perfect person to get the ax."

I look up at Malia. Another chip in her mask—this one around her mouth—reveals a fallen smile, not the hard frown she usually wears. Something flitters behind her, and I tear my gaze away in time for my stomach to drop about three stories. It's Malia's mom, serving the table behind us. And if the woman's wide-eyed gaze is enough to go by, she heard every word of Malia's confession.

"What?" The word crackles in the air, Malia's voice

cutting through the rest of the restaurant chatter, and I snap to attention. But I'm too late. Malia whirls in her seat, and her shoulders droop. "Mom."

Malia's mom places a final plate on the neighboring table, then crosses the distance between us in two long-legged steps. She stoops to put her arms around Malia who doesn't resist. A drop of moisture rolls down Malia's cheek, and her whispered words rustle the air. I push away from my table and weave my way through the patio seating area until I'm a safe distance away.

Sometimes, a girl and her mom just need to talk.

It's almost half an hour before Malia finally joins me at the restaurant entrance. Her face is red and blotchy, washed clean by her tears. For a second, my heart twists. If only Mom was alive, so we could sit together and have a big heart-to-heart like Malia and her own mother get to.

My heart trembles, but I twine my necklace around my fingers and press my mouth into a smile. "You okay?"

Malia's chin bobbles as she nods, but the cage that ensnared her gaze is gone. Her eyes are full of something else—something lighter, less burdened. "I think so."

"Good." I stand, shuffling my feet, waiting for Malia to offer something—anything—else. After all, I'm the only one now to know her secret. And she expects me to—

"Why did you stay?" Malia crosses her arms and stares at me, a spark flickering in her eye.

"I—um..."

Malia shakes her head, ebony mane swatting the air. An abundance of split ends stand out against the midday sun. When's the last time she's had a good haircut? "Sorry. I mean, uh—thanks, I guess. For waiting."

"No problem." I shrug, and we head toward the part of

the beach where the support group meets. Hopefully Jonah doesn't think we drowned or anything. "Listen, if you need anything—like, anything at all—ask me, okay?"

"Thanks. For real." A shadow crosses Malia's face, but whether it's from the swaying palm branches overhead or something deeper, I don't know. "You know you're sworn to secrecy, right?"

I nod, my stomach sinking. Jazz and I finally got everything out in the open, and now I have to start hiding things from her—again? Can I do it?

As if sensing my thoughts, Malia glances over at me. "I mean, I guess you can tell Jazz if you totally have to. And Brander doesn't seem like he'd be the type to squeal about it."

"No." I shake my head. "He wouldn't." And I would tell him about it—tell him about everything that's happened since he drove off last week. But he's gone, living the life in Nashville, too busy exploring his myriad options and working with Mike on a single to send more than a quick text.

I shake my head and press on beside Malia as the sun warms my face and neck. Brander is off living his dream—and, more than that, he's leading people to Jesus by doing what he loves the most. How can I fault him for that?

Chapter Twenty-Six

"ALOOOHA LAHAINA!" UNCLE KIMO, THE MOST irritating radio DJ on the entire island—maybe in the whole world—blares from the radio in Gramma's car. I groan. Can't she change the channel?

We're headed home after church a couple weekends after my talk with Malia, and I'm already hot and sticky, shoved in between Jazz and Macie in the backseat. It's bad enough that Macie's in a mood, insisting that she has to sit in the same row as Jazz—especially when Jazz and I need to talk. No use adding Kimo and his random ramblings to my list of problems.

And then the radio crackles. "Have I got a real treat for you all today." The DJ wheezes out a chuckle that sounds more like the crow of an asthmatic rooster. "One of our own, young pop sensation Brander Delacroix, dropped his first single this weekend, and it is my *plea*sure to be the first to spin this tune on the airwaves. So without further ado..."

My heart nearly jumps out of my chest as the volume of a backing track grows, a ukulele and synthesizer working together, fusing classic Hawaiiana with modern pop. Jazz elbows my shoulder—on purpose? Hard to tell, considering how cramped Gramma's backseat is, but I look over at her anyway.

"You like it?" She hardly does more than mouth the words, and I shrug.

"He hasn't even started singing yet," I say as Brander's voice fades in. It's still a little rough and scratchy, and it holds that rawness that makes it *real*. His heart seems to pour out of the speakers, especially when Grams reaches over and turns up the volume.

I bob my head along with the beat as the tune picks up and carries him into the chorus. He sings the words with what sounds like every drop of emotion he has in him.

Don't try to fix it, ooh
It's already fixed
Grace saved the day
Love found a way
To chase the lost
And heal their broken heart
And bring them back to shore

It's so...Brander. My heart swells at these words, words that pour straight from his very soul and into my heart. That song could almost have been written for me. I look over at Jazz as Grams pulls into the driveway.

"He found his calling." The words tangle on my tongue, but I can't deny them. Much as I wish they weren't true, that I could reach all the way across the Pacific Ocean, across half of the United States and bring Brander back, I can't.

And now, listening to this, maybe I don't want to.

We stay in the car, even Macie staying fairly still, until the song ends, and Grams shuts off the ignition. Macie tumbles out first, then me. Together, we help Jazz climb out. Her fingers tighten on my hand before I let go. "That was amazing." Her words are tentative, as though she's afraid they'll upset me.

And, in a way, they do. They squeeze my heart and turn over in my chest, reminding me of when the youth group had Brander all to itself, when he brought his guitar over to Gramma's to play and sing—for me.

When he kissed me, albeit on the forehead.

When he left.

But if it's God's will for Brander to become one of those overnight celebrities, to go around the world on tour, to reach thousands of people for the name of Jesus...well, who am I to mess with God's plan?

So I smile up at Jazz and Gramma and Macie and nod. "It was amazing."

And, truth is, it was.

"I have a challenge for you." Jonah's glint-eyed grin at support group on Saturday alludes to another one of his crazy, harebrained schemes. "Think about one of your favorite things to do on a nice weekend afternoon. Something you think everyone should experience at least once— something they might even *pay* to experience."

"Why?" Malia squints at Jonah and taps her pencil against her journal.

"Just do it." Jonah bounds to his feet and paces, Koa following him bound for bound.

Now that I'm not seeing Koa every day, it's always a surprise how much he seems to grow between group meetings. His soft, downy fuzz has been replaced by thicker golden hair, and his legs seem longer every week. I never thought I'd get attached to any animal other than a cat, let alone a dog, but I have to admit—I'll miss Koa when he finally goes to his forever home.

Which is going to be a lot sooner than any of us would like.

I bow my head, my stomach doing cartwheels at the thought of saying yet another goodbye, but Jazz nudges me and leans in close. "Koa's getting so cute. I can't imagine how excited that little squirt is going to be when he finally meets Koa." Her breath tickles my ear, and I can't help but nod.

Jonah must overhear Jazz, because he chimes in. "That's

exactly what I'm going for. Remember when we talked about hosting a luau for Lio and his family when we hand over Koa? Brander did great helping us get coverage for that event. We should make it a real blowout."

"When is it again?" Jazz winds the tail of her braid around her finger. "Did we even pick a date?"

Jonah shakes his head. "Brander advertised it as a Thanksgiving weekend celebration at the church. But what does everyone love to do during a holiday weekend?"

"Eat!" Jazz and that guy—Oke—say it at the same time, then share a smile.

"You should have a giant Thanksgiving dinner at the church then." Malia glances around, her phone nowhere in sight—that's a first. "I bet a lot of people would want to come if the food was good enough. Especially since it's for a good cause."

I bob my head in approval. Grams has been dropping hints about the impending holiday—what kind of pie do Macie and I like, do we want to do anything special?—but I've been doing a pretty good job of ignoring her. My first holiday without Mom isn't anything to be celebrated.

"What do you think?" Jonah stares at me, as though expecting an answer.

"Sorry, what?" I shake myself.

"Would your grandma be up for volunteering her culinary expertise? I happen to know that she makes a mean key lime pie. If your *tutu* pitches in, and we get enough other people to help cook, we can keep the cost down and hopefully bring in a lot of donations for Lio's family."

"I'm sure she'll be up for that." My shoulders unwind. Even if it is a holiday without Mom and Brander, at least it'll be fun.

"If my mom's not working, she could help." Everyone stares at Malia, as though questioning her suddenly supportive attitude. "What? It's not like she has anything better to do."

Oke nods. "I'll be there."

"Me, too." I shake my head as I say the words. What is happening to me? A few weeks ago, spending Thanksgiving with this bunch of oddballs would have been something akin to torture.

Now, the thought of it sends a warm ribbon of joy through my heart—everyone coming together to share the holiday, to celebrate the beginning of a grand adventure for Koa's new owner. And for Koa

And that's when a shadow falls across my sudden good mood. Because, in order to celebrate Koa's new life, I also have to say goodbye.

Again.

Sure, it's for a good cause, but still. I cast a glance at the mutt I've somehow come to love, and my heart turns in my chest.

Why does Goodbye have to be so hard?

My phone buzzes in my pocket later that afternoon while I'm wandering around the Kula lavender farm with Grams, Macie, and Macie's new BFF Kanani, the same Kanani who got Malia for a big sister. A cool upcountry breeze carries the scent of the blooming flowers toward me as I dig out my phone and jog a few paces away from Macie and Kanani's melodramatic reenactment of a scene from some Disney movie.

The number is strange—from the mainland—but I accept the call anyway and press the phone to my ear. "Aloha?"

"Hi." A deep, distinctively masculine voice rattles my ear, and I nearly drop the phone into a nearby lavender bush. "Is this a good time?"

"Brander? It's—it's always a good time." I cringe at the

ridiculous, rom-com-style upsweep of my voice, but I can't help it. I haven't heard Brander—other than on the radio—in weeks. "How are you? How's Nashville? Do you—" I stop before I can ask whether or not he misses me. *That*, I'm afraid, would be taking things too far.

"I'm doing great. Mom calls ten times a day to make sure I'm staying up on my schoolwork and that Dad and I aren't pigging out too much on all the fried chicken, but all in all—it's indescribable. You won't believe how many cool people are out here. I met this other guy at Mike's label who's crazy on fire for Jesus." He sighs. "It's fantastic."

"Sounds like it." A tiny part of my heart sags. Somewhere, deep inside, I hoped he was calling to say he hated the Nashville music scene, that he was hopping on a flight home. But—I clench my other hand into a fist, as though cementing my resolve—if what I've been hearing about Brander and his new single on the radio is anything to go by, he's doing exactly what God wants him to.

"You wouldn't believe how cool it feels. I played the Ryman last night, and I actually got to help lead this girl to Christ. She reminded me of you, trying so hard to be strong even when everything is falling apart."

"That's how you think of me?" I flinch.

What hurts more? The fact that, someday, I'll be nothing more than one of the many girls Brander's witnessed to over the years, or that he could see through my emotional mask all along?

"No. Sorry. I didn't mean it that way." Brander sighs. "This isn't turning out right at all."

"It's fine if you do. Think of me that way. I guess." I bite my lip. "But I'm doing better now."

"What do you mean?"

"I'm not hiding anymore—at least, not as much as I was. God and I've been doing some talking, and I think it's time for me to stop covering up my pain. It's not like doing that will protect my heart any more. Most of the time it makes me miserable."

"That's great. I've been praying that God would reveal that to you."

"You—have?" Maybe he hasn't forgotten about me after all.

"Olive." He laughs on the other end of the phone. "You're the one who never told anyone why you were afraid of dogs until I pried the story out of you. Ten years after the fact."

"You should've seen me at support group a few weeks ago." A playful bit of smugness creeps into my voice, but Brander doesn't banter back. In fact, he stays quiet. He didn't take that as a jab, did he? I frown.

"I wish I could have." His words are low, almost cautious. "I miss you guys. How's Malia doing?"

"Malia?" I shake my head. How'd we get on *that* topic?

"She looked like she was having a rough time when I saw her last. I've been hoping that someone could get through to her."

"That would be me."

"What?"

"Like I said, wish you could've been at youth group."

"No kidding." Brander sighs on the other end. "What happened?"

I fill him in, glossing over Malia's story as much as I can, but hitting all of the important points. I end by telling him about the plans for Koa's big Thanksgiving *luau*. "I think it's going to be good for all of us. My first holiday without Mom, Malia's first without a house, Jazz's first without a leg..."

"A lot can change in a few months, huh? Man." Brander sighs again, a touch of grit creeping into his tone. "Sometimes...never mind."

"What?" I clutch the phone, press it closer to my ear, as though that will help me hear straight through the line to Brander's heart and soul. Unfortunately, there's no such luck.

"Brander! Ready for action?" A soft, sultry woman's voice floats over the other end. "We need you in five."

"Sounds like you're pretty busy, huh?" I sigh and weave the chain of my necklace through my fingers as I walk through a row of lavender.

"Yeah. We're shooting today for a music video." Brander *hmm*s on the other end. "It's nowhere near as much fun as real singing."

"I bet you're great at it, though." I kick at a rock, the misty upcountry vapor wrapping around me as I climb a slight incline.

"Seriously? There are so many big names around here. I feel like a two-year-old on a toy ukulele."

I shake my head. "Don't be ridiculous. Everyone's talking about your song. They love it."

"Do you?"

"Of course." The words come easily, naturally. Because they're *true*. "It sounds...it sounds like it was written—"

"Brander!" Another voice, a guy this time, comes over the line, and Brander groans in my ear.

"I'm sorry, but I've gotta go. Mike—"

"I get it. Talk later?"

"Yeah. And hey—I'm sorry I haven't been able to call or text much. They keep me so busy around here I can't—"

"Bran*der*!"

"Okay, I've really gotta go now. Sorry. I—*aloha*, Olive."

"*Aloha*," I echo, the word rolling off my tongue as the line goes dead.

Aloha—hello, goodbye, and love. Which of those did Brander mean? Which did *I* mean?

Does it matter? I'll probably never see him again. Or at least, not for more than a few days during the holiday season.

When he's not on tour.

I stare at the row of lavender, the scent wafting through the air, wrapping around me and breathing comfort into my soul.

No matter how badly all of this hurts, I care about Brander. I want to see him happy, following God's plan for his life. And he's doing that. He's touching lives, touching *me*. Because, whether he'll ever know it or not, his single sounds like it was written for me.

And, as long as that song's playing on the radio, I'll think of Brander—not of the breakout pop star he's becoming, but the old Brander. The one who taught me how to make a shave ice, the one who showed me God's grace in a whole new way. That Brander that will forever be in my heart.

Like Mom.

Because I'm coming to learn—even when those we love are far from us, even when they're *gone*, they can be kept close in our hearts. They're not there to haunt us, to cause us grief or pain, but so their memory can live on. Forever.

Sure, I'll always miss Mom—and Brander and Koa—and even more people as time goes on. But, no matter if we're separated by an ocean or by an entire dimension, I can keep everyone close to me in my heart. And, as long as I'm alive on the earth, that's what I'll do.

Chapter Twenty-Seven

Thanksgiving Day

"OLIVE, CAN YOU GRAB THE MACADAMIA nut tart?" Gramma tosses the words over her shoulder as she bustles down the hall, arms laden with an abundance of other sweets.

"Sure." I jog into the kitchen and grab the confection before following Grams out to load up her car. The macadamia nut tart looks sort of like Dad's favorite pecan pie—except with macadamia nuts instead of pecans. Typical Hawaii.

Speaking of Dad...

I shift the pie plate to my other hand and pull my phone out of my pocket. I made Dad promise to video chat with me and Macie before we left for the church party, but it's time to go, and he still hasn't called.

And Dad's one of the most punctual people I know.

I peek at Macie, who's busy dancing around the front yard, out of the corner of my eye. She'll be crushed that Dad forgot our Skype date. But if I can distract her long enough, maybe she'll forget.

"Hey, Macie?" I slip the phone into my pocket and wave her over. "Can you go find me a pretty hibiscus to put in my hair?"

Macie's eyes grow wide, and she bobs her head. "Can I get one for me?"

"Sure. Grab one for Grams too." I give her a push toward the farthest hibiscus bush before placing the macadamia nut tart next to Gramma's pies—key lime, banana, and coconut cream. "This is the weirdest Thanksgiving ever." I shake my head at the offerings and turn to look at Gramma. "Where's the pumpkin?"

"Back on the mainland where it belongs." Grams winks at me and draws closer. "Need to talk about anything?" She chances a glance toward the hibiscus bush, as though checking to see if Macie is spying.

A wave of memories builds in my stomach—feathery images of Mom bending over the oven to pull out a perfectly basted turkey, holding hands around the table and giving thanks before the big meal. Thanksgiving has always been a special holiday for my family. But this year Dad didn't even bother to call.

"I..." I drop my head as new pictures come to mind—Jazz clambering around on her prosthesis, Macie making new friends at school, Brander's grainy picture on my phone screen the few times we've been able to video chat.

As much as I miss the old traditions, the relics of yesteryear—despite how much it hurts to know that Dad once again forgot to call, I can't help but smile. "I'm okay. I really am."

Is this that peace that passes all understanding? The one the Bible always talks about? Maybe—who knows? All I know is today's a holiday, the start of a new beginning for Koa and his little owner. It's a time to celebrate.

And that's what I'm gonna do.

When we pull in front of the church, Jazz and Malia are standing out front, arms crossed and doing what they do best—bickering.

I hop out of the car, the balmy air brushing my shoulders as I jog over to Jazz and Malia. "What's up? Didn't anyone ever tell you that holidays aren't for fighting?"

"No." Jazz crosses her eyes at me. "Especially when Malia isn't even going to try Aunt Ruby's special Spam stuffing."

"Spam *stuffing*?" I squeak and clap my hands over my mouth, then look at Malia. Her expression says everything I'm thinking. *Gross.*

Jazz takes one look at both of us, then bursts out laughing. "You two have no culture." She pulls me aside. "Wait until you hear—"

My phone buzzes before Jazz can finish, and I raise a hand. "Hold that thought. Dad's been supposed to call all day—this might be him." I pull out the phone and skim through my notifications. Not a call after all, just a text.

From Dad.

My heart sinks down to my toes, and I tap to read the whole message:

Dearest girls, so sorry for my forgetfulness. I wish you the happiest of Thanksgivings···perhaps we can Skype tomorrow? Love, Dad

I sigh and tap out a response, complete with one more heart emoji than I'm usually comfortable with. He *is* my dad after all—even if he's being a major space cadet—and it *is* Thanksgiving.

"Okay, what'd you want?" I slip my phone back into my pocket and glance up at Jazz. But, before Jazz can say a word, Jonah leans over the railing and waves his fist in a *shaka*. "Olive! Hurry up and get your grandma's pies in here. People are already here, and they're hungry."

I shoot him a thumbs-up and leave Jazz and Malia to their play-fighting as I cross over to Gramma's station wagon. Macie joins in to help, and we manage to get all of the pies inside in record time.

Malia and Jazz mount the stairs as I finish arranging the pies on the dessert table, and something warm flickers in my chest. Koa dashes between tables, weaving around our legs and yipping as we finish the preparations.

People file in, bringing covered dishes and bags of Krispy

Kreme donuts. "We kind of have an obsession here," Jazz whispers before clunking off to welcome Aunt Ruby.

It's nearly two o'clock—the designated turkey time—and the pavilion is packed when a beat-up red Jeep pulls in front of the church. "That's them." Jonah jogs over to where a cluster of kids from support group are hovering near the railing. The air is thick with the smell of Hawaiian-style pork and anticipation. Koa licks his chops, then sticks his button nose into the air as a family of native Hawaiians piles out. There's a husband and wife pair, a tippy-toed little girl, and a scrawny little boy with a vacant gaze—Lio.

"Okay, gang, this is it." Jonah dashes down the front steps and approaches the family as the rest of us wait at the entrance. He speaks in low tones with the parents, then squats and motions to Lio. The boy's eyes stay glossed over, but his mom gives him a gentle tap, and he takes a step forward. Jonah grins and leads them all up the stairs.

"Everyone gather round." He holds up his hands for attention, and the entire room falls silent. "Let me introduce the guests of honor. This is Lio Kane and his family, and we have a special surprise for them today. Jazz?"

Jazz tugs on Koa's leash and leads him over to Lio's family. Koa's nose gets to working overtime as he draws near to the new guests, and Jazz bends to unclip his leash. "Hey Lio, do you like dogs?"

Lio looks off into the distance and picks at his nose. Jazz's gaze falters for a moment, but she puts on a smile anyway. "This is Koa."

"Koa." Lio's voice is dull and flat as cardboard, but he takes a step forward. His parents look at one another, hope blossoming in weary eyes as Lio reaches out and pats Koa's head.

Malia nudges my shoulder, and we share a glance as Lio continues to pet Koa's floppy ears. The puppy is still a little wriggly, his tail wags faster than a jetboat propeller, but he's no longer doing his crazy-puppy-jumping-jack routine. My heart pinches. We trained him pretty well, after all.

I take another glance at Lio and his family. Even though this moment—this goodbye—hurts, it's so, so *right*. There's a tug on my hand, and I look down to find Macie beside me, a tear winking in her eye. "I don't wanna say goodbye to Koa. I love him."

"I know, squirt." I squat so I'm eye level with Macie and giver her curl a tug. "But even though you have to say goodbye today, that doesn't mean it has to be forever. As long as you remember the fun times you had with him, Koa will always be a part of you. And maybe you could even talk to Lio's family about coming over to visit."

"You think?" Macie's eyes light up, and she dashes over to talk to Lio's mom as Jonah bows his head to pray for the food. Macie screeches to a halt halfway across the floor and drops her head along with the rest of the group.

"Dear Heavenly Father, we thank You that we can come together today as one big *ohana* to celebrate all that You have given us. Please bless this food to our bodies, bless the hands of those that prepared it, and bless the rest of our time together."

Everyone joins in to say *amen* before an army of little kids—led by Macie—move to storm the dessert table.

"And now, real quick, before we eat, I have one more surprise for all the rest of you. A certain young member of our congregation, Brander Delacroix, was a huge help in promoting this event."

Jonah goes on to detail how Brander went viral, and my heart jumps. I chance a glance at Jazz. Last I heard from Brander, he was buried deep under a pile of publicity interviews. There wasn't so much as a mention of flying to Maui for the holidays. It would be foolish to hope...

"Ladies and gentlemen, without further ado, I present to you..." Jonah spreads his arms as though announcing the president himself. "Local Lahaina legend, Brander Delacroix!"

The pavilion erupts in cheers—and a few squeals from the girls—but all I care about is the person bounding up the church steps.

Brander, in all his gelled-cowlick glory, his parents hovering close behind.

His smile is the same as always. His warm gaze sweeps the pavilion as he waves, but it falters when it lands on me.

My heart flutters as he drops his hand and takes a step forward, almost as though controlled by invisible strings. He draws closer, his wide, gregarious smile fading to something more tentative. "Aloha." He's looking straight at me.

"Aloha," everyone choruses. Except me. The word is frozen in my throat like a block of ice.

He's really here.

For a moment, no one moves—not until Jazz shoves through the crowd and tackles him in a hug, swaying on her prosthesis and sending both of them toppling back into Brander's overstuffed pillow of a father.

Mr. Delacroix stumbles backward and laughs. "Good to see you didn't forget my son." He chuckles again and gives Jazz a gentle slap on the back as she rights herself. She grins and says something I can't quite catch before Brander gives her braid a tug and moves away to greet the others.

He makes his way through the crowd, polite expression never wavering, all the while drawing closer to me. Kids squeal and chatter, reaching for him and generally making as big a fuss as they would over a world-famous rock star. Brander's voice is warm, his laugh easy. He must be used to this by now, line after line of adoring fans waiting to chat after he plays one of Nashville's hottest venues. Maybe I shouldn't even—

"Hey." Brander steps in front of me, his eyes wide, gaze fluttering over my face.

I squirm a little inside. "I can't believe you're—I mean—"

"Yeah, I'm here." He reaches out and squeezes my shoulder, and the crowd around him dissipates as they drift toward the buffet line. "It's good to see you."

"Right back at'cha. How are you?"

"I'm great, now." He yawns and slaps a hand over his face. "Tired, though. The music business is weird."

"Yeah?" I lean against the railing.

Brander shoves his hands in his pockets and glances over his shoulder at his mom, who is presiding over an elaborate spread of sushi appetizers. "I told Mike I needed more time. To think and pray before I get any deeper into this than I already am."

"You mean..." A flicker of hope lights in my chest, and I do my best to snuff it out.

Brander sighs. Runs a hand through his cowlick. "I don't want to make any promises now, not when I haven't prayed about it yet. But maybe—I don't know." He shrugs. "Part of me thinks that God might rather have me leading worship right here in Lahaina."

My jaw drops. I hurry to snap my mouth closed before I end up looking like a hungry barracuda as Brander leans in to whisper to me. "You know that song? The one on the radio?"

"You know I do."

"I wrote it for you."

Before I can get out a single word, Brander rests his hand on my shoulder and propels me over to where Grams and Macie are waiting in line at the food table. As we approach, Jonah motions for Brander to join Lio's family. Brander flashes me a *shaka* and walks backward as he goes. I return the gesture, my cheeks growing warm.

Jazz sidles up to me, a slinky smile on her face. "Surprised?"

"Like you aren't? He never said a word about coming home for Thanksgiving. At least, nothing definite." And he for sure never remembered to mention that he wrote that song on the radio for me.

"I might have known already."

"What? You mean about Thanksgiving?"

"What else?" She reaches for a plate and piles it with something—could it be Ruby's Spam stuffing? "Brander asked me to help make it a surprise for you. Was it?"

No duh. I nod, any words left in my brain blocked by the fact that Brander cared enough to surprise me. And to write a *song* for me. And sing it. On the radio.

Later, as I sit at a table surrounded by Grams and Jazz and Macie, all of these people I've come to know as my *ohana* over the last few months, I'm filled so full of that *aloha*—that warm spirit of the islands—that I'm nearly bursting. Or maybe I feel that way because I've got three pieces of macadamia nut pie rumbling around in my stomach.

Either way, I can take comfort in the fact that I'm learning, slowly but surely, that life isn't perfect.

It's messy and awful and everyone has secrets they hide.

But, even through the sadness, the pain, and the heartache—even when we're apart from those we love, even when we're forced to say Goodbye, life can still be beautiful.

Wonderful.

A bird trills as it flies overhead. The pounding of ocean waves builds in a dramatic crescendo as Brander strums his guitar, playing his song—my song. The words weave through my heart, filling me with indescribable hope.

No matter how different this Thanksgiving is, no matter how much I hate Goodbye, today feels right. Somewhere amid the warmth and joy spilling from this pavilion, the peace and gratitude spilling out onto the shoreline...

I can't deny that I am finally *home.*

Author Note

There are some stories that tug on an author's heartstrings, wrap themselves up in a writer's brain, and beg to be written. And—when the eager scribe finally puts pen to paper (or fingers to keyboard)—the words just *flow*.

Sand Castle Dreams was NOT one of those stories. In fact, the book you hold in your hands now is my third attempt at a *Porch Swing Girl* sequel. For my first draft, I tried writing a story solely about Jazz...for all of about ten-ish pathetic chapters. I actually finished draft number two (again, from Jazz's point of view but with a completely different storyline) only to realize, thanks to a gut-wrenching phone call with my editor, that I simply couldn't write an entire book from Jazz's perspective.

Then, when everything seemed to be going wrong and I was struggling to stay in control, Jesus swept in. (Doesn't He have such good timing?) He spoke to my heart and showed me what I'd been doing wrong. That, instead of placing myself in God's hands and trusting Him to show me the way, I was trying to make it on my own.

Some writers pray every day before their fingers even touch a computer keyboard—they ask for guidance and wisdom in their writing, and they trust that their Heavenly Father knows best.

I sat down every day, wondering what I should write, wondering why I was struggling to find the story that would suit Olive and Jazz, and wondering what I was doing wrong. And then I realized—I hadn't surrendered my writing to the One who gave it to me. (I'm still not the best at this, but I am learning!)

Enter this story—what is now *Sand Castle Dreams*—a story I didn't even know I had in me. A story that somehow managed to worm its way into my heart. As I wrote *Sand Castle Dreams*, I learned so much—about myself, my characters, and the world at large. God spoke to me in ways I'd never expected or imagined. He showed me that having an independent, perfectionistic spirit can *hurt* me as an author almost as much as it helps. He showed me a small snippet of His will for me as an author. He showed me how to surrender—how to trust Him with my dreams.

God has revealed to me through this publishing journey what is really important—serving Him. At the end of my life, nothing else matters but what I did for Christ.

And, while that's a hard lesson for me to remember when I'm pounding the keyboard, pushing to hit my word count, working to make a deadline, it's one of the most valuable lessons I've learned in my eighteen years of life on this earth.

And now, as this story makes its way out into the world, my earnest prayer is that I have succeeded in crafting a story that touched you, helped you, or entertained you in some small way. (Because we all know how crushing it is to read a second-rate sequel, right?)

Banana Bread Ice Cream Sundaes

From the kitchen of Tutu Bonnie

Olive's grandma believes that more is always...well, MORE, when it comes to dessert. Even those of us who—like Olive—aren't a big fan of bananas will enjoy this take on the tropical treat. This recipe puts a spin on the classic quick bread by topping a warm slice with ice cream, caramel sauce, fresh bananas, and whipped cream—yum!

WHAT YOU NEED:
(Recipe makes one loaf)

- 1/2 cup cooking oil
- 1 cup sugar
- 2 eggs, beaten
- 3 ripe bananas, mashed
- 2 cups all-purpose flour
- 1 teaspoon baking soda
- 1/2 teaspoon baking powder
- 1/2 teaspoon salt
- 3 tablespoons milk
- 1/2 teaspoon vanilla extract
- 1/2 cup chopped macadamia nuts
- Caramel sauce (jarred, or your favorite family recipe)
- Ice cream (vanilla, or go bold with coconut, chocolate, or macadamia nut)
- Bananas (for slicing)
- Heavy whipping cream or canned whipped topping
- Extra chopped macadamia nuts (optional)

HOW TO MAKE THEM

1. Preheat the oven to 350°F

2. Beat oil and sugar together. Add the eggs and banana pulp and beat well

3. Add the dry ingredients, milk, and vanilla. Mix well and stir in macadamia nuts. Pour into a greased and floured 9"x5" loaf pan

4. Bake at 350°F for 1 hour. Let cool slightly

5. If using, whip the heavy cream, adding sugar to taste, until it reaches the desired consistency

6. Place a slice of banana bread in a bowl and top with the sliced bananas and ice cream. Drizzle with caramel sauce and top with whipped cream (or canned whipped topping). If desired, garnish with chopped macadamia nuts.

Discussion Questions

1. Olive decides she'd rather go back to the comfort of Gramma's house in Hawaii than create a new life in Boston with Dad. Do you agree with this decision? What would you have done if you were in her situation?

2. Jazz is determined to make it back onto the swim team, despite losing her leg over the summer. Would you be brave enough to make such a bold goal so soon after a life-changing operation? Have you or someone you know ever had to deal with an event in your life that turned it completely upside down? How did you find the courage to go forward?

3. Instead of sharing her heart and emotions with those closest to her, Olive tries to hide her feelings and uses little white lies to get by. Do you find it difficult to open up to people about personal subjects? How can you get more comfortable dealing with difficult topics?

4. Olive is unreasonably afraid of dogs because of a traumatic incident that happened when she was very young. Have you ever experienced something like this that has altered your outlook on a particular subject? What did you do to help overcome that fear, or what did others do to help you?

5. Malia's dad lost his job in part because he started taking extra time off to support his family. Do you think he should have been a more diligent worker, or did he do the right thing in leaving work to cheer on his daughters? Was there any kind of balance that he could have found that would allow him to do both?

6. Olive's dad forgets his promise to talk with the girls on Thanksgiving morning. Do you find this kind of behavior acceptable in a parent, given the circumstances? If you were Olive, would you confront Dad later?

7. Macie is saddened by the thought of saying goodbye to Koa at the end of the book, but the girls know that the pup will be going to a place where he can make a big difference. Have you ever had to sacrifice something special because you knew it was for the best? How did that make you feel?

8. Do you think Brander will move to Nashville and pursue a career in music? Do you think he should? Why or why not? Have you ever faced a decision that could change your life and possibly even your family's life and wavered, not knowing what was best? What helped you make that decision?

A Sneak Peek at Book Three
Barefoot Memories
Coming April 1, 2020

Chapter One

New Year's Eve

"HAPPY NEW YEAR!" MY LITTLE SISTER Macie reaches over me on the couch to grab a stray party horn, then blows it. Right in my ear.

I yelp and jump off the couch, then wink across the room at my best friend, Jazz, before ruffling Macie's topsy-turvy ponytail. "Backatcha, squirt." It is New Year's Eve after all. Why let something like a burst eardrum spoil the evening?

Macie giggles and hops to the ground, nearly colliding with Gramma, who steps into the room with a platter piled high with goodies sure to give Macie even more of a sugar rush than she already has.

Jazz's gaze finds my own, and we wind up on either side of Gramma as she places her treat tray on the coffee table. "Thanks again for having me over, Tutu Bonnie." Jazz grins at Grams as she reaches for a pineapple upside down cupcake, and I do the same. When Macie and I first came to live with Grams on Maui earlier this year, it seemed weird for Jazz to call Gramma Tutu—the Hawaiian word for Gramma. But now we're one big *ohana*—family—connected by love if not by blood.

Strange, the things a person gets used to.

My gaze strays to the framed photo of Mom hanging in

the hall. Will I ever get used to celebrating the holidays without her?

Thankfully footsteps sound in the hall before I can ride my train of thought right down the road to a pity party, and Dad appears in the doorway wearing a garish sequined tie over his usual weekend uniform of dark-wash jeans and Harvard University t-shirt. He's practically lived in the getup—minus the tie, of course—since he showed up on Gramma's doorstep a couple of weeks before Christmas.

"Who got the party started without me?" He winks, then crosses the room to grab a handful of Gramma's famous macadamia nut caramel corn.

"Nice look, Dad." I snort at his disco-ball tie and pretend to cover my eyes. "At least now we don't have to bother watching the ball drop—you *are* the ball."

"Speaking of letting things drop..." He flashes a grin that makes the hair on the back of my neck stand up straight. The last time Dad "let something drop," he ended up dumping Macie and I at Gramma's while he ran home to put our house on the market.

And now? Who knows what he has to say. As if she can sense my nerves, Jazz sidesteps closer to me, her prosthesis knocking against Gramma's polished floors. I lean in to whisper to her, but Dad clears his throat again.

"I know the last year has been hard on all of us. We've all had a rough go of it. But now that a new year is—"

"Sorry to interrupt." Jazz reaches out to squeeze my hand, then shoots me a glance out of the corner of her eye. "But do you want me to leave? This sounds kind of personal."

"No way!" I squeeze Jazz's hand back so hard her fingers twitch. "You're family. You're *ohana*. You're my other sister. Whatever Dad has to say, you should hear it too." *Besides, I'll roll over and croak without your moral support.*

"Continuing on then." Dad brushes his hands together and smooths them over his hair. "I'd like to attempt to make up for some small portion of where I went wrong this last year. But to do that, we need to spend more time together. As a family."

Goosebumps tug at my arms, despite the warm Hawaiian breeze wafting in from the open front window. Family togetherness is a good thing, right? Unless Dad plans on dragging me and Macie back to Boston with him.

"That's why I've decided to stay here, if that's all right with you, Bonnie." I train my gaze back on Dad in time for him to deliver that zinger.

"What?" My mouth falls open, and—so a quick glance around the living room reveals—so has everyone else's.

"You're leaving Harvard?" Gramma's eyes goggle like fishing lures in the choppy waves at Ka'anapali Beach. "You got your tenure last year."

Dad shakes his head and takes a breath. "Not leaving permanently but going on sabbatical. So I can stay here, with all of you."

"*Really*?" Macie bounces on her toes and clasps her hands over her chest, then gives another toot on her horn. "Then this is gonna be the best-est new year ever."

"That's wonderful, Alex." A smile replaces Gramma's gaping, gasping mouth, and her gaze flickers with warmth. "How long will you have here?"

"I'm not exactly sure yet. I'll admit, this was a bit of a last-minute decision." Dad's eyes meet my own, and I smile his way, even though my stomach is churning beneath the surface of my New Year's cheer.

Ever since Dad showed up for Christmas, we've been getting along about as well as I get along with dogs. Marginally.

It's not Dad's fault he tries too hard to patch over the holes that got torn in our family when Mom died. But...

I sigh.

"Right, Olive?" Jazz elbows me straight in the ribs, and I wince, refocusing on the festive scene before me. Macie is still dancing around with her horn, Gramma is on her way to the kitchen—probably for more snacks—and something tells me Dad's waiting for an answer. From me.

"Uh, sure." I smile wider and shrug, then pull Jazz aside the second Dad starts prancing around the room with Macie. "What exactly did I agree to?"

"That you'll get Macie a puppy for her birthday. Since the whole family's here and all." Jazz's voice is deadpan, but the light in her eyes flickers and dances.

"You *are* kidding, I hope." I've had enough changes in the past six months, I don't need to add something as unpredictable as a dog to my plate.

Jazz snickers. "Of course I'm kidding. We made sure your dad knew he wouldn't disturb us while we did school."

"Gotcha." Ever since Jazz lost her leg to cancer this summer, she's been doing school online. Since she needed help catching up her grades—and I wasn't exactly itching to be the new girl at a new school—I joined her in her homeschooling efforts. "I can't believe school's starting up again. It seems like we barely got on our break."

"Yeah." Jazz's face grows dark, a second before my phone blares its jaunty ringtone—a certain hit single by a certain new Christian music star.

"It must be Brander." I reach into my pants pocket. "He said he'd try to get in on the fun in between sets."

I never could have dreamed that Brander Delacroix, the island's most music-loving, God-fearing teenager would have headed off to Nashville, but viral videos have a strange way of throwing a monkey wrench in people's lives. A freak encounter with the right viewers sent a clip of Brander singing into the national spotlight, and now it looks like he's staying there.

But for how long?

"Are you going to answer that?" Once again, Jazz breaks through my haze, and I flip the phone out of my pocket. There must be unusually high melancholy levels in the air tonight—a byproduct of all of the "Auld Lang Syne's" being sung around the world?

I shake my head, blink hard a couple of times, and answer the call—a video chat, actually. Within seconds, Brander's face appears on the screen. "Happy New Year!"

"Not for us." Jazz steps closer and waves into the camera, then glances at her watch. "Not for another…six hours."

"Oh. Right." Brander shrugs, and his trademark coffee-colored cowlick bobs atop his head. "My set's coming up pretty soon, but I wanted to make sure and catch you guys."

"Thanks for doing that." I quirk an eyebrow at the phone's camera. "So this is the last concert. Does that mean you're coming home soon?"

When Brander left on a blowout tour with some of the biggest names in Christian music, he'd planned on being home in early January. But even in the few short months that Brander's been in the industry, we've all learned one thing—time is precious and schedules change faster than the tides.

"Well…" Brander's almond-shaped eyes grow even narrower, and he hangs his head. "It sounds like I've got some loose ends to tie up in Nashville with Mike and the label."

"*Seriously?*" Jazz groans. "But we were all going to go down the road to Hana next weekend. That's what Olive's calendar says."

Before he left, Brander got me a calendar that had a scattering of the boxes filled with adventures for the three of us to go on after he returned from his tour. My stomach twists at the thought of having to throw all our plans out the door because of something as silly as loose ends.

"I'm really sorry." Brander's gaze darkens. "I wasn't too thrilled about it either when Mike told me. But I'll try to make it home soon."

Jazz and I both nod and—in my case, at least—attempt

to smile. We chat for a few precious minutes before Brander peers into the phone, as though trying to see over Jazz's and my shoulders. "Is that one of Tutu Bonnie's famous treat trays?"

I nod, and Jazz licks her lips. "Dontcha wish you were here?"

A cloud passes over Brander's face, obscuring his smile for a moment. "Speaking of Bonnie, is she around? I was hoping to say hi."

"Sure. I'll grab her."

I do, and Grams and Brander spend a couple minutes catching up—sounds like something about a mutual friend on both of their prayer lists—before a commotion rises on Brander's end of the phone.

"Sorry. Gotta go. That is the intro for my set." Brander's eyebrows twist, and he peers into the phone to wave at the three of us. "Have a great rest of your night. And happy New Year."

"Happy New Year!" Jazz, Gramma, and I all say it at the same time, right as Macie and Dad step back into the room, both of them headed straight for Gramma's treat tray.

Jazz and I join them in their quest for sugar, and we all head out for a stroll along the beach out front before settling down around the coffee table again. Even though Dad seems a little uncomfortable amongst us girls, we manage to get a good debate going on whether or not he should wear a Hawaiian shirt now that he's going to be a "long-term tourist."

After a while, though, we're yawning more than talking. One by one, we fall silent—sucked into the age-old void of sleepiness mingled with nostalgia. Soon the only sound is the echo of Gramma's wall clock, every tick moving us closer and closer toward midnight.

A cluster of candles flicker on an end table, and the darkness beyond the open front window seeps in to the living room, wrapping each of us—except Macie, who's sacked out in Dad's lap, snoring like a model train engine—in our own velvet curtain of memories.

As if drawn by invisible strings, I slip out of the living room and creep upstairs, where I grab a half-full notebook from my desk. Before Mom died and the world as I knew it erupted, I used to keep a semi-consistent journal. Maybe I'll get back into that this year.

But until then...

I flip it open and skim through the pages until I find what I'm looking for.

December 31st

Funny how last year at this time life was just normal. And now...

A wave of tears builds deep in my chest, but I swallow it down and read

I'm not usually a New Year's Resolution kind of person, but this year is different. I'm almost sixteen—time for me to start planning for the future. What better time than now?

To be Completed This Year
1. *Get my driver's license*
2. *Read Jane Eyre. All of it.*
3. *Get an Instagram account. (But what would I post?)*
4. *Look into Harvard undergrad admissions—start with Dad*
5. *Volunteer somewhere?*
6. *Come up with something cool to get Mom for her big 4-0 B-Day*

I sniff and slam my journal's cover closed before I can read any more. Here I am, a year later, and I've only checked one thing off of my bucket list—the Instagram account. And my few posts never got over a dozen likes. Mom barely made it to her fortieth birthday, and it was a pretty pathetic affair, spent in a sterile hospital room with a handful of half-inflated balloons.

"Olive!" A commotion sounds from the living room, and I glance at my watch—only five minutes until the New Year arrives. "Where are you? Come on!"

Minute footsteps pitter-patter up the stairs, and I shove the journal in my desk drawer as Macie barges into the room. "You're going to miss the New Year!"

A smile overtakes my wavering frown as I let Macie take me by the arm and drag me downstairs, where Jazz snaps a party hat onto my head and Gramma hands me a horn.

We stand clustered together, watching on Grams' staticky TV screen as the Times Square ball makes its descent. A warm breeze bursts in the front window as the ball reaches the ground and a hoarse cheer erupts from the crowd gathered on the ancient television.

Another wave of tears wells in my chest, and I close my eyes—alone for a brief moment amid the clamor of cheers and Happy-New-Year wishes.

God, I don't have time to write out any New Year's resolutions right now, but I know You're listening. And this year, I'm only making one resolution.

I'm going to do whatever it takes to get life back to normal—old normal, new normal, doesn't matter. But I'm ready to stop hurting and start healing. Amen.

And then, despite everything that's happened in this last year, I throw up my hands, blow into my party horn, and give a surprised Gramma a smack on the cheek.

It's the New Year, after all—a fresh start after the most painful year of my life.

Things can only go up from here.